BARGAINS WITH BEASTS

UNBROKEN MAGIC

STACIA STARK

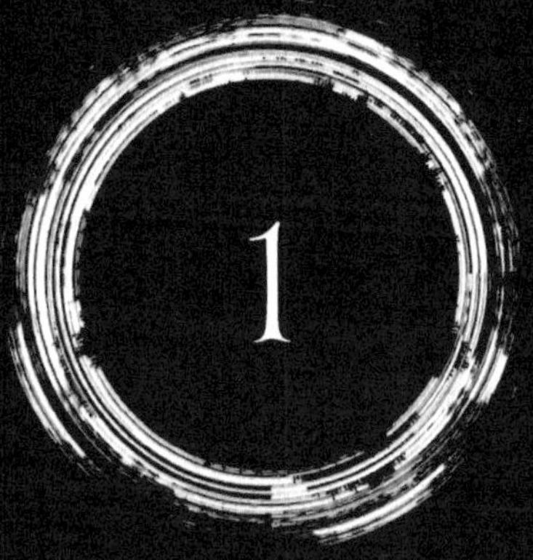

EVIE

It wasn't exactly a stranger to bad days. But today might go down in history as one of the worst.

Not only had Nathaniel kept the little fact that I was his mate from me, but so had both Danica and Kyla. Fury mingled with humiliation, and all I wanted to do was drink until I could no longer hear their excuses ringing inside my head.

Unfortunately, from the look on Mere's face, that was unlikely to happen.

She sighed. "I'm sorry, Evie. I know this is a lot, but there's something else you need to know."

I lowered my drink. "What is it?"

"Kyla went after the sword. I assumed you were going too, so I didn't stop her."

The world receded until I felt as if I were floating above my body. "She went alone?"

Mere nodded, wiping at the same smudge on her bar, over and over. "She said she'd heard from Aubrey and the seelie king is moving up his schedule again."

Aubrey probably attempted to call me when I was in the underworld. When he couldn't reach me, he'd called Kyla, assuming she'd fill me in.

Instead, she'd gone alone.

"Of all the stubborn—" I got to my feet and pushed the stool back under the bar. "I'm going after her."

Vas went still. "I'm coming too."

"No." I cut him off. "You have a kid on the way. This is for Kyla and me to do."

Only, Kyla had obviously decided I wouldn't be helping her. She'd also obviously decided our friendship was over.

My memory provided me with the image of her wounded eyes when I'd confronted her, and I ran my hand over my face.

After the fight we'd had, I couldn't blame her. But it was stupid and reckless. We weren't prepared to put the plan into motion together, let alone by ourselves.

"I've got to go."

"How can we help, Evie?" Vas looked tortured. Next to him, Mere looked like she wanted to send him, but she had clamped her hand around her lower belly.

"If we don't come back, let everyone know who has us and why. That's all I need. I've got this."

They let me go, but neither of them liked it. Unfortunately, that meant I had to return to the underworld.

My mind was looping around the same thoughts over and over again. We weren't prepared. We weren't prepared. We definitely weren't fucking prepared.

I stopped at Aubrey's. He paled when I told him what had happened. "She went alone?"

"Yeah. Don't worry, I'm going to kick her ass when I find her. If she's still alive."

Guilt stabbed into my gut. If she wasn't alive, it was all my fault.

"I gave her the map," Aubrey said, and I closed my eyes. "But I made a copy." He took my arm and led me to the closest chair, guiding me into it. Then he turned and murmured to one of his servants.

"I wanted to have a backup for my own records," he admitted.

"In case you decide to take the throne?"

He sighed. "A lot more would go into it than a decision to take the throne and a map of his castle, but yes."

The servant returned and handed me the map. "I need to go."

"Wait. I have a few things for you. I'd hoped to give these to Kyla, but she was a little...wild when she arrived, and I didn't get the chance."

Aubrey riffled through the hall closet and pulled out a backpack. He wandered away, although I could hear him muttering. When he returned, he patted the backpack twice. "There are a few things in here that should help. You'll know how to use them."

"Thank you. If we don't make it back..."

"You will. You better make it back, Evie Amana, and you better bring Kyla home with you, or I'm coming after you. And I'm not yet prepared for war."

I nodded. Then I leaned up and kissed his cheek. His eyes glittered as he watched me turn to go.

"Good luck."

I drove to Gary's, where I parked my car and poked through the backpack Aubrey had given me. My mouth dropped open as my hand brushed a tiny jar of pixie dust. It could heal even mortal wounds if applied quickly enough. This jar was worth almost ten thousand dollars, although the human population had no idea it existed. If they learned of it, the next thing we knew, they'd be farming pixies for their dust.

I still had the key Entaris had given us. I shoved it into one of the inside pockets of the backpack, then popped the trunk and pulled out the first aid kit Nathaniel's wolves all carried in their cars.

Gary watched me quietly while I stocked up on pain charms. I'd told him what had happened, and he was chewing on his gray lips with his sharp teeth. He loved Kyla too. I picked out some lapis lazuli, which was excellent for tracking spells if Kyla and I got separated after I found her.

"Thanks, Gary."

"Good luck, kid."

I got back into the car and drove toward the portal

to the underworld. I didn't want to return, but I didn't have much choice.

This time, Danica was in the garden.

"Evie." A faint smile crossed her face, as if she thought I was here to apologize or some shit.

"Kyla went after the sword. Without me."

Danica paled. I ignored the horror in her eyes.

"I'll forgive you if you give me Angelica's ring," I said.

Danica glanced down at the ring, and I saw the moment she figured it out. "You think it'll help. You don't need to pretend to forgive me. Kyla's my friend too." She slipped it off her finger. "Here. Take it."

I didn't bother answering. I just pushed it onto my own finger and hauled ass back toward the portal.

NATHANIEL

I smiled at the mage.

He'd known I was coming and had gone on the run. It hadn't taken much for my wolf to hunt him. In truth, the monster inside me was almost disappointed by how easy it had been.

But no one could hide from me for long.

I watched as he raised his hand and an ugly brown ward appeared.

Then I stepped through it.

He let out a choked sound that pleased my wolf. My people didn't make it known that Alphas could call on the power of the pack when necessary. There was no point tipping off our enemies. But my pack was large. Powerful. Angry.

I could feel them, all of them. Which told me my wolf was dangerously close to the surface. Regardless of how each of them felt about Evie as a person, they all felt the same violent outrage that the mages would dare come after my mate.

"How did you get in here?"

I shook my head at Albert. "That's not what you should be asking. You should be asking how much I'll make you suffer before you die for targeting Evie."

Surprise flashed through his eyes. He'd thought I had come here as retaliation for attempting to stoke a war between various werewolf packs. He thought I'd come to threaten him, maybe punish him, for the reputational damage he'd caused us among the humans.

I gave him a slow smile, and he trembled. "Evie is my mate."

His trembling turned to a full-body shudder, and my wolf silently howled his victory. We'd kill this threat to our mate. And then we'd convince her to return to our territory. To our home. Where she belonged.

I allowed the wolf to take over, only shoving him aside when I needed to travel back to my territory.

Hunter gaped at me as I stepped into the house. He immediately dropped his eyes, although not before I saw his own wolf peek out at the scent of the blood covering me.

"You killed Albert."

His voice was carefully neutral.

"Yes," I growled, still on the killing edge.

Ryker stepped into the room. "There's something you need to know. Vassago just called."

"And?"

"Kyla went into the seelie realm. Evie went after her."

That fucking sword. I'd always planned to be there to make sure they didn't cause a war—or worse, end up dead. But they went after it alone.

"You can't follow her," Ryker said. He stiffened when he felt my gaze on him and kept his own eyes down. "Tomorrow is the full moon. She's your mate. We just lost a pack member. There's no way your wolf will stay in control."

I watched him. My wolf pondered whether he should live. Hunter stepped into my line of sight. And that was how I'd chosen my dominants. Because they were loyal to me, but even more importantly, they were loyal to one another. That loyalty was good for the pack as a whole.

My wolf agreed. Ryker would live. But we *would* be finding our mate.

I'd known Evie would run. That was okay. I was

going to prove we belonged together. Right after I saved her life, kissed her lush mouth, and spanked her ass.

I threw my head back and howled my fury.

2

EVIE

I had everything I needed.

At least, that's what I was choosing to believe. The ring would help significantly. I'd worked a look-away spell once before, making myself appear invisible to an ex when I pranked him. But that was only good for a few minutes before I would be a shaky, weak mess. Turns out, convincing the human brain that you weren't standing in front of them took a lot of power.

The ring would solve that problem.

After Danica had handed over Angelica's ring, I'd borrowed extra clothes and weapons, packing them in the backpack. I might be pissed at my sister, but I wasn't an idiot.

Most of the time.

And I was distracting myself from the terror that made my hands shake. Kyla had been gone for too long.

"Of all the stupid, reckless, *insane* things to do," I muttered as the portal came into view.

I parked in Cate's Landing, slammed my door closed, and opened the back door, pulling out the bag Aubrey had given me. I'd had a quick look but hadn't had time for much more. All I could hope was that there were enough of his little "tricks" that, combined with my own power, Kyla and I would both stay alive.

I was going to kick her ass *so* hard when I found her.

Panic clawed through my chest. What if I *didn't* find her? Kyla had a head start on me. What if she'd gotten into the kind of trouble that I couldn't help her with?

No. I refused to think that way.

Stuffing the bag from Aubrey inside my backpack, I zipped it up and slung it over my shoulder. My heart rate tripled as I popped the ring into my mouth. Danica had warned me how strange it would feel to suddenly be invisible, and I took a deep breath through my nose. It was disconcerting not to be able to see my own hands as I locked Liam's car and slipped the keys into my pocket.

And then I was walking toward the portal, my palms sweating. I *hated* being unprepared. But Kyla had been right about one thing—if Taraghlan was planning to move the sword, we had to strike before it was even more difficult to steal.

I stepped into the portal, skin burning. A few

moments later, I was in the seelie realm.

I very carefully avoided glancing at the dense forest to my right. That forest had almost killed me once, and if I looked for too long, I'd find myself wandering toward it, eager to lie down on the soft grass among the wildflowers.

A lush meadow stretched out before me, and I broke into a light jog down the dirt path that would take me to the castle. I knew what I'd find when the path curved to the right, but it was still impressive.

I might hate Taraghlan, but even the least romantic person in the world would admit his castle was like something out of a fairy tale. It gleamed welcomingly, the towers and turrets stretching toward the sky, where they caught the sunset, reflecting it across the land. The surrounding moat was as blue as the ocean. As I approached, I caught sight of jewel-like rocks strewn across the bottom, as if the seelie king had thrown them out his window in a temper.

Taraghlan's guards wore white, and all of them seemed alert, their gazes sharp as they examined anyone who approached. They were stationed on the bridge leading to the castle and every six feet or so along the moat.

I slowed my steps, careful not to draw their attention. Carriages carrying various well-dressed fae were coming and going, and the guards were checking each one. My stomach clenched. How the hell had Kyla snuck in without being seen?

Or maybe she *had* been seen, and she was currently being tortured for information while I dithered here.

That thought was enough to make me launch into action. I pulled the map from my backpack and studied the castle in front of me. According to Entaris and Tilella, I needed to skirt the creepy forest and mosey around to the back of the castle, where I'd find the seelie king's emergency exit, beneath his moat.

I sucked in a deep breath, eyeing the forest.

Nathaniel wouldn't hesitate if he were here. I was pretty sure he wasn't scared of anything. My chest tightened. Later. That was a thought for later. Because if I allowed myself to picture the frustrated fury on Nathaniel's face, if I allowed myself to mourn what I'd *thought* we had, I'd be useless to Kyla.

I strode toward the forest. Last time I was here with Meredith, we were almost killed by a fluffle of bunnies. Vas and Bael had swooped in to help us, but the only reason the forest had allowed us to leave was the demon fire Vas had curled threateningly around his hand.

If I used my new fire trick, would the fire be invisible? And if it *was* invisible, would the forest be threatened?

I felt the forest shift the moment I stepped off the path. I could *feel* it paying careful attention to me. With a glance over my shoulder, I focused.

My hand lit up, and the forest went still. "I don't want to hurt you, but I also don't have time to be chased by your killer bunnies," I said in a low voice. I had no doubt it could hear me.

I stepped deeper into the forest. I'd only have to walk around the edges to get to the spot I needed, but I had no doubt that the forest could kill me regardless of how deep I wandered.

Already, I could feel my lids growing heavy. There was a spot beneath a tree to my right where the grass was so thick it would almost feel like a mattress...

No. I snapped myself out of it and brought the ball of fire close to that tree. I could *feel* the forest's annoyance, but my head was suddenly mine again.

Allowing my fire to disappear, I made my way toward the back of the castle. I cursed as I stood on a stick and it snapped, the sound louder than a gunshot to my ears. One of the seelie guards turned his head toward me, and I froze.

"I know that was you," I told the forest. "If you draw attention to me, you won't like what comes next."

Yes, I was threatening a sentient forest. Life was weird.

I could practically feel the forest pouting, but I slowly continued on, and the forest stopped exaggerating the sounds my steps made.

Eventually, I was standing at the spot I'd marked on the map. I surveyed the castle. The moat was about ten feet wide at this point, and while there were a few guards on duty here, the seelie king obviously didn't figure anyone knew about his little escape route. That thought gave me the warm fuzzies. He'd betrayed us in the worst possible way. Now *he'd* know exactly how it felt.

It was petty, but I'd love to be a fly on the wall when he learned we'd stolen his precious sword from right under his nose.

Of course, for that to happen, we had to find the sword *and* somehow stay alive.

I peered through the gap in the tree branches, surveying the tunnel entrance in front of me. As I'd been warned, it was invisible, the entrance impeccably tucked away within the walls of the moat. Taraghlan was hiding his little exit in plain sight, so it looked like just another of the huge stone blocks containing the water. If he'd been an honorable king, this little secret would have stayed just that—a secret. Instead, he'd been sold out by people who were determined to stop him from wreaking havoc on the realms.

Counting the stone blocks, I narrowed my eyes as I got to the seventh from the right. That was it. If Entaris and Tilella were truly helping us—and this wasn't a trap—I'd crawl *through* the block, then drop down into the tunnel below.

Guards were positioned on this side of the castle, stationed every ten feet or so. One of them stood next to the unmarked entrance. His eyes were heavy-lidded—almost sleepy, but I wasn't fooled. His gaze was just as sharp as his colleagues'.

How had Kyla gotten past him?

Taking a deep, steadying breath, I strapped my backpack tighter around my shoulders and raised my ward—impenetrable and noise-canceling. My vision narrowed until all I could see were the guard and the tunnel behind him. He was standing in front of the stone block and a little to the right. I was going to have to crawl past him.

Without my silence ward, there was no way I would have been able to do it. But I rolled my shoulders and dropped to my knees.

I crawled forward. The guard shifted to the right, and I froze. His knee was inches away from my shoulder. If he stepped any closer, his leg would brush my body and it would all be over.

Did I dare move?

I was stuck, barely breathing, inches from the entrance. If I didn't get out of here, I was worse than dead.

Time slowed. I lowered until I was almost on my stomach, inching my way forward. The guard sighed, scratched his butt, and then straightened, moving a few inches back to the left.

I took my chance and shot forward. I felt the moment my boot brushed his, and then I was rolling, getting to my feet as he glanced down, clearly puzzled.

But I was already running. I glanced back to see him leaning back against the wall.

I pumped my legs faster and hurtled down the tunnel and into the seelie king's castle.

NATHANIEL

"When my guard said you were demanding an audience, I assumed he was mistaken."

Finvarra watched me with his eerie gold eyes, amusement flickering through them. As much as I might want to trade barbs with the unseelie king, I had more important things to worry about.

"I need to borrow your book."

He raised one eyebrow and leaned back in his chair. I'd helped myself to a seat in his library, my wolf howling mournfully inside me as we caught the scent of our mate. Evie had been the last to sit here.

It was taking every ounce of my hard-won restraint to keep my expression neutral when I wanted nothing more than to launch myself at the king. He was powerful enough to kill me, but I could make him hurt before I died.

His eyes gleamed as if he were reading my mind. Impossible, thanks to my built-in defenses against magic.

"Which book would you be referring to?" Finvarra waved his hand, gesturing to the shelves surrounding us. "I have so many, you see."

"You know which book I mean. The silver one. The one that turns the user invisible."

"The one *your* teenage pack member was using to frolic across Durham?"

"Yes."

"And why would you imagine I'd loan you something so important?"

Kyla had told me where the unseelie king's cousin had found the book before she'd stolen it. If it were that important, surely Finvarra would have kept it in his own castle, not buried among the rest of his junk at one of his other estates.

"Kyla went after the sword. Alone."

Finvarra went still. Something alien sparked in his eyes, and he tilted his head in a way that reminded me of my wolves when they were on the hunt.

"I thought your mate was planning to join her on that little excursion?"

Little excursion. He'd bargained with *my* wolf when she was desperate, ensuring she would need to risk her life to find that sword.

Frankly, the realms would be better off if both fae kings killed each other.

"They had a...disagreement, and Kyla went alone."

I was watching the king closely enough to catch the way his hand tightened on the arm of his chair. "Of all the stubborn, bullheaded, single-minded—"

With a flash of my teeth, I cut him off. "News flash, all those words mean the same thing. The fact remains that the seelie king is moving the sword. Kyla obviously saw her chance and took it. Evie went after her, but I don't know how far ahead Kyla was. I'm leaving for the seelie realm now, but in order to get into the palace, I need the book."

Finvarra studied me for a long moment. "If you have any thoughts about keeping it, know that I will come for you with everything I have. And I have a lot."

My wolf didn't appreciate the threat. It urged me to sink my claws into the unseelie king's guts and watch his organs fall to the floor—

"If you're done with your murderous haze..." Finvarra gave me a look full of smug satisfaction.

We will kill him at a later time. When he least expects it. When we have rounded up our allies and are ready for war.

I could feel my wolf's approval of that plan.

"Let me remind you that if Kyla dies, you don't get your precious sword. She's the *only* person who bargained with you. The rest of us would like to watch you die. Slowly."

"That seems like an overreaction, although not entirely unexpected from your people." But he was thinking about it, I could tell. He knew as well as I did that if Kyla attempted to take the sword and failed, Taraghlan would move it to a more secure location. If that happened, the chances of Finvarra stealing it before it was used to run him through were greatly diminished.

As much as I would enjoy hearing Finvarra's scream as he died, I needed him alive until I had Kyla safely home and Evie safely in my bed. Where she belonged.

"Each moment you ponder this situation is another moment in which you could be losing your sword. And my wolf could be losing her life." I didn't mention Evie. Finvarra didn't care. But without Kyla, he was screwed, and he knew it.

Finvarra clenched his jaw, but he lifted a stack of books from the table next to him and held one of them out to me. The cover gleamed silver, as if it were made of molten metal. I plucked it from his hand before he could change his mind.

"Four of Taraghlan's spies were found in my territory yesterday. From all accounts, one of them holds information Taraghlan doesn't want me to know. He sent a messenger requesting the opportunity for a prisoner swap." Finvarra stretched again, the movement like a lazy tiger in the sun. I had a feeling Taraghlan was likely to underestimate him. To his detriment.

"You think he'll want to swap today?"

"I will contact him and state that I wish to discuss the matter in person. Neither of us will agree to meet in our own territories, so it will likely be somewhere in your realm. That will ensure a slice of time when he is away from his castle. Now that he no longer has his little portal maker by his side, it will take him some time to return."

"How do you know he'll agree?"

Finvarra smiled. "Because I already know what information the spy has, and he would do almost anything to prevent me from learning it."

This was an unexpected gift. I'd continually underestimated just how badly Finvarra wanted this sword.

"Thank you."

He simply stretched out his legs. "Enter my territory without warning again, and it will be war. Do you think I'm unaware of how your own power works, Alpha? It's not just your pack who lend you their will, it's any wolf who has sworn loyalty or fealty."

And exactly how had he known that? I studied him back, considering just how much of a threat he posed to my pack.

"We'll revisit this another time," I said finally.

He gave me a sharp nod. "Return the book immediately once you have retrieved the sword."

Neither of us bothered with any further conversation. Tucking the book under my arm, I stalked toward the door.

3

EVIE

I'd thought I was brave.

But from the way my hands shook and my knees quaked as I stood at the edge of the tunnel, I was rethinking that position.

The tunnel itself was dimly lit. But that light disappeared about three feet in. I rolled my shoulders, wishing I could create my own ball of light. But Entaris had warned us to be careful when using magic down here. He'd said any disruption in the power levels would draw the attention of all different kinds of nasties. As much as I would like to waltz in here fully warded, with my hand lit up with my power, I couldn't risk it.

Darkness stretched out before me. I popped the ring out of my mouth, and strode down the corridor.

A few minutes later, I wasn't feeling any more settled. But I could see the glow of more light ahead.

Slowing my pace, I cupped the ring in my hand, ready to stuff it back into my mouth if I needed to.

By the time I was just a few steps from the end of the corridor, I was so tense my muscles hurt. Taking a single step into the room, I froze.

Kyla had obviously been here. I wasn't sure what the creatures had been before they attacked, but now they lay in pieces, clawed apart. A hunk of white fur was all that had been left behind.

I studied the scene. The creatures had likely dropped down from the ceiling. She'd carved through them within moments.

Well, since Kyla had taken care of this trap, I could continue walking. Even with the evidence of her capabilities, I couldn't help but worry.

Pushing open the next door, I broke into a jog, making my way down the next long corridor. This one curved to the right, and I slowed to a walk as I followed it, until I was standing in the next chamber.

My eyes met Kyla's.

Something tight in my chest unfurled, and my eyes stung.

Alive. She was alive. Unfortunately, she was also bound to a huge wooden pole in the middle of the room. The thick ropes were wrapped around her arms and legs, and from the way her hands had begun to lose color, they'd tightened as she'd attempted to break free.

"What the fuck did you think you were doing?" I

demanded.

She rolled her eyes. "Can we go over this later? I'm a little...tied up."

"Cute." I stepped toward her and studied the ropes.

"You can't use your magic," Kyla said. "Remember?"

"Those ropes are magically reinforced. Otherwise, you'd be free by now."

From the sour look on her face, she'd been attempting to cut through them for hours.

I pulled my Applegate-Fairbairn fighting knife and tried to slice through one of the coils holding her leg in place.

"I shifted my claws," she said. "Nothing will get through the rope."

"Then we have to use my magic. You've been here for too long. Besides, if your claws can't get through it and my knives can't get through it, we have no other options."

"Fine." She turned her head and stared at the wall. I scowled. How the fuck was *Kyla* mad right now?

I was the one everyone had lied to.

We didn't have time for hurt feelings. If we were going to get out of this alive, I had to keep my head in the game.

Pulling in a deep breath, I studied the ropes and reached for my power. It immediately responded, as if it had been waiting for this moment. The ropes were seelie magic. I didn't know how I knew that, but it was as if being in this realm made it easier for me to reach for that thread of power. I grabbed the rope curling over Kyla's shoulder and focused. I had no idea what I was doing, but I pictured the rope dissolving in that spot until it snapped.

"It's working," Kyla said.

"I can see that."

She clamped her mouth shut, and guilt panged through me. There was no need to be an asshole.

"Why did you even bother coming after me?" she gritted out.

"We made a deal."

Her silence spoke louder than any words. I ground my teeth. "I need to focus for this to work."

I concentrated on the next rope, this one over her biceps. As soon as that strand broke, Kyla had the use of her right arm.

Something scuttled in the dark behind us. My gaze met Kyla's. Her eyes had gone wolf.

"What is it?"

She swallowed. "Scorpions. From the Middleground. I recognize the scent."

I worked faster. Kyla kept her ice-blue gaze behind me, and I knew she'd alert me when she needed to.

"They're coming," she bit out.

I'd gotten her right leg free. "Can you shift?"

"I tried earlier. The rope tightened until I didn't have enough room."

One more rope left.

"Duck!" Kyla roared.

I dropped to the floor as something flew at me from the right. Kyla snarled and lashed out with her free hand, her claws slicing through its neck.

I backed up, taking in the creatures. They were bigger than a large-breed dog, eight-legged, their backs covered in what looked like blade-proof armor.

"Our king will be pleased…" one of them hissed, and I shuddered.

"They can fucking talk?"

"Oh yeah," Kyla huffed out. "They had plenty to say when Danica and I killed them in the Middleground."

"Right. Your bestie Danica. Lots of bonding experiences going on between you two. Did you compare notes when you were lying to me?"

"Yeah, we talked all about how you're an unforgiving asshole."

I clenched my fists. One of the scorpions scuttled toward me, and my A-F was in my hand before I realized I'd moved. I sliced at its skull, stumbling as it merely ducked and rammed its head into me.

I fell on my ass. But at least from here, I could see its vulnerable underbelly. I stabbed and dragged the knife toward me, gagging at the smell of its guts. They slid out in a wet pile, and the scorpion screamed. I kicked out at it until it fell off me, writhing.

The other scorpions didn't seem all that concerned about their two dead friends.

"Hungry," one of them howled.

"Don't let them sting you," Kyla said. "It's

poisonous. Get me free, and I can help."

"How the fuck do you suggest I do that?"

"If you don't do it, you're dead."

"I can kill them with my power."

"But what if the consequences of using magic in this place get worse based on just how much magic you use?"

"The scorpions are already here. How much worse can it get?"

She snorted. "Are you seriously asking that question? There's a big difference between cutting through some rope and burning eight scorpion creatures alive."

She had a point. If the scorpions were in response to the power I'd used, would killing them with power attract something worse?

I reached out a hand. Kyla grabbed it and directed it to the rope. I concentrated, but two scorpions flew at me, leaving me no choice but to dart away.

"To your left," Kyla screamed, and I dove to the right, barely dodging a poisonous tail.

They were playing with me, but I was outnumbered. I couldn't risk using my Beretta. Bullets would likely ricochet off their armor, and that was a stupid way to end up dead.

"*Move*, Evie!"

I slashed out with my knife.

Missed.

I was surrounded on three sides, Kyla at my back.

"Free me," she snarled, her voice more wolf than human.

"This wouldn't even be fucking happening if you hadn't rushed off alone half-cocked."

"Maybe after your temper tantrum, I couldn't trust you to have my back."

"Are you fucking kidding me?"

"You told me to stay the fuck away from you."

Three scorpions danced toward me, and I shied away, rolling beneath the one to the right, slicing through its chest.

"Temporarily!" I snapped. The scorpion leaned closer, sharp teeth snapping at my face. I shoved my knife in deeper. "While I came to terms with the fact that you'd been lying to me every day while we were working together."

"How was I supposed to know it was temporary?"

Blood splattered my face, and the scorpion screeched. I kicked it away, but another had already taken its place before I could even get to my feet.

And then Kyla was there.

"What the fuck?"

She slashed out, only using one clawed hand. Another screech sounded as razor-sharp claws separated the scorpion's head from its body. I dropped down, slicing into another neck.

Something dug into my thigh, and I screamed, turning. It wasn't a poisonous tail, but one of the scorpion's claws had gotten lucky.

Kyla kicked it in the head. The scorpion flew, hit the wall, and ended up on its back like a dead cockroach.

Three left. God, it felt like this would never end.

"Get up," Kyla demanded.

I stumbled to my feet, blood dripping down my thigh. Her left arm hung unnaturally by her side. She'd dislocated it to get free of the last rope.

"Get behind me," she said.

I shook my head. Kyla cursed, but this time, she didn't wait for the scorpions to attack. She launched herself at one of them, claws gleaming.

Her one-armed attack was a thing of beauty.

Two left.

One for each of us.

Except, my vision was blurring. I blinked furiously. The scorpion danced before my eyes. It was in front of me with my next blink. I had no choice. I pulled my Beretta and dropped back to the floor, shooting up into its belly.

Its scream turned into a gurgle. Kyla turned to me, her eyes wide. She'd dispatched the last scorpion.

"How bad is your leg?"

"Well, if it had been my femoral, I'd be dead by now," I mumbled, slumping to the floor.

"Shut up." She used her good hand to drag the backpack closer, riffling through it until she found the first aid kit.

"Magic," I said.

"I know. You had no choice."

"No. Aubrey." Fuck, why could I barely talk? Maybe I'd lost more blood than I'd thought.

She pulled out Aubrey's bag of tricks, relief clear on her face as she dumped everything on the floor.

"Pixie dust," I said.

She nodded, taking the tiny jar and trickling it onto the wound in my thigh. I bit into my lower lip as fire erupted, traveling up toward my hip. But my head was already clearer.

"Don't use it all. We might need it later."

Kyla didn't look happy about that, but she nodded, tucking it back into Aubrey's bag. I used the wall at my back to get my feet. Pixie dust was almost mythical, the expense so incredible that few people had ever seen it. Not only could I feel the wound in my thigh knitting back together—a nauseating feeling I never wanted to experience again—but the pixie dust would be slowly replacing my lost blood.

"Evie?"

My thoughts had drifted away from me again. Hopefully, my missing blood was replaced sooner rather than later.

"We need to fix your shoulder," I said.

Kyla nodded. Then she turned and slammed it into the wall. With a pop, her shoulder was back in place.

I leaned over and threw up.

She wrinkled her nose and waved her hand toward the dead scorpions, blood, and entrails strewn in front of us. "That didn't do it, but the shoulder did?"

I wiped my mouth. "I'm sure it was cumulative."

Our eyes met. My lips trembled. Tiny lines formed around her eyes.

We cracked up.

There was literally nothing funny about our situation. If anything, things were dire.

I laughed harder.

Kyla leaned over, her good hand bracing on her knee as she chortled.

I wiped at my eyes. Ludicrous. We were both ludicrous.

"Okay," I said with a deep breath. "Let's get the hell out of here."

NATHANIEL

Getting past the guard on the tunnel wasn't an issue. The book kept me invisible, and my wolf rose to the surface, ensuring I stayed entirely silent. Of course, I was willing to tear out the guard's throat and drag him into the tunnel with me if I had to.

I could scent Evie as I prowled down the tunnel, the light guiding me toward her. Kyla's scent was fainter, but still layered beneath the odor of old magic.

I broke into a jog.

I was responsible for the fracture in their

relationship. Kyla had learned that Evie was my mate, and I'd immediately ordered her to keep that information to herself. I'd justified it with the argument that Evie couldn't blame Kyla when she learned I'd ordered her silence. But Evie wasn't a wolf. She had no idea of the compulsion that would have stopped Kyla each time she wanted to fill her friend in.

It hadn't occurred to me to order Kyla not to go after the sword until we were ready. And that was a mistake on my part. She was impulsive, yes, but I knew each of my pack members—some of them better than they knew themselves. Kyla had a deep well of protective loyalty within her. She would die for her friends, and yet the moment she and Evie fought, she'd assumed their friendship was over.

She'd likely seen this as a chance to remove any threat to Evie before disappearing from her life completely.

I was sure Evie would have plenty to say about that.

Now that I had a moment to breathe, I could admit the part I'd played. I still stood behind my decision not to tell Evie she was my mate. I'd needed her to see me as a man, not a potential jailer. If she'd learned of who she was to me, learned just how much my wolf needed her, she would never have come near me. We would have remained strangers. Now, at least, I knew she cared for me in some capacity. Even if it was reluctant attraction.

When it came to Evie, I'd take anything she had to offer.

Light gleamed from the end of the corridor. My wolf leaped to the forefront of my mind.

The first chamber held nothing but the creatures Kyla had obviously ripped apart. Pride curled in my gut, but I didn't have time to study the scene. Slamming through the next door, I hit the corridor behind it at a jog.

I could smell Evie. Kyla. Blood. And enemies.

My jog became a sprint. A snarl left my throat as I looked at the carnage in front of me, taking it in. Thanks to the scents left behind, it was easy to understand what had happened. That rope had held Kyla. Evie had arrived, and they'd killed the scorpion creatures. But Evie had lost so much blood, my wolf howled its rage inside me.

My mate was wounded. So badly, she could be dying right now. I stalked past the bodies and eyed the rope. My wolf searched it for traces of magic, but whatever Evie and Kyla had done, it was now inert.

I walked warily through the hanging strands of the rope before pushing open the door on the other side of the chamber. Kyla had been in here for hours. They couldn't be too far ahead of me.

I picked up speed.

4

EVIE

We moseyed down the corridor. I'd known the footprint of the seelie king's castle was massive, but this hallway was stretching on for what felt like miles.

I glanced at Kyla. An awkward silence spread between us. She looked as miserable as I felt.

"I know you couldn't tell me," I said finally.

"Do you really? Then how come you've barely looked at me, except for when we both almost died?" She shook her head. "You don't understand."

"Then make me understand."

"Nathaniel doesn't give orders often. He doesn't enjoy knowing people have no choice but to do what he says. He once told me he would rather know if people disagreed with his orders. That way, he could tackle the problem head on."

Sounded like Nathaniel.

"But he gave you an order."

"Yeah. I found out you were his mate, and of course I was planning to tell you. We hadn't been friends for long, but I figured you deserved to be told, regardless.

"Nathaniel stepped into the room and said he was sorry. He looked tormented, and some part of me knew what was coming. He ordered me to never talk to you about being his mate until you already knew. He also said I wasn't allowed to hint, nudge, or even allude to the fact that Nathaniel could have a mate."

That son of a bitch. I ground my teeth as Kyla went on.

"The moment he finished speaking, the order took effect. I'd never experienced that level of compulsion before. Whenever I even thought about attempting to tell you, my throat closed up. I physically *couldn't* tell you, Evie. I'm sorry that I lied to you. And I'll regret it for the rest of my life. But lying to you was torture."

I kicked out at the wall. "I'm sorry. I knew it wasn't fair to blame you the moment you told me about his order, but hearing how it worked now... I should've listened properly. It was just...a lot."

"You'd just been blindsided by it. I get it." Kyla studied me. "Did you talk to Danica?"

I sucked in a furious breath. "Yeah. She spouted some bullshit about how it was for the best, and how Nathaniel convinced her I would run. All *I* know is that she should've been loyal to me first."

"Don't be too hard on her, Evie."

I narrowed my eyes, and Kyla held up her hands. "All I'm saying is no one *wanted* to lie to you."

"No one except Nathaniel. And he's going to pay."

She opened her mouth. I shot her a warning look. "Don't even think about defending him."

She clamped it closed and shrugged. "Fair enough." She slid me a look. "Friends?"

"Friends. Of course. God, Kyla, I'm sorry."

"I'm sorry too."

"I'm still pissed at you for coming alone."

"Look on the bright side. At least we're getting the sword before Finvarra's deadline."

"I would've preferred to be better prepared."

Kyla shrugged. "It's not ideal, but part of me is glad we'll get it over with. I've hated having it hanging over our heads."

"Yeah. There is that." We both surveyed the door at the end of the corridor, which was blocked by several huge boulders. They were going to be a pain in the ass to move. I'd learned enough about werewolves to know that even though Kyla could lift them without a problem, her arms were only so long, and getting a good grip on them would be an issue.

Kyla froze. Her eyes went wolf. "Uh-oh."

"What the hell are you two thinking?" The low, furious voice made me flinch.

We both whirled. Nathaniel stood behind us. He wore jeans, a blue T-shirt, and a dark scowl.

I glanced at Kyla. "You didn't scent him?"

She waved her hand toward the blood and *other things* smeared all over both of our clothes. "Have you gotten a whiff of us recently?"

I turned back to the bane of my existence. "More importantly, what are *you* doing here?"

And how the hell had he convinced Finvarra to give him that book he was holding?

Nathaniel leveled us with a hard stare. "Chasing after my woman who ran, *as expected,* and my wolf, who should have known better."

Both of us bristled. Kyla narrowed her eyes. Nathaniel opened his mouth, and I stepped in front of her. "If you ever order her to lie to me again, I'll kill you."

"Evie."

Our eyes met and held. "Tell me you can't hear the truth in my voice."

His eyes hardened. "That's where we're at?"

"Oh yeah. That's where we're at. We have this under control. You can leave now."

Kyla cleared her throat delicately. "Under control *miiiight* be a slight exaggeration."

I scowled over my shoulder at her, and she lifted one eyebrow. "We can't use your magic without facing all kinds of deadly creatures, and you've already nearly died once."

"A cut to my thigh does not equal almost dying."

A strong hand took my elbow. I attempted to shake Nathaniel off, but he wasn't having it. "Let me see where you're hurt."

"I'm not hurt."

"Show me, sweetheart."

"Don't call me that. We fixed it. Aubrey gave us pixie dust."

He examined my face, as if attempting to determine whether I was lying. Finally, he nodded and let me go. I refused to acknowledge how much my body craved the feel of his hands on me.

"We need to talk."

"We don't have time for a powwow, Alpha."

"Keep pushing me, Evie. See what happens."

If I could've used my power, I would've given him a display he never would've forgotten. Instead, I had to settle for giving him my best death glare.

A solitary curl chose that moment to escape my messy bun and bounce off my cheek. Nathaniel's lips twitched.

I would not dignify his amusement with a response. I stuck my nose in the air and turned away.

"Mature."

"I don't need your commentary right now. If you're going to hang around, why don't you put your muscles to good use and move those rocks?" I waved a hand toward the boulders blocking the door.

A muscle jumped in Nathaniel's jaw, but he seemed to realize I wasn't ready to talk about how badly he'd hurt me. What he didn't realize was that I wasn't ever going to be ready. He stalked past Kyla, who gave him a dark look of her own.

"What did you expect?" she muttered.

He ignored that, which was a good choice on his part. I definitely did not pay any attention to the way his T-shirt stretched over his back muscles as he leaned down to grab the boulder. My mouth also did not go dry as I surveyed his biceps when he lifted said boulder and carried it out of the way as if it were a feather pillow.

Kyla gave me a knowing look, and I narrowed my eyes at her. With a grin, she stepped away to help Nathaniel.

I knew my limits. If I'd had access to my power, I could've helped. Instead, I pulled out the map, studying it while they cleared the way.

"Done," Nathaniel said a few minutes later. His T-shirt was damp with sweat, and it clung to his spectacular chest.

Asshole.

"We need to decide our next move," I said, returning my attention to the map. "There are three spots the sword is most likely to be. The safe, which seems too obvious to me." I frowned. "Unless that's exactly what Taraghlan *wants* people to think..."

"Where else?" Nathaniel asked.

I hated that I had to work with him right now. All I wanted was to be alone so I could lick my wounds in private.

"Evie?"

Why did his voice have to be so gentle?

I swallowed. "Half of this place is a dungeon. Taraghlan is keeping his enemies here. There's a possibility he's hidden the sword in that part of the castle. The other option is the armory. Maybe Taraghlan is hiding the sword with his other weapons."

Kyla leaned over my shoulder and studied the map. "We need to split up."

"No."

"Absolutely not."

For the first time since Nathaniel had torn out my heart, we were on the same page.

"Think about it, you guys. The three best options for the sword are in different directions. We need to get gone before Taraghlan figures out we're here. We don't have time to be precious."

She had a point.

"I'm heading for the safe," Kyla said. "You go to the dungeon, and Nathaniel can—"

"I'm not leaving Evie."

Kyla's eyes met Nathaniel's, and her gaze dropped. I curled my lip at him. "We don't have time for this."

Nathaniel merely looked at me. "If you'd allowed me to talk to you when you learned I was your mate, I would have explained just how much control my wolf takes when it thinks you're in danger."

I most definitely didn't want to hear about that.

"Fine. Kyla, you head for the safe. We'll head for the dungeon. If neither of us finds the sword, we'll all circle around to the armory and meet there."

Kyla pulled out her own map so she could memorize her route. She'd head left after this door when the corridor split. Nathaniel and I would head right. If none of us found the sword, we'd meet at the armory, which was north of where we were standing.

Kyla studied the map while I dug into the backpack and pulled out the two pieces of lapis lazuli I'd brought, fixing a spell to them.

"If you find the sword, throw this into the air," I told Kyla. "It will alert us, and we'll make our way to you. If you see it light up, it means we've found the sword. Follow it until it leads you to us. It'll darken if you're going in the wrong direction."

She nodded and took the stone. I still wasn't happy about us splitting up, and from the frown on his face, neither was Nathaniel. But even he could see the wisdom of getting this done and getting the hell out of here.

"Be careful," I told her.

"You too." She flicked her gaze to Nathaniel, and I shook my head. No, I wouldn't be letting him back beneath my defenses.

We all tensed as I opened the door. When nothing jumped out at us, Kyla prowled to the left. I moved to the right. Nathaniel fell into step beside me, and I ignored him. Being left alone with him was going to be hell.

When I'd kissed him, when I'd slept beside him,

when I'd let my guard down around him…I'd thought I'd seen beneath the Alpha wolf. Thought I'd seen the man beneath.

The worst part? My traitorous body refused to get with the program. It held an awareness of what it felt like when he took my mouth as if it were made for him. It knew exactly how good it felt when he wrapped me in his arms and stroked my hair.

"Talk to me, Evie."

"No."

Another door waited at the end of this corridor. According to the map, there were three chambers we would need to get through in order to get to the dungeons—each separated by a corridor. I stalked toward the door, wishing more than anything that we could just get this whole thing over with.

"Why not?" Nathaniel growled.

"Because I trusted you. And you took that trust and smeared shit all over it."

The bastard sighed. *Sighed.* As if *I* was being unreasonable.

"I was right. You would've run."

"You don't know that. And by encouraging everyone to lie to me, you took away the chance for me to make my own decision."

He reached out to catch my arm, but I was already pushing through the door.

I froze, my instincts on high alert.

The chamber was empty. But I didn't buy it for

a second. Next to me, Nathaniel went still, lifting his face to sniff at the air.

"Anything?"

"No."

A silver door beckoned from the other side of the chamber. I scanned the chamber again, my instincts telling me something was off. "I think we should haul ass."

"Agreed," Nathaniel said.

Look at us, working together like professionals.

I sucked in a breath and shot toward the door.

"Evie!"

Something whistled past my head. I dropped to a crouch and whipped my head to the right. A three-foot-long crossbow bolt was buried in the wall.

I flattened my body as the next bolt almost struck me in the head. And then Nathaniel was there, pulling me to my feet.

The wall on our left had slid open, revealing hundreds of steel bolts, all poised to shoot.

"They fire with movement," Nathaniel ground out, keeping his body between mine and the metal bolts.

"I'll use a ward."

"You know we can't risk it. You're too powerful." Pride flickered in his eyes when he said it, and I tried to ignore the warmth that slid through my chest.

Surveying the bolts, I slowly sucked in a breath. "We'll have to zigzag."

"There are too many of them." Nathaniel's eyes were filled with steady resolve. "We go together. You stay to my right."

He wanted me to use him as a human shield.

"No."

The magic responsible for the bolts obviously decided we'd been in our spot for too long. Another bolt shot at us, breathtakingly fast.

I ducked. Nathaniel waited until it was within a foot of him and stepped neatly to the side. I had a feeling he was doing some complicated calculation regarding speed and velocity in his head.

"Listen to me, Evie," he said. "I need you to do what I say."

"Not if it means you get skewered!"

"We don't have a healer here. You get hit, and you're dead."

Panic made my voice sharp. "You're not disposable."

He gave me a grin. "Werewolf, sweetheart. I'll heal. You won't."

"I'll use my fucking power."

"We can't risk it."

Another bolt flew past, close enough that I could feel the wind of it on my face as Nathaniel nudged me out of the way.

"We can't stay here," he said. "We go on three."

His eyes were all wolf. There was no point arguing with him. All I could do was move my ass and hope the reflexes Edward had sharpened would keep us both alive.

I was so angry with him, but the thought of him dying here, in this fucking castle...

"It will be okay," he assured me, reaching for my hand. He squeezed. "One, two, three."

We launched forward. Bolts immediately whistled toward us. Nathaniel's wolf reflexes were a hundred times better than mine, and I let him push me to and fro, slamming me to the floor when a bolt came too close.

We were within three feet of the door when the bolts came even faster. There was no real way to avoid them.

Nathaniel shoved me away from him, pushing me toward the door.

And a bolt impaled his chest.

EVIE

I screamed. A deep, guttural sound that came from a part of me I hadn't wanted to accept. "No, no, no, no."

I flattened myself as another bolt whistled past. Nathaniel's expression was blank—a clear sign the Alpha was in immense pain.

He still managed to glower at me. "Go."

"Not without you, jackass."

I raised my hand, ready to lay waste to the bolts. Nathaniel shook his head. "No. We're almost there."

Getting to my feet, I darted to the left as another bolt disturbed the air between us.

Blood poured from Nathaniel's chest. I had no idea how he was still walking, but he put himself back between me and the bolts.

I choked out a sob.

"It's going to be okay," he soothed me.

I scowled in his direction. He had a bolt sticking out of his chest, and he was attempting to make *me* feel better?

We had to get out of here. Nathaniel wasn't playing—he wouldn't let me get hurt. He'd continue to put himself between those bolts and me until he was dead.

Without warning, I shot toward the door. I hadn't done any calculations, but I had reasonably good instincts. I paused, lunged forward, took a step backward, and zigzagged. Nathaniel followed me, a rough growl leaving his throat.

I hit the door and pushed it open, reaching for Nathaniel. He made it into the corridor and dropped to his knees.

"Need to remove it," he said.

"Okay. Don't worry, we still have some pixie dust."

"No. For you."

Ignoring that, I examined the bolt. "The end is fucking barbed. Oh God, I'm going to have to pull it all the way through."

My hands were fluttering in front of his chest. He caught them both in his, waiting until I met his gaze.

"I'll break off the front. You pull it from the back. I can't reach."

My throat was so thick I couldn't swallow, but I managed a nod. Nathaniel drew in a deep breath, grabbed the front of the bolt, and snapped the metal in two.

Werewolf strength.

The groan that left his throat made the tears I'd been suppressing flood down my cheeks. I moved around to his back and studied what was left of the steel pole.

"You can do this," Nathaniel said softly.

I knew I could do it, but I was unprepared to hurt him this badly. It had to be done so he could heal, but the thought of causing him this much pain made me want to vomit.

"Brace yourself against the wall," I said, and my voice sounded like it was far away.

Nathaniel raised his hands, pressing them against the wall.

"On three," I said. I grasped the pole in both hands. Just that tiny movement made Nathaniel stiffen, fresh blood dripping down his back. The edges of my vision darkened, and I blinked a few times until I'd gotten a hold of myself.

If this didn't work, I was using my power, and fuck the consequences. I wasn't going to torture Nathaniel needlessly.

"Think about how angry you are with me," he gasped out. "Maybe that'll help."

"Not funny. One. Two." I grabbed the pole and hauled with all my might.

The pole slid out, and Nathaniel collapsed to the floor.

"Fuck, fuck, fuck," I chanted. I dragged the

backpack off my shoulders and rummaged until I found the pixie dust.

Nathaniel was in no state to argue as I ripped his shirt open over his head. I had to get the dust deep into the wound, or it would only be healing his skin and the outer edges of the wound instead of the *hole* in his chest.

I raised my head. Nathaniel's wolf stared at me. "I need you to let him pass out."

"We will not leave you alone," the wolf said. This was the first time I'd had an actual conversation with his wolf. I'd deal with how weird it was later.

"I can't do this to you unless you're unconscious. Please. Just for a little bit."

"No. Do it, mate, so we can heal."

"Please," I begged. "Please don't make me hurt you like this."

His wolf just closed his eyes. I knew he wasn't unconscious. I clenched my teeth. "You're just as stubborn as Nathaniel."

His lips twitched.

Hesitating would only draw this out longer. At least wolves didn't need to worry about infection. I pulled the knife from my ankle sheath and pressed it into Nathaniel's wound, widening it enough that I could pour the pixie dust right into the worst of it.

The bolt had gone through a lung. How the fuck had he stayed standing?

"I leaned on our pack," he said, doing that weird

anticipatory mind-reading thing he sometimes did. Our eyes met, and Nathaniel was back in charge. "Speeds healing."

Ignoring the *our pack* part, I returned my attention to the wound and began slowly pouring the pixie dust into it. I knew just how badly this hurt, but Nathaniel didn't make a sound. Each time I looked at his face, his eyes were on me, a strange kind of tenderness in them.

"Why won't your wolf make you pass out?"

"My wolf adores you. He'd do anything you asked. But he will never leave you alone and in danger."

I didn't know what to say to that, so I just kept working on his wound. Nathaniel shifted, clearly in pain, then forced himself to be still once more. "I would be shot by those bolts a thousand times if that's what it took for you to talk to me," he said softly. "To feel your hands on me."

"I'm torturing you," I snapped. "This isn't *romantic.*"

He gave me a faint smile. "I'm sorry, you know."

I poured more pixie dust, my head spinning with relief as his healing accelerated. I could no longer see parts of his lung.

"Are you?" I attempted to keep my voice cold, disinterested, but it cracked. I swallowed around the lump in my throat, but the burning behind my eyes told me if we continued this conversation, I'd turn into a blubbering mess.

Because it wasn't just rage I felt. The rage was

easiest to lean into. But beneath all the fury and frustration, all I felt was betrayal and *hurt*.

And yet the sight of him in pain... Knowing he'd hurt himself so badly to keep me safe... It *killed* me. Deep inside, I knew it wasn't just because I was his mate either. It wasn't just his wolf that needed to protect me. It was Nathaniel.

My eyes filled. Nathaniel grabbed my arm, stilling my hand, which had been trickling the dust.

"Enough."

I lifted my gaze. He cursed, raising his other hand to my cheek. I flinched. He hesitated, but he kept his hand where it was. "I'm sorry for lying to you, Evie."

I sniffled. "You'd still do the same thing again."

"Yes. But I'm sorry I hurt you."

I pulled at my hand, but Nathaniel clearly had no plans to let it go.

"My only excuse is that I've been tied in knots since the moment we met. I'd never expected my wolf to choose a mate before I could. But the moment I saw you, the moment I heard your laugh, the moment I watched you wield that smart mouth...all I felt was relief. Because sometimes the man disagrees with the wolf, and all I could think was that I would have chosen you a thousand times without hesitation."

I sucked in a shaky breath. "We didn't...hang out after we met. We met months and months ago, and it was only when the kids started disappearing that you contacted me."

His gaze was frank, open, and…tender. "Because I don't deserve you. I've killed innocents, Evie. I've made decisions that hurt the few to protect the many. My hands are stained with blood, and I'd do it all again to keep my pack safe. You're sunshine, and I'm the shadows, and I have no business being anywhere near you. That was one of the reasons I made your sister swear not to tell you. I knew you were my mate, and I knew you'd disappear if you found out. You'd been through so much, and all my wolf wanted was to protect you. To know where you were and to keep an eye on you, even if it was from a distance."

"So, when you told Danica not to tell me, it was because you never thought you'd act on the mating?"

He nodded. "With the kids…I knew you'd figure out what they were up to. But the moment you were in my territory, I felt as if the missing piece of my soul had slid into place."

"You didn't think you were worthy of me?" I stared at him. That was ridiculous.

"I'm not. But the more time I spent with you, the more I needed you. You made me feel like more than just the werewolf Alpha for the first time in years. You made me feel like a man. A man who could maybe even have love."

My heart stuttered, and he gave me a sweet grin. "Only love could make me act like a complete idiot."

His hand was so warm on my face. I glanced at his wound to find it mostly healed—the pixie dust and wolf healing it together.

"Never lie to me again, Nathaniel. I can take it from anyone but you."

He sat up. I attempted to push him back down, but it was like pushing against one of the boulders that had blocked our way. "Never, Evie. I swear to you, I will never lie to you again. No matter what."

My eyes flooded. He pressed a gentle kiss to my cheek, and then *I* was the one lying down, and he was poised over me, his gaze hot.

"What the hell are you doing? You're still hurt, you idiot."

He laughed. "There's that smart mouth." He played with one of my curls. "You were worried about me."

"Well, yeah."

"Because you feel it too."

I sighed, reached my hand up, and ran it through his hair. "Yeah. I feel it too."

It would be easier if I didn't. I'd certainly never planned to feel like this, especially when it came to the werewolf Alpha. But he'd burrowed his way into my heart.

He lowered his head, giving me plenty of time to push him away.

I didn't.

His mouth was firm and warm against mine, coaxing me into kissing him back. I wrapped my arms around the back of his neck, and he groaned.

I froze, jerking my head away.

He slipped his hand around the back of my head and held me steady. It obviously hadn't been a groan of pain, because Nathaniel plundered my mouth, his tongue stroking mine, claiming me.

Our kiss was a mutual apology, a healing, and the beginning of something new, all at once.

"Be mine, Evie. I'll be yours too. And I promise, I'll be the best mate you could have ever hoped for." His voice was gruff, hoarse, and I didn't hesitate.

Truthfully, part of me had known the moment I'd seen him down here, ready to protect both Kyla and me.

I'd known he would come. Because I knew, no matter what, no matter how angry we were with each other, for the rest of our lives, he would come for me. And I'd do the same for him.

"I'm still going to need more independence than most werewolf mates," I managed to get out. A large part of me wanted to agree to anything he asked, just so he'd keep looking at me that way. But it was important to set the ground rules.

He tucked a curl behind my ear. "I can't promise to always be reasonable when it comes to keeping you safe, but I promise I'll try. I'll learn. I'll do whatever it takes to make sure you're happy."

I sighed, handing him back his shirt. So much for staying strong. I was weak when it came to this man.

"This has to be a partnership, Nathaniel. We work together. No more secrets."

He'd already promised, but I had to be sure.

"A partnership…" He smiled. "We'll be a team of two. You'll see, Evie."

I held out my hand. "Partners."

He took it, squeezing gently. "Partners."

NATHANIEL

My wolf was more content than he'd ever been before.

I'd allowed him to come to the surface as my wound took the majority of my attention. He'd been determined that we would stay conscious, that we'd guard Evie no matter what.

As much as we tended to disagree, we would always be in agreement when it came to her safety.

My wound burned as it knit together. Evie still looked tormented each time she looked at it, which made me want to shake my head at her.

Didn't she know I'd take a hundred of those bolts for her and still count myself lucky that I'd been the one to keep her safe?

"Okay." Evie shoved the remainder of the pixie dust into her bag. "We're packed, you're no longer bleeding like a stuck pig, and we only have one more of the seelie king's chambers of hell left before we'll hit the dungeons." She chewed on her lower lip. "I wish we hadn't separated. I'm worried about Kyla."

"I would know if she was hurt."

"One day you'll have to tell me how that works."

I'd tell her anything she wanted.

Evie smiled up at me, and I held out my hand once more. Something warm unfurled in my chest when she took it. Her other hand was tucked down by her side, her knife held loosely, ready.

I'd seen how badly she'd wanted to use her powers in that chamber. The fact that she'd trusted me, had allowed me to protect her, made my chest puff out with pride.

We got to our feet, and I ignored the pain as my wound continued to burn. Evie gave me a look that told me she knew exactly what I was doing. But she let it go.

"We should probably talk about Albert," she said, her mouth turning down.

My mood darkened. Hearing the mage's name made my mind return to the look on Evie's face when she told me how he'd been undermining us.

"He's done damage, hasn't he? With his little scheme. Paying a reporter to target you while simultaneously attempting to provoke a war was low, even for him."

I merely smiled, and Evie's eyes widened. "Why do you look so..." Her mouth fell open. "You didn't."

"Oh yes, I did."

"You killed him?"

"He should have died months ago."

She looked adorable with her mouth hanging open like that.

"The power vacuum…"

"He tried to have you murdered. He threatened our pack." I studied her face. "Are you…upset?"

"No. I mean, kinda. To be honest, I wanted to kill him myself. So did Danica. In fact, I'm sure there's a long list of people who want him dead." Her face creased in thought. "That could help us for sure. The humans and the mages may not know you were responsible for a while."

I shook my head. "They'll know."

She grimaced, likely picturing the kind of death Albert had suffered at my claws.

We turned and walked toward the door at the end of the long corridor. My nose told me no one was waiting to jump out at us from the walls, but I still stayed alert.

"I have another question." From the side-eye she gave me, she didn't think I'd want to hear it.

"Ask it."

"Did…did Liam know I was your mate?"

"No."

"Does he know now?"

I shrugged, my wolf not happy that Evie was even thinking of the other man.

"He wasn't right for you. Even if you hadn't been mine."

She gave me a look that told me she was searching for patience. "I *know* that. But I don't want to hurt him either. We were friends before this."

My wolf insisted she didn't need to be friends with him. I pushed the thought away. While I'd always known what my wolf thought, its ideas about the world, about *Evie,* had never been this clear before.

Tomorrow was the full moon. My control was… thin.

"Wolves understand the mating urge, even if they haven't experienced it themselves. Liam will be sad," I said. "Usually, the pack Alpha would step in to help him through it. Since I'm the one you're mated to, Hunter will check on him and ensure he is okay."

"I'm staying friends with him," she insisted.

I kept my face expressionless. "I would never suggest you didn't."

She gave me a look that told me she knew I was full of shit.

We reached the end of the corridor and the silver door waiting for us. I picked up Evie's hand once more, pressing a kiss to it, before shifting my body in front of hers. "Are you ready?"

"Let's get this done."

6

EVIE

Nathaniel grinned at me as he shoved his body in front of mine, ready to open the door. That grin was so disarming, I almost tripped. I wanted nothing more than to jump into his arms, to press kisses down his throat, to let him bend me over and—

Nathaniel groaned. "Whatever you're thinking... stop. You're killing me."

"Before you open that door, show me your chest," I demanded.

"Evie."

"Partnership. Remember?"

I knew full well he was humoring me, but he allowed me to take a look. It was almost miraculous, really, considering he'd had a hole all the way through his body. Right now, the wound was still nasty, leaking blood, but at this rate, it would be completely closed within the next half hour.

I'd wanted to bandage him, but he'd flat-out refused, insisting we didn't have enough time. I knew the truth. He was saving our medical supplies in case Kyla or I needed them.

He couldn't help himself.

Part of being mated to an Alpha wolf was going to be picking my battles. My stomach fluttered at the thought. I was really doing this.

It turned out, giving up a slice of my independence was worth it if it meant I got Nathaniel in return. I had no doubt our mating would be full of fireworks as we learned what both of us would and would not accept, but...

I was looking forward to it.

"Okay. Let's go."

Nathaniel opened the door and stepped into the chamber. I did the same. His hand swung out and landed against my chest, stopping me from moving any closer. I opened my mouth, but he'd frozen in that eerie way the wolves sometimes had, his head angled in a manner that was all predator.

I followed his gaze.

Well, this wasn't ideal.

"What. Is. That?" Nathaniel ground out.

I gaped. "Something that I thought only existed in myth. I shouldn't be surprised that Taraghlan has a fucking Chimera in his castle."

We both stared at the creature, as if the longer we

stared like idiots, the greater the chance it would fade out of existence.

It didn't.

The Chimera lay on its side, its lion head snoozing, while its goat head eyed us with a malicious expression I never would've imagined a goat could make. Its tail was the body of a snake. A snake wider than my thigh, with its own head watching us. Its tongue darted out, tasting the air, and I shivered. Snakes had always creeped me out.

"I'll take the lion," Nathaniel said grimly. I didn't bother arguing. From the considering look he was giving me, I had a feeling it was taking everything in him not to tie me up and leave me in this corridor while he dealt with all the parts of the Chimera.

I stepped toward the Chimera, and Nathaniel slid his body in front of mine. "Wait," he said. "We need a plan."

"I have a plan. I'm going to stab at it with my knife. If that doesn't work, I'll shoot it."

His mouth twitched, but he managed to flatten it, sending me a stern look. "Now that I have my mate, I'm not going to lose her."

Half of me wanted to call him out on that *my mate* stuff. The other half wanted to jump him. Ugh.

From his slow smile, that's what he'd been going for.

I ordered my hormones to settle down. "We, uh, need to watch out for the snake head. It'll be vicious and fast."

"Okay. You circle around behind it and distract the goat head. I'll take the lion and then help you with the snake if it's still alive. Ready?"

All this talking was just making me antsy.

"I've *been* ready."

Nathaniel dragged me to him, and his lips crashed down on mine. "Stay alive."

Letting me go, he turned and stalked toward the Chimera. I followed him.

The lion head opened its eyes as we approached, each of us from opposite sides. The goat's eyes flashed red, and it bared its teeth at me in a distinctly un-goat-like way. Nerves fluttered in my belly. There was something about it that freaked me out.

I wasn't sure exactly why I was practically tiptoeing toward the Chimera. It knew I was there. I pulled my A-F and slid closer.

The tail lashed out.

"Evie!"

I ducked and rolled. The snake part of the Chimera was blazingly fast. It immediately swung back around and hurtled toward me again.

No wonder the goat didn't seem worried about me. The snake could keep me at bay for as long as the lion head needed to take care of Nathaniel.

I risked a glance in his direction. He'd obviously realized he'd need his wolf form, because he'd stripped off his clothes. The lion head lunged at him, and he shifted in midair as he leaped aside, his claws slicing down its head.

One of the heads had to control the snake tail. If we killed that head, it'd be easier to take out the other one. Unfortunately, I had a pretty good feeling the goat head was the one that was really in charge here.

I watched as the snake cut across the stone floor. It had limited reach, thanks to the way the lion head was currently attempting to take a bite of Nathaniel. Unless the lion head cooperated, the snake could only sweep back and forth along the floor in front of me. And if I got close enough, I'd be able to avoid it and kill the goat.

This would be a hell of a lot easier if I could use my power.

Fucking Taraghlan.

I took a few steps closer. The snake sliced through the air, and I ducked and rolled again, sliding in close to the goat head. I buried my A-F in its gut, and the goat snapped at me. The snake hissed and swung my way.

Nathaniel roared a warning.

"I've got it."

I lunged backward, and the snake lashed at me. Rolling to the right, I launched myself to my feet.

I sliced my A-F through the snake, and I fell, off-balance. The snake head fell on top of me.

I didn't flap my hands and shriek "Ew! Get it off! Get it off!" but it was close.

Both the goat and the lion heads howled as blood sprayed.

Without the snake, I could get closer to the goat. I sent a quick glance at Nathaniel in time to see him rip out the lion's throat.

The goat snarled at me, more canine than goat. But with the lion dying next to it, it couldn't do much as I shoved my A-F into its eye and twisted.

I stepped away and surveyed the Chimera. "Two out of three," I preened. "Does that make me the heavy hitter in this relationship?"

Nathaniel wandered over to me, his wolf's head almost level with my chest. He licked my cheek, chuffing as I squirmed away.

"Gross!"

He was suddenly a man, and he grinned at me. My face flamed as I took in his naked form.

My eyes dropped to his bare chest. The werewolf Alpha was all hard muscle, with not an ounce of extra fat anywhere. I'd seen him training with his wolves, and I knew he didn't do it so he looked good.

That was a side benefit.

My gaze continued down his chest to his abs. I wanted to trace each bump with my tongue. Then I'd linger on that V that pointed directly to his—

He groaned.

Our eyes met and held.

His smile was slow, hot, wicked. "Your eyes have gone a little…glazed," Nathaniel purred, taking a step toward me.

"We don't have time," I whispered. Or whimpered. Whatever.

"We don't. But I've been making a list of all the things I'm going to do to you when I finally get you alone and no one's trying to kill us."

He stepped closer, and it took everything in me not to let my gaze drift back down.

"God, the way you look at me," he said, and his eyes were suddenly all wolf.

My cheeks heated, and he grinned. Then he turned and strolled back toward his clothes. And I got my first look at his ass.

I sucked in a choked breath. Nathaniel glanced over his shoulder and winked at me. I forced myself to look away, fanning my face.

"The, uh, dungeons are just through that door," I managed to get out.

"Good," Nathaniel purred in my ear.

I jumped. I hadn't heard him coming up behind me. He nipped playfully at my neck, and my thighs clenched.

We could be walking into anything. And yet, my hormones were so fired up, all I could think about was the way his hands had felt on me when we were in his bed. The way he'd expertly played with my body, his mouth driving me to—

"Evie?"

"Nothing. I wasn't thinking about anything."

"Uh-huh." He gave me a pleased smile. I sighed, picked up my bag, and wiped the blade of my knife along my jeans. They were ruined anyway.

"According to Tilella, there will be guards in this part of the dungeon. We need to take them out quickly, before they warn anyone else that we're here."

"How many guards?"

"They work on a rotation. Every twenty minutes or so, a few of them do the rounds. But Tilella said there aren't currently many prisoners, so it's not as well guarded as it usually is. The guards are well trained, though, and I'll have no choice but to use my magic if they spot us and try to take us down. We should probably use the ring."

I didn't mention the book. It was stuffed in my backpack and much more unwieldy than the ring.

"Okay," Nathaniel said.

I popped the ring into my mouth and reached for him. The moment I touched his hand, he turned invisible as well.

Nathaniel pushed open the door with his free hand, and I clutched my knife in mine. Another corridor stretched out in front of us, only this one boasted hundreds of cells on either side. It was dank and dark, the air hanging heavy with the stench of mildew, rot, and decay.

Our footsteps echoed on the stone floor. There was just enough room for Nathaniel and me to walk side by side, and I peered into the empty cells as we passed them.

"Where could the sword be?" I whispered around the ring in my mouth.

I felt Nathaniel shrug. "The guards could have it, wherever they're stationed."

"Is it just me, or—given what we know about the seelie king—shouldn't these cells have prisoners in them?"

"They should. I doubt Taraghlan has suddenly turned over a new leaf and decided to show mercy."

The fact that Nathaniel understood my garbled mess of words was impressive.

My steps sounded loud on the stone floors. "So, where the hell are they?"

We continued walking until we approached the end of the corridor. I was officially creeped out.

I caught movement out of the corner of my eye and jumped backward, pulling my knife. Nathaniel thrust me behind him, and we both stared at the lone prisoner.

Even half-starved and covered in filth, the seelie woman was beautiful.

I spat the ring into my palm, and she didn't even jump. She stared back at us, but her eyes were glazed, as if she wasn't really here.

I couldn't blame her.

Crouching in front of her cage, I waited until her eyes lowered to once again meet mine.

"What's your name?"

She licked her lips, and I pulled a bottle of water from our bag, sliding it through the bars.

Her eyes lit up, and she grabbed for it.

"Be careful," Nathaniel said. "Drink slowly."

She obeyed him, taking small sips. The way she relished the water made me want to kill Taraghlan even more desperately.

"My name is Hellaphine."

"I'm Evie, and this is Nathaniel."

She shot Nathaniel a wary look. I couldn't blame her. That muscle was ticking in his jaw, and his arm muscles bulged as he gripped the bars to her cage.

"He won't hurt you. His wolf is upset to see you treated like this. He wants to protect you."

Surprise flashed through her eyes, and she got to her knees, placing the water bottle next to her.

"How did you end up here?" I asked.

Hellaphine pushed her long, tangled blond hair over one shoulder. "I was part of the rebellion. His Majesty's spies caught me distributing information about his betrayal of our allies, and I was immediately arrested." Her lower lip trembled, and she bit down on it. "I'll be moved soon."

"Moved where?"

"I don't know exactly. But I'm the last one left. There were others here, and they were taken, one by one. The guard said I'll be tortured, experimented on."

My body went hot and cold all at once. "Experimented on?"

She twisted her mouth. "The king has an *arrangement* with humans. Anyone who annoys him is sent to their laboratory. It's a fate no one wants to risk, and it's how he keeps his advisers in line. I'll be going to the main lab, apparently. Because I'm powerful enough." Desolation was written all over her face.

My breath caught in my throat.

Holy shit.

I turned my head, meeting Nathaniel's eyes. His expression was grim, but he nodded. The seelie king was working with Humans for Equality. Handing over his own people to be experimented on.

"What does he get out of it?" I asked.

Hellaphine shrugged, reaching for her bottle of water again. She took small sips, as if to savor it, and I handed her another one. The gratitude in her eyes made my throat burn.

"I don't know. He gets to make his enemies suffer."

"There will be something else in it for him. He could have you tortured by his own guards," I mused aloud. Hellaphine flinched, and I winced.

"Sorry. We're currently looking for the labs. We're going to shut them down."

Tears rolled down her cheeks. "My sister. She was taken to them. Months ago. I didn't know she'd been sent away until one of the guards told me. Please, find her."

My gut twisted. I had a sister of my own, no matter how pissed I currently was at her. And the thought of her being taken away and experimented on while I was stuck in this dungeon…

Nathaniel placed his hand on the back of my neck and squeezed lightly, bringing me back to the present. I took a deep breath and examined the bars. "We're getting you out of here."

Hellaphine's eyes widened. She shook her head. "No."

"No?" My voice was incredulous. From the way Nathaniel's hand had tensed where it rested against the back of my neck, he didn't understand either.

"I know you're planning to stop these humans, but I can't risk my sister. I have to find her. If they take me to her, at least we'll be together."

"You can't help her if you're caught."

"I can. You'll find us both." More tears dripped down her face. Her eyes were no longer dazed and lost. No, they were filled with a dark determination. "You have to understand. She went to the main lab too—she's more powerful than me. She's my baby sister. It's my job to protect her."

The backs of my eyes burned.

I had a big sister. And I knew, deep in my bones, that Danica would make the same choice. Goddamn it.

Nathaniel's voice was a low caress as he leaned over my shoulder to murmur in my ear. "What if we can track Hellaphine? She could lead us straight to the lab."

Hellaphine's eyes widened. "Yes," she said

immediately. "Yes, do it."

"They could kill you as soon as you arrive," I said. "The moment we leave this realm, we can no longer help you."

"But my sister could still be alive. She's the one who matters."

"I have a big sister. I wouldn't want her to throw her life away."

She gave me a shaky smile. "But if she was taken, you'd do the exact same thing. Wouldn't you?"

Without hesitation.

Hellaphine nodded at whatever she saw on my face. "Can you do it? Can you track me?"

"I can. But if I use my power, it's going to attract something nasty. His Majesty has wards in place that detect magic and respond accordingly."

"We'll leave immediately after," Nathaniel said. "And whatever it summons will follow us."

A door clanged. I shoved the ring into my mouth and reached for Nathaniel, my heart rate tripling.

While I had gone still, in the way a rabbit was when caught by a flashlight, Nathaniel was motionless in the way of a giant predator, deciding whether he would strike.

"I'm telling you, I heard voices," one of the guards insisted.

"Probably the prisoner talking to herself. They all go crazy eventually."

Fury thundered through me, but I allowed

Nathaniel to pull me into his arms. He held me a few inches above the stone floor and slowly moved backward. I couldn't blame him for picking me up. He moved silently, like a panther, while I'd likely scuff the floor with my shoe or something. Even now, I was conscious of my every move. People made noise even when they were trying to be quiet. I wanted to sniff, itch my cheek, clear my throat, crack my knuckles…

"No one here," the second guard said with a sneer. "Like I told you."

The younger guard's eyes narrowed, and he stalked toward Hellaphine's cage.

"Who were you talking to?" he demanded.

"No one."

Compared to the woman we'd met just a few minutes ago, this was a completely different person. Funny what hope could do for a soul.

The guard cursed. Then he pulled his sword and began sweeping it through the air around him. He wasn't stupid. He was making sure no one was here.

Nathaniel tensed, took another step backward, and slowly placed me back on the floor.

Uh-oh.

The older guard rolled his eyes. But he stalked over to the cage and gave Hellaphine a look that made my blood run cold. She dropped her gaze.

"You wouldn't be hiding anything from me, would you? You know what happens to bad prisoners."

She shook, and I memorized his face.

"Tell me what you're hiding, and I'll tell the humans to go easy on you. Maybe they'll play with your liver once you're dead, and not while you're still alive."

That was it.

I raised my hand, but Nathaniel was already moving. He popped into existence and ducked beneath the guard's sword, his claws slashing out.

A thin line of red appeared, spreading across the guard's throat.

I blinked. One moment, the guard was alive, and the next, he'd dropped to his knees, clutching at his throat as his blood spurted onto the stone floors.

I took the ring out of my mouth and braced, ready to leap forward and take the older guard.

Nathaniel shot across the corridor, and the guard screamed. I glanced down.

His claws were already buried in the older guard's gut. I had a pretty good feeling one of them had just punctured the guard's liver. Above all else, Nathaniel was a protector. The full moon was tomorrow night, and he hadn't taken kindly to hearing the threats spilling from that guy's mouth.

I sighed, sheathed my knife, and walked past the guard who'd fallen, already dead. The other guard's eyes met mine, pleading for mercy.

I just shrugged. "I maybe would've helped you before I learned what a scumbag you are." I glanced at Hellaphine. "Did he hurt you?"

Her face had gone deathly white. I had a feeling we'd gone from saviors to possible threats. Well, it couldn't be helped.

She nodded, and some of the color returned to her cheeks. Her eyes sparked furiously as she stepped closer to her bars. "He hurt me many, many times," she spat, sealing the guard's death sentence.

Good for her.

"Where is the sword?" Nathaniel growled.

The guard whimpered. "I don't know what you're talking about."

Nathaniel twisted his claws. "I'm sure you know all about the golden sword. I'll give you a quick death if you tell us what we want to know."

"Armory," the guard gasped out.

Nathaniel twisted his claws again, and then he removed them, slashing across the guard's throat.

I dodged out of the way of the spray. Hellaphine looked like she might pass out.

"Sorry you had to see that," I said.

"No apologies necessary," she said softly. "Believe me."

I handed Hellaphine our last bottle of water. "Drink that, and then give us the bottles back before we go, so the other guards won't know you cooperated with us. I'll need to figure out how I'm going to do this."

Nathaniel's gaze burned into me as I turned, swinging the backpack off my shoulder. His eyes held pride. His hand was still covered in blood.

"Don't get too excited," I muttered. "This might not work."

He gave me a slow smile. "Yes, it will. I know you, and you'll do whatever it takes."

I didn't know what I'd done to give him such unshakable faith in me, but I wasn't going to argue.

Hellaphine's eyes shone as she watched Nathaniel, and something that felt a lot like jealousy wormed its way into my belly.

What the hell was wrong with me?

"Evie?" Nathaniel murmured, and I shook my head.

"Don't worry."

From the look in his eyes, he *would* worry.

I gazed at the lapis lazuli, a sudden thought occurring to me. What was this but a bastardized tracking device? I couldn't give it to Hellaphine—the guards would for sure check her for any weapons or other objects when they moved her. But I could tie the spell to the stone, ensuring it would work across realms.

It would no longer work for Kyla and me, but Nathaniel would be able to find her. Plus, if she were here, I knew she'd be telling me to stop deliberating and help Hellaphine.

"I need some of your blood," I told her.

She nodded, holding out her hand. I found a clean throwing knife and made a shallow cut in her forearm, before turning her arm over until a few drops spilled onto the stone.

My heart stumbled. This was one of those times when I had to use my power, but my imagination provided me with all kinds of repercussions—most of them involving Nathaniel dying in front of me.

He was suddenly there, his arm wrapped around my waist. "You can do this. I'll keep you safe."

"It's not me I'm worried about," I gritted out.

He pressed a kiss to my cheek. I scowled, but the feel of him pressed against me was helping me summon my courage.

I concentrated, reaching for the strand of power that would help me with this spell. It wasn't a large amount of magic—or particularly difficult—but it needed to be precise.

My power leaped forward, as if it had been waiting for this moment. I clamped down on it, only allowing the smallest tendril free.

Control.

There.

I reached for the stone and poured my power into it as I twisted the spell. When my eyes opened, the stone glowed.

I let out a shaky breath.

"The lapis lazuli will alert me when you cross into our realm, and I'll be able to track you. But it's likely that the lab has some kind of ward in place that prevents this sort of thing. They've stayed hidden for years at this point."

She took a deep breath. "I understand."

"How does it work?" Nathaniel asked.

"It'll glow like this when Hellaphine's in our realm. We can place the stone on a map, and it will show us an approximate location. It's not exact, but it'll help."

His smile was all bemused pride, and I wanted to preen. Unfortunately, there was no time for that.

"We need to go before we lure whatever is coming here," I said.

Hellaphine's eyes filled. "Thank you."

"Don't thank me until we find you."

"You've given me the first glimpse of hope I've had since my sister was arrested."

"What's your sister's name?"

"Kostana."

I gave Hellaphine what I hoped was a confident nod. She smiled back at us.

We continued walking down the corridor, and my chest clenched at the sight of so many empty cells. The seelie king was handing over his own people to be experimented on and killed. *This* was how he was keeping them in line. All a dictator needed to do was present someone with a fate worse than death, and suddenly, that spark of insurrection was extinguished by a flood of self-preservation.

Picking up our pace, we pushed through the next door. I could practically feel the king's wards targeting us for our use of magic. It was only a matter of—

The floor beneath us was turning to liquid.

"Fuck."

I glanced at Nathaniel. His eyes were wild as he reached for me.

But it was too late.

The floor was too fast. I threw the lapis lazuli to him.

He caught it automatically, his body still in the air as he flew toward me.

He slammed into my ward. His roar shook the walls.

The floor sucked me down.

NATHANIEL

y roars echoed throughout the chamber. As soon as Evie fell through the floor, her ward disappeared.

And so did her scent.

I'd turned before I realized my wolf was in charge. It was currently clawing at the floor, attempting to dig through the stone to find our mate.

Enough.

My wolf ignored me. He had decided I had no business telling him what to do after the way I'd failed to protect our mate.

If you dig through the stone, you risk the foundation collapsing and hurting our mate.

A mournful howl sounded from deep within me. I allowed it free rein and then ruthlessly cut it off. With my wolf so close to the surface, I could feel Kyla making her way toward us, which meant she still hadn't found the sword.

My hand tightened around the lapis lazuli, and I barely prevented myself from crushing it. This was why Evie had thrown up that ward. Because if she didn't make it, she wanted me to protect this stone and take down the labs.

She still didn't understand.

It was taking everything in me not to turn the stone to dust. If Evie died, I wouldn't give a fuck about the labs, the seelie king, or the sword. My wolf would rampage through this world until someone managed to put me down.

We'd thought this was the lowest level of the castle. But we'd been wrong. That meant that unless Evie was buried alive—and I'd *know* if that was happening—she was currently directly below me.

Stairs. I had to find stairs.

Kyla and Evie each had a copy of the map. But my wolf had memorized our mate's scent. I just needed to get down a level, and I would be able to locate her.

And I would teach her to never sacrifice herself like this again.

EVIE

I hit the floor with a thump that winded me. My bones ached, and I groaned.

I cut off the groan as knowledge seeped into me.

The knowledge that I wasn't alone.

Nathaniel would get to Kyla. The lapis lazuli would ensure they could get out of here and track Hellaphine.

Nathaniel would be livid when his wolf finished its tantrum and he realized what I'd done. But I had no regrets.

At least, I didn't until I caught sight of the creature in front of me.

I sucked in a strangled breath and hauled myself to my knees.

The Nothir slid toward me, a strange kind of malevolence gleaming in its lone eye. It had the body of a worm, with six barbed tentacles that it used as arms. One of those tentacles opened, revealing a hole of a mouth, filled with sharp teeth. A tongue slid out, tasting the air.

Nothirs were usually lurkers, hiding in caves, holes, and crevices—primarily in the Middleground. They weren't predators, but they *could* be insanely territorial. They would consume anything, using their tentacles to drag wounded creatures off to their lairs, where they would take their time...

Nope, nope, nope.

Wiggling Angelica's ring off my finger, I shoved it back into my mouth. The Nothir let out a strangled hiss as it lost sight of me. Then that tongue slid out once more. Of course, it was scenting me. And since

I was covered in blood and various other disgusting fluids, it wouldn't exactly be hard for it to figure out where I was.

I spat the ring back out. No point risking swallowing it when the Nothir could scent me anyway. This would come down to which of us wanted to survive more.

This creature had a brain the size of an apple. It was all instinct. I could kill it. I had to get back to Nathaniel.

But I was so tired. And everything hurt.

I had to finish this quickly.

The Nothir moved closer, its wormlike body slithering across the stone between us. Behind it, a flight of stairs taunted me. Kill this creature, get up those stairs, and find Nathaniel and Kyla. That was all I had to do.

Studying the Nothir, I paid careful attention to its range of motion. It could move quickly backward and forward. But when I took a large step to the side, it had to stop and turn its head in my direction so its body could follow.

Excellent.

Maybe I could finish this without having to add to my bruises. Pulling my Beretta, I aimed into the center of the Nothir.

Bang. Bang. Bang.

The shots were loud enough to make my ears ring in the small chamber. The Nothir screeched, lunging toward me, and I darted to the right, narrowing my eyes.

Plunk. Plunk. Plunk.

Three bullets hit the stone. The Nothir had pushed them back *out* of its body.

I aimed at its head this time, but—as expected—its tentacles closed over its mouth and eye, and my bullets ricocheted. I ducked. It would be fucking embarrassing if I was taken out by my own bullets.

I tucked my Beretta away and reached for my knife. The hilt of the A-F felt slippery in my clammy hand.

So much for getting this done quickly.

I raised my A-F. The Nothir moved toward me, attempting to box me in against the wall at my back. I ducked and rolled, giving myself space to move. It hesitated, turning slowly, and I studied it.

When it moved in a straight line, it was surprisingly fast. But it had trouble spinning around. I could use that.

It had almost finished turning when I moved again. It let out a screech, obviously frustrated, and one tentacle slashed out at me.

"You missed."

I wasn't sure if it understood me, or maybe it was just the sound of my voice that pissed it off. Most creatures could understand when they were being taunted, even if they didn't know the exact words being used.

The Nothir hissed, and this time, two tentacles whipped toward me.

Nathaniel would be losing his damn mind by now. I needed to get this done.

After the way the Nothir's body had repelled my bullets, I knew I needed to cut off its head. And that meant removing some of those tentacles.

Another tentacle joined the first three. The Nothir was almost facing me now. I shied away from the tentacle and swiped my A-F at it. The blade sliced cleanly through skin and sinew like it was paper, and the Nothir let out a sound that made me want to clamp my hands over my ears. Noxious yellow blood splattered me.

Slam!

I flew back, hitting the wall with a thud. Dazed, I made it to my knees.

Fuck.

I hit the floor, barely avoiding the next tentacle. The Nothir was smarter than I'd given it credit for, and those tentacles were surprisingly wily. It had used one of its back tentacles, smashing straight into the side of my face.

Now I was pissed.

"Do you know how upset my wolf is going to be over this?"

The Nothir charged toward me. I darted a step to the left, then lunged to the right, slashing out at the next tentacle.

Two down.

Circling the Nothir, I took a running start and leaped onto its back.

Its skin was smooth as marble, which did not make it easy for me to scramble up to its neck. Stabbing my A-F into its back, I used it like a handle, pulling myself up.

The Nothir bucked, but its remaining tentacles couldn't reach me. I yanked out the A-F, gagging as putrid yellow blood sprayed across my head. The Nothir slammed itself into the wall in an attempt to knock me loose, but I was already stabbing deep once more, this time right into the joint between its head and its body.

Its movements were slowing. Reaching into my ankle sheath, I pulled out my other knife and began to cut deep.

Thankfully, it didn't take long for the Nothir to collapse. Blood loss hit everyone eventually. It was unconscious by the time I cut off its head.

Sliding off its body, I catalogued my wounds. My face hurt, but I didn't feel concussed. Although it had taken me by surprise, it had been a glancing blow.

I stumbled toward the stairs, practically crawling up them.

"Nathaniel?" I called.

A distant roar.

The stairs ended at a blank wall. I stared at the wall for a long moment, heart rate tripling.

I would not panic. I would *not*.

Another roar. Nathaniel was on the other side. There had to be a way out. I refused to rot down here in this antechamber with nothing but the Nothir's body to keep me company.

Slamming my hand into the wall, I jolted as it vibrated. It shook again, and I took a deep, steadying breath. That was Nathaniel on the other side. He would rip this wall apart if he had to.

"I'm fine," I called. I couldn't hear him, but with his senses, it was likely he could hear me. "I'm going to figure this out. Just give me a second."

I studied the wall in the dim light. No door handle waiting to pop out. Running my hands over it, I ignored the frustration that wanted to take over.

Slowly, methodically, I inched my hands over the smooth wall.

There.

A hinge. Problem was, I had no idea how to open it.

The door rattled again. "I'm okay," I reassured Nathaniel.

He merely growled.

The door shuddered again before it finally slid open, and my mate was standing in front of me, looking very put out.

My chest unlocked. I could suddenly breathe again. A choked sob stuttered from my throat, and then Nathaniel was there.

His arms came around me, squeezing until I squeaked. But I was holding on to him just as tightly.

"I'm sorry," I told his wolf, who glared at me. "I had to."

His growl was terrible. I raised one hand and stroked his cheek, until his eyes darkened once more, and it was Nathaniel I was talking to. He didn't look any happier.

"Pull anything like that again," he said, his voice soft in a way that made the hair on the back of my neck stand up. "And I'll tie you up and leave you in my house while *I* search for the lab."

I pushed at his chest, but his arms were clamped around mine. I knew I'd terrified him, but I needed to nip this bullshit in the bud before it bloomed.

"Don't threaten me," I said, my voice just as soft. "It won't get you what you want."

"It's not a threat. I'm the werewolf Alpha. People of all power levels owe me a favor. If I wanted, I could keep you away from danger."

I punched him in the gut. If it hurt, he didn't let me know. His eyes had gone wolf again.

"You ever try to keep me from doing what I was born to do, and I will *leave* you. Do you understand me?"

"When I saw you sucked under, when you threw that rock at me, I thought I'd lost you too. I nearly rampaged, Evie. Something I haven't done for over seventy years."

"You'd never do that."

He bared his teeth in a sharp smile. "The moment I met you, no one else mattered."

I didn't believe that. He shook his head at me. "You truly don't understand. You're the other half of my soul. My wolf is *yours*."

If he'd continued with the threats, I would have ramped up our power struggle. But the desolation and terror in his eyes made me suck in a steadying breath. As I got a handle on my own fear and fury, his wolf seemed to calm.

"Where you go, I go," Nathaniel said. "Do you think I'd continue to live without you?"

"We haven't, um, mated," I said. "Your wolf would survive."

He shook his head at me. "My wolf has no consideration for the formalities of it all. He was yours the moment he saw you. And so was I."

I'd done him a disservice by taking his fate into my own hands. If Nathaniel had done that to me, I'd be ripping him a new one.

"What are you thinking?"

"I'm thinking I'm a hypocrite."

His eyes widened.

I huffed out a breath. "You have a point. I shouldn't have set the ward. Honestly, I could've used you down there. And I would've hated it if you'd left me like that. It's going to take me a while to get used to compromising. But I'll work on it. I promise."

Nathaniel pondered me for a long moment. Then he lowered his head and brushed his mouth over mine. "That's all I ask," he said against my lips. "I found which direction Kyla is in. Let's head for the armory, grab the sword, and get out of here."

"Sounds like a plan."

He loosened his arms long enough for me to take a step back. His eyes darkened. "You're hurt."

I raised my hand to my bruised face. My fingers slid through yellow goo, and I swallowed, barely suppressing the urge to gag. It smelled like rotten meat.

"I can't believe you hugged me," I muttered.

He just smiled. "You definitely need a shower."

"Now there's an understatement." I hauled the backpack off my back, pulled out the map, and handed it to him. I knew where my strengths lay, and I was bad at directions at the best of times. I'd fallen through the floor to a lower level, made it up these stairs, and I was assuming we were still close to the dungeons. But this castle made no sense half the time.

Nathaniel's brow creased in thought as he studied the map. The expression was so cute on him, I wanted to jump him. He slowly lifted his head and raised one eyebrow, likely scenting that interest.

Shoving my hands on to my hips, I gave him my hard stare. "Mind your business."

His lips twitched, but he returned his attention to the map. Within a few minutes, we were strolling down the next corridor, torches flickering on either side of us.

"Taraghlan sure managed to make this place creepy as hell," I muttered.

Nathaniel was silent, clearly still thinking about the ward.

I sighed. "I couldn't take the thought of you getting hurt again. You want to protect me, and I get that, but I want to protect you too."

My mind replayed the sight of him skewered with that metal bolt, and I shuddered. Nathaniel's expression softened.

"I was put on this earth to protect you," he said. "My wolf exists to keep you safe."

"That's all good and well, but if you want our mating to work—"

"Oh, it will work," he said, a hint of warning in his tone. I ignored him.

"Then you have to let me protect you, too."

He didn't like it. But he let out a sigh and pulled me close to him. I listened to the steady thump of his heart against my ear, and my eyes grew heavy.

"Well, well, well," Kyla said from behind us. I whirled, and her pointed glance took in just how close I was standing to Nathaniel. "I leave you two crazy kids alone for a couple of hours and look what happens."

I grinned at her unrepentantly. "What can I say? He convinced me."

Nathaniel just laughed, pulling my hand up to his mouth and pressing kisses along my wrist.

"You smell like a cross between shit and vomit," Kyla said. "You truly must have Nathaniel wrapped around your little finger if he's willing to put his mouth anywhere near you."

"Charming," I muttered. "I killed a Nothir."

She raised one eyebrow. "Aren't they slow as hell?"

I glowered at her. "Only when they're turning. And their tentacles are fast."

She grinned, clearly pleased to have gotten a reaction from me. "Since none of us had any luck, I'm guessing the sword is in the armory. It should be through that door," Kyla said, nodding toward the door at the end of the corridor.

We all turned and trudged toward the door. Nathaniel pushed it open.

"All I can hope is that this golden sword is *actually* gold. Because if we have to search through thousands of swords— Well, fuck."

We all stopped and stared at the hydra. Stared at its many, many heads. "Oh goodie," I said dully. "More snakes."

Kyla shrugged. "Three of us, nine heads."

"I'll take the right side," I said.

"I'm in the middle," Nathaniel said, surprising no one. Of course he'd want to be where he could intervene if either of us needed him. I gave him a look that said I knew his game, but he was already stripping off his clothes.

One of the hydra's heads slithered toward us, and

my mouth went watery. I really *hated* snakes.

Kyla sighed. "Something tells me it'll be best if I'm wolf for this. You want to try shooting the thing, Evie?"

"The last creature I shot ate my bullets and spat them back out," I muttered. But I pulled my Beretta anyway, aiming at the closest head.

The hydra moved so fast it was a blur. My bullet hit the wall behind it.

"The gun is out. We need to cut off its heads. There's a problem, though."

"What kind of problem?" Nathaniel was studying the hydra as if its existence personally offended him.

"I'm pretty sure it can regrow those heads."

Nathaniel took that information like he took everything else—in his stride. "In that case, we'll need fire. We cauterize the necks, and they can't grow back."

"I can do that, but there's a chance we'll attract another nasty creature or the castle will spring some other trap in response to my magic."

Exhaustion barreled through me at the thought. I wanted out of this fucking place.

Nathaniel wrapped his arm around my shoulders as we all surveyed the hydra. It was staying put, clearly only willing to attack us if we attempted to get past it.

"There's no other way to the armory?"

Kyla shrugged. "I think the map is out of date. There's a reason I stumbled across you guys."

I wasn't going to risk backtracking and dealing

with those fucking bolts.

"We try without magic first," Nathaniel said. "If the heads grow back, Evie can burn them. We'll deal with whatever comes next. Together."

That calm certainty radiating from him was just one of the reasons why he was such a good Alpha.

"Okay," I said, my A-F in my hand. "Let's do this."

Kyla and Nathaniel immediately began stripping off their clothes. A few moments later, they were in their wolf forms. We spread out, approaching the hydra from three sides.

"Now," Nathaniel ordered, and we lunged forward as one.

I aimed for the head that was the farthest on the right, hoping it would be difficult for the other two heads to get to me.

Slash, slash, slash.

Fuck.

I had okay reflexes, but the hydra heads were fucking fast. Each time I sliced at it, it reared back then struck at me with a hiss.

"Evie!"

I ducked as the head whistled past my own head.

"Eyes on your own page," I called to Nathaniel. He'd transformed long enough to scream at me, and now he was in a strange half form I'd never seen before, with his claws out, slashing at the hydra.

This wasn't working. They were too fucking fast.

The wolves were having more luck than I was.

They were fast, too. Kyla latched on to the closest head and tore out its throat. The other heads screamed as one, and the hair stood up on the back of my neck. And then she was slicing through the head with her claws.

We all ducked back long enough to watch.

The head regrew.

I sighed.

A bump was appearing right where the hydra's other necks met its body. Within a few moments, an extra head was hissing at us.

"And then there were ten," Nathaniel said, his expression grim.

We definitely needed my magic.

Nathaniel lunged at the hydra, dodging between two snapping heads. He buried his clawed hand into the neck of the head on his right, swinging himself up. I gaped at him. He was sitting on the hydra's back, nimbly dodging its attempts to remove him.

"I cut, you burn," he called.

Kyla began running in circles on the left, snapping out at the heads and distracting them. Nathaniel's claws were wicked fast, and I called my magic to me. He sliced through the head below him, and I reached for my fire, aiming it directly at the neck.

The hydra screeched louder this time. I held my breath, but the head didn't regrow. The second head was attempting to push through the hydra's scales, but I immediately cauterized it before it could fully form.

We were down to eight.

Now that we knew what we were doing, the other heads were much easier to manage. The hydra attempted to shake Nathaniel off again and again, but he dug in, stabbing his claws into it with brutal efficiency. Those claws were viciously sharp, and he somehow managed to take out two heads in the span of a couple of seconds.

My head spun a little as I burned the remains.

Six.

Kyla had taken out another one. I immediately aimed my flames at the empty spot on its neck.

Five to go.

Nathaniel took out another one. We were falling into an easy rhythm now.

Four.

A howl cut through the hydra's screams. I finished burning the closest head and glanced toward Kyla.

Fuck.

I was running before I knew I'd moved.

The hydra's head had clamped around her leg, teeth cutting deep. It was dragging her closer to two other heads, which were waiting to rip her apart.

Nathaniel's roar gave me goose bumps. The head that had taken Kyla down was busy dragging her, and I sliced through its neck, immediately burning what was left.

I didn't have time to burn the second head as it formed. I was too busy dragging Kyla's wolf form from the fight. She snapped her teeth at me, and I glowered down at her.

The hydra's teeth were still stuck in her leg, the head adding to Kyla's weight as I pulled her.

"Leave it," I snapped. "The moment we remove the teeth, you'll pour blood."

Kyla snarled, and I went still.

She was all wolf.

I lowered my gaze, but I didn't have time for dominance games with pissy werewolves.

"You want to live? Leave it alone." Hopefully that would get through to her wolf.

Nathaniel was growling behind me, and panic punched me in the gut.

Turning, I sprinted toward him. He'd been doing what he could to damage the remaining heads without risking another regrowing. The moment he spotted me hauling ass toward him, another head dropped to the floor.

Three.

My power poured from me, and I fought to keep the flames aimed solely at the hydra's neck. The flames felt almost alive, and I ruthlessly suppressed the urge to engulf the entire creature in my magic.

Nathaniel was still riding the hydra, currently clawing through the next head.

It screamed, a high, enraged sound as that head fell to the floor. I reached for the embers of my power.

Two.

I hadn't used enough of this power to know how to wield it in a way that wouldn't burn me out. Nathaniel's eyes met mine, and I had a pretty good feeling he knew just how little I had left.

He barely ducked beneath one of the last two heads. Without Kyla, they only had him to focus on.

I got close enough to the hydra that one of the heads lashed toward me. Nathaniel let out a growl, but the hydra had presented its head in the perfect position for him to cut through it.

I ground my teeth as I burned it.

One left.

Except Nathaniel had already taken care of that too. It flopped to the floor, and I managed to cauterize the final neck just enough that it didn't regrow.

I stared at Nathaniel over the huge body. He stared back.

Both of us sprinted toward Kyla.

8

EVIE

Kyla was one pissed-off wolf. Thankfully, Nathaniel only had to let out a soft growl, and she snarled, dropping her gaze.

"What do we do?"

Nathaniel brought his hand over the back of my neck once more, but even the feel of his comforting warmth couldn't soothe me.

"Is she all wolf?" I demanded.

"She'll be fine," he said. I must have looked doubtful, because he squeezed his hand gently until I was gazing up at him.

"She's a werewolf, and she's hurt. She's hungry and pissed off, and she doesn't appreciate being injured around any other wolves, even when one of those wolves is her Alpha."

Kyla growled. Nathaniel fixed her with a stare. She showed him her teeth.

He merely angled his head, and she dropped her gaze again.

That was pride flickering over Nathaniel's face. He was impressed by her dominance, even as his instincts demanded he shut it down.

"I'll remove the head," Nathaniel said. "You pour the pixie dust."

It made sense since I sure as hell wasn't strong enough to unlatch the hydra's grip on Kyla.

Nathaniel pried the teeth open, sliding them from Kyla's leg.

She snapped her teeth at him, lightning-fast. I couldn't blame her. That must have hurt like hell.

Nathaniel deftly wrapped his hand around her nose and jaw, clamping her mouth closed. His other hand held her down as the blood sprayed.

"There you go, darling," he soothed, leaning down so Kyla could better soak up his scent. "It's all going to be okay." He sent a glance in my direction. "Pour, Evie."

I leaned close, peering into the wounds. Thank God for the pixie dust. I sprinkled the last of it into the huge holes, watching as they slowly closed.

Kyla whined, and I glanced at her. "I know it hurts like hell. Almost done."

We all waited as her flesh knitted back together. Kyla shuddered, and Nathaniel crooned to her. Finally, Nathaniel let her go, giving me a look that told me, without words, that I needed to step back.

We gave her some room, and she lurched to her feet, teeth bared.

"Shift," Nathaniel told her, his voice hard.

I turned to grab her clothes, and by the time I returned, Kyla was standing shivering in the cool air.

That wasn't a good sign. "Don't you run hot as a werewolf?"

"She needs to eat," Nathaniel said, his expression grim. "What did you bring with you?"

I rustled around my backpack until I found some jerky, handing it to Kyla.

"That'll do," Nathaniel said. Kyla just began stuffing it into her mouth, clearly exhausted.

We were all tired, hungry, and grumpy. My power felt like a tiny spark compared to the fire that usually burned, waiting for me. And thanks to the fact that I'd just had to use that power, we had to be on the lookout for any further surprises from the castle.

"Armory is through there." Nathaniel gestured, and we all gave the hydra's body a wide berth as we stepped around it and opened the door.

This corridor was shorter than any we'd traveled down so far. Nathaniel pushed open the door at the end, and we all surveyed the armory.

One entire wall was devoted to shelves stacked with swords. They'd been placed on the shelves blade-first, and from the look of the hilts, they covered every kind of sword from American Civil

War swords to swords that looked as if they'd come straight from the Ottoman Empire.

But it wasn't just swords. One of the shelves held a collection of daggers, while one whole corner was devoted to crossbows, which had been stacked messily on top of one another.

"Wow," I said, stepping closer to inspect a Tibetan sword with an intricately carved ivory hilt. "Danica would have a total lady boner if she were here." I frowned, taking in what had to be a few thousand swords. "This is going to be like looking for a needle in a haystack."

"Yeah," Kyla said, obviously feeling better after the jerky. "Or, you know, a sword in a room full of other swords. Who keeps their weapons like this, anyway? I should clean Taraghlan out just for this alone."

"We take the sword only." I narrowed my eyes at her. "Please don't make *me* have to be the voice of reason for this little trip."

"Let's split up," Nathaniel said. "I'll take this half of the room. You two take that half. What exactly are we looking for anyway?"

"It shouldn't be all that difficult," I said, scanning the closest shelf. "It has a golden hilt, which is engraved with scenes from the first wars."

Interest sparked in Nathaniel's eyes. "Cool."

I shook my head. "You are such a guy."

His eyes darkened, and he opened his mouth.

"Nuh-uh," Kyla said. "I'm still recovering from blood loss. I don't need to vomit up that jerky too."

I wrinkled my nose. "Charming."

We sorted through the blades. While some shelves were stacked neatly enough that we could tell they held no gold at a glance, other shelves looked like something out of a rummage sale. I attempted to be methodical as I picked through them, but a low-level anxiety was burning through my gut at the thought of whatever nasty creature would be waiting for us next.

I'd had no choice but to use my power against the hydra, but...

Something itched at the edge of my mind. I went still.

"What's wrong?" Nathaniel asked, proving he was paying close attention to me even as he searched through the swords. A ball of warmth settled in my stomach.

"Nothing." I was pretty sure.

I wished I could take a picture of this place for Danica. Even as mad as I was with her, I still wanted to show her the things I found most exciting. And didn't that describe life with a sister in a nutshell.

More itching in my mind. I turned toward the knives, stilettos, and daggers, suddenly feeling as if I were sleepwalking.

"Found it." Kyla held up a sword, and I spun back to her, noting the golden hilt, engraved markings, and of course, the sheer power that seemed to radiate from it now that it had been found.

"This is definitely the golden sword," Kyla announced, as if Nathaniel and I had been struck blind in the last few moments.

Triumph thundered through me. At times, I'd doubted whether we'd be able to steal this sword. Sure, I'd been all in, but I'd still found it difficult to believe it was possible. I shouldn't celebrate just yet, though. We still needed to get it out of this castle.

"Seems too easy." Kyla slitted her eyes. "After everything we've been through, all the times we almost died, and all the creatures *we* had to kill, the sword is here—in plain sight?"

"I imagine Taraghlan was relatively certain no one would make it through his little labyrinth of terror," Nathaniel said dryly.

"Why am I not surprised overconfidence is yet another one of his flaws?" I smirked. "Either way, it's ours now, and I, for one, am glad we don't need to kill anything else for this thing."

"For now," Kyla said darkly. Our eyes met, and her mouth trembled until she was grinning, holding out her hand for a high five. We slapped palms, and Nathaniel handed her a dusty scabbard for the sword. While she slid the sword into the scabbard, I lowered my mental shields, allowing that little voice to speak to me once more.

The blade of the dagger seemed to catch the

light—just in case I'd missed its presence in my head. I picked the strange artifact up and studied it.

"And I've got Misty," I said.

It was almost comical, watching Kyla's mouth fall open.

"What the fuck is the Mistilteinn Dagger doing here? Danica gave it to the Merqueen."

"Yeah, well, they must have made some deal with the seelie. Although I'm surprised it ended up *here*." I smiled. "It can make itself appear like a normal dagger. I bet Taraghlan has no idea what it does."

Nathaniel took it from me. "What exactly does it do?"

"It's the dagger of truth. It glows red when people are lying."

He nodded and handed it back. I sighed, unsurprised by his nonchalant reaction. Nathaniel had always been an expert at determining whether people were lying. He'd once told me his wolf could pay attention to microexpressions that his human side would miss. Not to mention, his senses allowed him to pick up on things like an increased pulse rate or shallow breathing.

Nathaniel might not think this was a big deal, but I was practically doing a happy dance. Oh, the people I could interrogate with this thing.

I studied the dagger. It had once spoken in my head, turning blue when I touched it. Now, it seemed almost like a regular dagger. I couldn't feel anything from it.

"We take the sword only," Kyla mimicked me, putting on a Valley Girl accent.

"You make it hard to like you sometimes."

She just raised an eyebrow. I scowled.

"Misty doesn't count."

"Uh-huh. We need to get out of here."

I tucked Misty into my ankle sheath. I'd lost the knife I'd carried into this castle when we'd fought the hydra.

Nathaniel was studying the map. "Should we go back the way we came?"

The fact that he asked gave me the warm fuzzies. It was a little thing, but Nathaniel was used to making most of the decisions for his pack. His every order was followed. But with me, he was attempting to be a team player.

I shook my head. "That way has the bolts." I glanced at Kyla. "Did you pass a room that shot steel bolts at you?"

She gaped. "No."

Decision made. Obviously, the seelie king had put more effort into defending the route to his dungeon. After meeting one of his prisoners and hearing what she had to say, I found it easy to understand why.

"We'll go that way."

No one argued.

Kyla had killed her way through the castle, but

she'd faced one fewer chamber than we had. I raised my eyebrow at her as we trudged through blood and gore.

"Kobolds," she muttered. "Vicious little shits. Almost cost me my right paw."

By the time we'd made our way back to the spot where we'd separated, my energy was flagging. My head throbbed, and all I wanted to do was curl up in a ball and take a nap. I'd even lie on the stone floor if it meant I could rest.

Thoughts of vengeance had to keep me going. "When all this is over, when we've found the lab and destroyed it, I'm going to release proof that the seelie king was handing over his subjects to be tested on," I said.

Kyla let out a low whistle. "You think people will believe you?"

"I'll make sure we have irrefutable proof. He may be a king, but he still needs his subjects to follow him. Half of them are disgusted that he turned on the demons and allied with Lucifer, putting us all at war. Once they find out he was handing over his own people, he'll be judged by the court of public opinion."

"There's a good chance it'll make him more dangerous."

"Oh, it will. So, we'll need to prepare accordingly."

Nathaniel nuzzled my ear. "You're a little strategist."

I raised one eyebrow. "I've always been highly intelligent. You just weren't paying attention."

"Believe me, when it comes to you, I'm always paying attention."

His voice was a low purr. My toes curled, and I shrugged awkwardly before I could do something embarrassing, like blush.

Nathaniel grinned and ruffled my hair. His hand got stuck in some kind of mysterious goo, and he pulled it back with a grimace, wiping it on his jeans.

Maybe I needed to go straight to Vas after we were through here. He'd never attempt to mess up my hair again.

Kyla smirked. "You two are very cute and all, but we're here. We all need to turn invisible and get the hell out of this realm."

Nathaniel pulled Finvarra's silver book out of the backpack and handed it to Kyla. I popped the ring into my mouth and took his hand. We hadn't yet suffered any repercussions from me using my power—maybe because we'd been so close to the exit. But that didn't mean there wasn't some kind of surprise waiting for us.

We all stepped through the last door and into the main corridor leading into the castle. A different guard was on shift now, and he tensed as my shoe scuffed the floor.

Nathaniel launched himself forward, his movements utterly silent. A moment later, the guard was slumping to the floor and Nathaniel was dragging his unconscious body deeper into the corridor. He positioned him on his side, tucking him against the wall, and then held out his hand for me to take.

We all made our way to the end of the hallway.

"Oh shit," I muttered.

No wonder no one had noticed Nathaniel attacking the guard.

Kyla made a choked sound. "Is that what I think it is?"

I stared up at the sky. Then I spat out the ring, wiped it off, and slid it back onto my finger. Super hygienic.

"If you think it's the roc I lured into this realm, then yes, it sure is." I waved my arms. "Hey, you big murderous bird, get over here."

"What the hell are you doing?" Kyla hissed.

"Saving our asses."

I needed to wield an illusion spell. I'd never tried anything like this before, but I knew how to do it. In theory.

I only had the barest hint of my power left, but it would have to do. If there was ever a time for a Hail Mary, this was it.

Closing my eyes, I reached deep into my power, pushing away all the fear that wanted to cripple me. I didn't have time for it.

When I opened my eyes, my hair was blowing

back from my face in a silent breeze. Nathaniel's eyes had turned a pale blue, and he was staring at me.

He tensed as I stepped out of the corridor, but he didn't try to stop me.

Shouts sounded as the guards spotted me. Turning toward them, I waved my hand, creating the spell on the fly. My power streamed from me, and I heard Nathaniel suck in a sharp breath behind me.

One by one, the guards' faces all became mine. Their hair turned blond and curly, and their bodies took on my form.

The roc swooped. I ducked back into the corridor and shoved the ring back into my mouth. The roc shrieked its rage, and then it was arrowing toward the guards, all of those who looked just like me.

Sweat dripped down my back. I had nothing left. I turned, stumbling, and then I was in Nathaniel's arms as he sprinted toward the portal.

9

EVIE

We had the sword. And we were all still alive.

Kyla gripped the hilt as if it were her lifeline. In many ways, it was.

"I'm taking this to Finvarra before anyone realizes we have it," she said.

I studied the sword. It was glowing gold in the sun. "I'm coming with you."

Kyla opened her mouth to protest, but I gave her a look. After a brief hesitation, she shrugged.

We both knew Kyla wasn't her best self around Finvarra. I could say the same for Finvarra, but he'd had centuries of experience plotting and planning. If Kyla weren't careful, she'd end up in some other awful bargain with the unseelie king.

Nathaniel didn't look pleased, but there was no doubt he needed to stay behind. Finvarra and Nathaniel weren't exactly buddies.

"Are you sure you're okay? You don't have any power left."

"Finvarra won't hurt me."

Nathaniel nodded, taking the backpack I held out. "I'll be waiting for you." He leaned closer, and awareness thundered through my body. I knew what that tone meant, and my hormones were celebrating.

Lust curled through my belly. I wanted him with a kind of desperation that would have embarrassed me if I didn't know he wanted me the same way.

Kyla had driven, so I followed her in Liam's car. Since I was covered in various body fluids, I'd pay to have it cleaned before I returned it. I needed to talk to him soon. Now that I'd accepted that I was his Alpha's mate, I wanted to make sure he was doing okay.

I jolted as a red truck swerved into my lane with no warning. "Asshole."

My reflexes were slowing down. I needed to rest…

"Focus, Evie."

The Duke Gardens came into view, and I parked, following Kyla's loping stride to the portal. A few humans were standing near the fence, staring curiously at the red-pink portal. Kyla showed them her teeth, and they backed up as she scaled the fence with one hand, her other hand clenched around the sword. Her knuckles had turned white, and I couldn't blame her. She was so close to finally ending her bargain with Finvarra.

I climbed the fence and followed Kyla through the

portal.

Finvarra allowed us immediate entry to his library, where he was cradling a glass of something dark. His eyes brightened, shining an eerie gold as he took in the sword. Placing his glass on the table next to him, he swept his gaze over the two of us.

"Difficult day?"

Kyla opened her mouth. I elbowed her, and she clamped it closed, striding forward and handing the sword to Finvarra.

He took it, face blank as usual. But his eyes fired with vengeance as he surveyed the golden hilt.

"Our deal is now complete." Kyla recited the words formally. She hissed, holding up her hand. The bronze mark was slowly fading. Relief made my head swim.

Finvarra watched her for a long moment. "Something tells me this is not the end for us."

They stared at each other for a long moment. I fought the urge to back away.

Kyla just nodded at Finvarra and turned, stalking out the door.

"Nice work," I told her as we walked out of the castle. "I thought you were going to try to rip his throat out for a moment there. Either that or…"

She gave me a look as we strolled back toward the portal. "There is no *or*."

"Uh-huh. To be honest, that felt anticlimactic."

Kyla just grinned, although it was strained. "I still have to steal that fucking sword off him or the realms burn," she murmured. "I'm sure *that* will be suitably dramatic."

I winced. "Any idea how we're going to achieve that?"

"There's no *we* involved."

"Excuse me?" Planting my hands on my hips, I turned to survey her, ignoring the unseelie guy who stalked past us and through the portal.

"I've thought about it. Finvarra's not stupid. We go into his realm together, and he'll know something's up. No, I need to convince him to invite *me* in."

I thought about it. "Uh, how exactly are you going to do that?"

"You heard the man. 'We're not done.'" She cracked her knuckles. "He has no idea just how right he is about that."

I'd almost feel sorry for Finvarra, if he hadn't forced her into the deal in the first place. He was going to learn exactly why he shouldn't have fucked with Kyla. I was looking forward to the fireworks.

NATHANIEL

I opened my front door and stepped into the noise and chaos of the pack.

Ryker had warned me that a few of them had gathered here to wait for me, needing to know their Alpha had returned from the seelie realm unharmed.

If I were an Alpha like Frederik, I would take

offense at the mere suggestion that I wouldn't return alive. But after so long running this pack, I knew it wasn't an insult. My pack had been built on mutual respect and loyalty. Beneath the dominance games and power plays, we also *cared* about one another.

"Nathaniel's here," Naomi announced, as if the wolves couldn't scent me. I smiled at her, and she hugged me.

"Glad you're okay."

I nodded, slowly making my way toward the kitchen, greeting wolves as I went.

It wasn't often that I truly felt tired. But I couldn't remember the last time I'd looked forward to laying my head on my pillow this much.

If I was tired, Evie must be exhausted. It had been difficult to let her go—knowing she was going to see fucking Finvarra. My wolf paced in my mind at the thought of the unseelie. It was bad enough that Kyla had to deal with him. I didn't want Evie anywhere near him. But I understood why she needed to go with Kyla.

"Gabriel is in town," Xander told me, offering me a plate of food.

I took it. Tobias smiled at me, and I gave him a thankful grin. But my mind was on Gabriel. He was the man in charge of the Mage Council. It had been his father who'd first started the council over seventy years ago, and Gabriel was a known recluse. If he'd left Chicago to come to Durham, it was for a good reason. "I'm guessing he's looking into Albert's murder."

"Yeah, and I don't think it's going to take him long to turn his attention to you, given the way Albert was ripped apart," Naomi said.

I glanced at her. She dropped her eyes. I let my gaze rest on her for a long moment before picking up my fork.

"Albert attempted to make the humans turn on us," I growled. "He sacrificed his own mages and had one of them plant a coin on Evie so Fenrir would target her."

My jaw ached, and I realized I was gritting my teeth.

"No one blames you for killing him, boss," Ryker said, taking a seat at the island next to me. "But we're still going to have to figure out how we'll deal with Gabriel. It's rare for him to leave Chicago, and he's already sent a message *kindly requesting* you meet with him. Alone."

I smiled at that. Gabriel hadn't kept his mages in line by acting impulsively. If he wanted to meet with me, it was because he had a plan.

"Tell him we can meet," I said.

Xander gaped. "Are you…sure?"

"Oh, I'm sure. You and Ryker take care of the security concerns when he gets back to us."

"Done."

Getting to my feet, I nodded to my wolves. "I need a shower."

What I really needed was a few moments alone

to calm my wolf, who was convinced Evie and Kyla shouldn't have gone to Finvarra alone. Evie had been so low on her power, and Kyla was a recently injured, starving wolf who had been mostly feral not all that long ago.

They could handle themselves. In fact, together, they made one hell of a team. Still, I couldn't help but listen for every car that drove near my territory, hoping one of them would be Liam's.

10

EVIE

The sun had already set by the time I drove into wolf territory. Kyla waved at me when I turned off. She'd said she wanted to go straight to sleep, and I couldn't blame her.

Pulling up to Nathaniel's house, I sat for a moment, attempting to motivate myself to get out of the car.

Nathaniel's door opened. That was all I needed. I got out of the car, practically sleepwalking up to his front door.

Nathaniel gave me a long, searching look.

"I'm okay," I assured him. "Just tired."

"And hungry, I bet," Tobias called. "Come eat, Evie."

I smiled. Food was Tobias's love language. I stepped into the warmth and brushed past the Alpha. Nathaniel had showered, and he smelled fresh and clean...like *home*.

I wanted to burrow into him, but I also didn't want to dirty him up again. Unless we were talking in a sexy way, of course, because I was down for—

"Where did you go?" Nathaniel had stepped in front of me.

"Sorry. Just tired. Mind wandering."

He pushed a hunk of my hair behind my ear. It was covered in blood, yellow goo, and various other substances, but he didn't seem to mind. He gently lowered his head, brushing his lips against mine.

"Now that I have you in my home, where you belong, and you've agreed to be my mate, all I want to do is take you upstairs and prove you're mine."

My body flushed hot, and I elbowed him, giving a nod toward the kitchen where Tobias had gone silent. He'd definitely heard everything Nathaniel had said.

Nathaniel just laughed, wrapped his arm around my shoulders, and led me into the kitchen.

My face flamed. Naomi smirked at me, while Ryker, Hunter, and Xander kept their eyes on their plates. Smart men.

Tobias took one look at me up close and gaped. I hesitated. "I can go clean up first," I said.

"No," Nathaniel said as my stomach chose that moment to let out a howl. "I want you to eat."

Tobias gestured for me to take a seat, and Ryker immediately scooted over so Nathaniel could sit next to me.

"I was just telling everyone about what happened

below the seelie castle. And our plan for HFE," Nathaniel said.

"I still don't see why we have to be involved in Evie's war," Naomi muttered.

Nathaniel went still, his head cocked in a way that didn't bode well for Naomi's health. I'd never seen him turn that kind of look on her before, and I elbowed him to draw his attention. "Can you pass the butter?"

I didn't need the butter. His wry look told me he knew that. But he was focused on me. Naomi's mouth twisted in a way that made it clear she was grateful for the distraction and hated that I'd been the one to make it happen.

Tobias had made spaghetti and meatballs with fresh garlic bread. I took a bite and let out a contented sigh.

Nathaniel grinned at me, and it was clear both he and his wolf were pleased that I was eating.

"HFE convinced the seelie king to give them his prisoners in exchange for who knows what," I informed Naomi around a bite. "If they can do that, something tells me they might not have any issues convincing an Alpha wolf to hand over a second who was getting too powerful. There are a lot of packs in this country."

Naomi shook her head, even as a faint line appeared between her eyebrows. "An Alpha wolf is programmed to protect his pack."

"Really? 'Cause I didn't see much of that protection

when I was speaking with Frederik."

Nathaniel tensed at the reminder of my little visit with his enemy, and I absently petted his shoulder. He gave me a bemused look.

Tobias leaned against the counter. "We have a responsibility to help those who are being preyed on," he said softly.

No one argued with him. I took a deep, steadying breath. "I have werewolf DNA," I said. "Along with a bunch of other things. Basically, I'm a freak."

Nathaniel went still. I knew that look. He was pissed. I just shook my head at him. "I'm a cute freak, but I'm still a freak. If HFE was playing with werewolves back when my mom was taken, who knows what they're doing now? We have to cut the head off the snake, or it's just going to keep regrowing like that fucking hydra." I scowled at the reminder.

Xander gaped at me. "You fought a hydra?"

"I mostly distracted it. Nathaniel and Kyla did all the work."

"No, we didn't," Nathaniel said. "She used her power to keep the heads from growing back."

Ryker grinned. "I want to hear all about that."

"Later," Nathaniel said. "For now, I want everyone ready. Evie used a tracking spell which will allow us to know when one of the seelie prisoners is in our realm. As soon as we know where she's being taken, we need to strike."

"We have to hit all the labs at the same time," I

said. "We can't risk even a single HFE member getting free."

"We may be a large pack, but how exactly are we going to do that?" Naomi asked. Interest flickered in her eyes, though, and I knew I had her.

"I'm going to reach out to the demons, the seelie, and the witches."

"Not the unseelie?" Ryker asked.

Nathaniel growled. "We've had enough of Finvarra for a while. If we play this right, we can take down HFE with a little cooperation from our friends."

Ryker frowned. "Are you sure? Because we could probably use—"

Nathaniel slowly turned his head. "Who is Alpha?" His voice was very soft. "Because the last time I checked, it wasn't you."

Something prickled along the back of my neck. *Wrong. This was—*

"Well?"

Ryker's expression had turned blank with shock. Rage flickered in his eyes before it was carefully banked. "You are."

"That's right."

Ryker dropped his gaze. The room was silent for a long moment. Obviously, there was some kind of undercurrent I wasn't aware of. Something that had happened between them recently.

Tobias was staring at Nathaniel as if he'd grown another head. Obviously, Nathaniel was stressed. He was probably exhausted too. I knew I was.

"Eat," Nathaniel ordered me.

I rolled my eyes but dug in.

Half an hour later, I was moaning around Tobias's homemade tiramisu. "Of all the perks of living with you, this has to be the best," I told Nathaniel.

Tobias sent me a grin. The other wolves had filed out, and he'd cleaned the dishes, wiped down the counters, and set the kitchen to sparkling again. He disappeared into the butler's pantry, and Nathaniel leaned close. "There's a much bigger perk…"

I choked on my tiramisu and elbowed him, conscious of Tobias just a few feet away.

"You know, I could probably come up with a cleaning spell," I told Tobias when he returned. "Save you some time."

He shook his head. "I enjoy it."

I stared at him. "Really?"

"It gives me something to do with my hands. I can be…anxious."

"Well, the offer is open if you change your mind."

I scraped my bowl clean and sighed, patting my belly. "That was incredible."

Nathaniel held out his hand, helping me off my stool. I didn't need help, but it pleased him.

"Come, mate," he murmured in my ear, his warm breath making me shiver. "You need a shower."

I sent him a saucy look over my shoulder as we walked upstairs. "Is that an offer to scrub my back?"

His grin made him look ten years younger. His eyes gleamed at me, and for a moment, all I could do was stare. I wanted to see that expression on his face every day and know that I was the one responsible for putting it there.

Nathaniel's hand slid to my butt. "Do you need some help making it up the stairs?"

I grinned back at him. "I think I can handle it."

The moment we got into his room, I stripped off my shirt, suddenly desperate to be clean.

Nathaniel's bathroom was huge, and I eyed the bath. Next time. For now, I needed—

"Holy shit." I'd caught sight of myself in the mirror.

Nathaniel loomed behind me, his gaze on mine. I took in the blood still covering most of my face and neck, the chunk of hair missing from above one ear, and the mystery fluids that had turned into a disgusting, glue-like substance.

"I may need to cut it off and start again," I said.

"Never." Nathaniel grinned at me. "Besides, I have this."

He lifted his hand, revealing the hideously expensive but incredibly useful cream I used in my hair.

I gaped at him. "You..." Turning, I peered at his shower. All my toiletries were here. Shampoo, conditioner, body wash, even my razor.

"You did this today?"

"No. I did it the moment I learned you'd gone to

the seelie realm, while I was waiting for my dominants to organize themselves."

"Someone was sure of himself," I said. I wasn't sure whether to be touched or annoyed by how prepared he was.

"I needed the hope," he murmured, his huge body pressing up against mine as he flicked on the shower. "My wolf needed to know that, no matter what happened, you'd be in my territory, in my home, and in my bed."

Nathaniel grabbed my hand and turned me, dropping to his knees to untie my boots. It was strange, seeing the Alpha on his knees, but no one who looked at him would ever think of him as submissive. Not with the way his wolf stared up at me as he pulled off my boots.

Sliding Misty out of the sheath on my ankle, he set it on the bathroom counter and unstrapped the sheath. My jeans were next.

"I can do it," I whispered.

"Allow me. Please."

When I was standing naked in front of him, Nathaniel just stared at me, his eyes glittering. "You are so fucking beautiful."

Warmth exploded in my belly. "I know you've already showered, but...you want to join me?"

"Of course." He pulled off his own clothes while I stepped into his shower.

Multiple shower heads pounded me from every

direction, and I moaned. The water at my feet turned dark with blood. I scrubbed my face, rinsed it, then washed it once more.

Large hands pulled me out of the stream of water. The lavender and vanilla scent of my nighttime shower gel wafted toward me, and then Nathaniel's hands were stroking, rubbing, smoothing away every trace of the seelie realm.

I sighed, arching my back as he found a particularly tight knot in my shoulders.

Then he was shampooing my hair, his fingers caressing every inch of my scalp.

"Rinse."

He shampooed again, then once more, until the water at my feet was clean. If not for my magic cream, my curls would be a frizzy mess after so much shampoo. Nathaniel added conditioner, and I sighed.

"You have magic hands."

"You ain't seen nothing yet, sweetheart."

I laughed, and he lowered to his knees once more, his hands sliding to my thighs, caressing every inch as he massaged the shower gel along my skin. I gasped as even the backs of my knees turned sensitive. Needy.

I stared down at him, a little bewildered by how he'd turned such a random spot into a pleasure zone. Nathaniel laughed at whatever he saw on my face.

"I knew having a mate would be life-changing, but I never knew it could be...fun."

Fighting back a smile, I attempted to look stern.

"I'm glad you're amused."

Nathaniel guided me to the bench on one side of the shower, then continued his exploration down my legs, lifting my feet and massaging each one until I groaned.

"Such delicate feet," he murmured, pressing a kiss to my big toe. Then he was pushing my thighs apart, and my breath caught at the sight of him kneeling in front of me, his eyes glittering, cheeks flushed.

We stared at each other for a long moment. Long enough that my chest ached and my throat tightened with the realization of what we were about to do.

He'd truly be my *mate*.

The thought of someone like me with a mate felt almost ludicrous. And it wouldn't have worked with anyone else. But with Nathaniel, I felt like we *would* be a team of two. Us against the world.

"What are you thinking?"

I filled him in, and he smiled. "Always. It's you and me, Evie."

He turned his attention back to my thighs, pressing kisses along the sensitive spots that made me shiver. I arched, and he tutted, his huge hands holding me still for him.

"Be a good girl, and you'll get your reward."

I reached for him, but he'd already dropped his head once more, and his tongue gave me one, firm swipe.

The sound that left my throat made him chuckle,

and I groaned again at the vibration against my clit.

"You're so wet for me," he murmured.

"I want you."

I attempted to pull him close, but he stayed exactly where he was. "I've been thinking about the way you taste, remembering all those high-pitched little noises you made for me before we were interrupted that night."

We'd been interrupted by an attack on the pack. Hopefully, nothing would interrupt us tonight.

"I don't make high-pitched little noises."

Nathaniel gave me a shit-eating grin and lowered his head once more. He slipped one finger inside me, followed by a second, and he expertly caressed my clit with his tongue until I was writhing on the shower bench.

He lifted his head long enough to say, "Those kinds of noises."

I would've blushed, but I was too busy tightening around him, the world narrowing until a meteor could have hit the house, and I probably wouldn't have noticed.

"Come for me, mate," Nathaniel ordered. His teeth scraped my clit, and he crooked his fingers inside me, hitting *that* spot as his tongue danced along the sensitive bundle of nerves.

I gasped out a curse, and my head fell back as I shuddered, pleasure coursing through every inch of my body.

Nathaniel continued playing with me until I was so sensitive, I was pushing him away. I cracked my eyes open enough that I caught his pleased grin, and then I was in his arms as he hauled my limp body off the bench and beneath the water.

A quick rinse, and then he was steering me out of the shower and patting me dry with a huge, fluffy towel.

"I can do it."

"Allow me."

He dried every inch of me. When he was done, he swiped at himself with the towel and then picked up my curl cream.

I narrowed my eyes at him, still a little put out by his confidence that he'd convince me to see the error of my ways. "Did you move *everything* into your rooms?"

"Our rooms." He studied the bottle. "How does this work?"

Shaking my head, I took the spelled curl cream from him, combed it through my hair, and washed my hands. He played with one of my curls.

"It's so long when it's wet. It comes halfway down your back."

He nuzzled my neck, and my belly tightened. Dropping the cream on the counter, I wrapped my arms around his neck, pulling him down for a deep kiss. He was hard and thick against my stomach, and I shivered with anticipation.

Nathaniel hoisted me up, his huge hands palming

my butt as he walked into his bedroom and laid me on the bed. Gently. Reverently. He stared down at me, and his wolf appeared briefly in his eyes.

"It feels almost unreal that you're here. It's difficult to believe that you're finally mine."

I pulled him closer until his face was inches from mine. "Believe it." I leaned up so I could kiss him, and he let out a growl, pressing me back into the pillow.

My breath caught. "I want you."

"You'll have me."

"Now."

"Be. Patient."

"I don't think so." I hooked my leg behind his waist and arched, rubbing against his cock. He took my mouth with a groan, grinding against me.

"More," I demanded.

"Wicked thing."

Nathaniel wrapped one hand around my wrists and held them down, turning his attention to my breasts. I moaned as his tongue flicked one nipple, then the other. His teeth scraped gently, and I tensed, attempting to reach for him. The way he held me down just plain did it for me.

Huh. Who would've thought?

He was kissing his way down my body. "I want to taste you again."

"Please, Nathaniel. I need to feel you inside me."

He let out a groan of his own. And then he was positioning himself at my entrance, and we both gasped as he slid inside me.

I'd known he was big, but the way he filled me up…

Thankfully, he took his time, pulling out, then sliding in a little farther. Gliding one of his hands down to my clit, he gave me a gentle stroke that made me melt, and he used that moment to seat himself fully inside me.

We were actually doing this. And none of my fantasies could live up to the reality of Nathaniel poised over me. Of the feel of him slowly moving within me.

"Fuck, you feel so good," he growled, bending at an unnatural angle so he could take my mouth. He cupped my breast in his other huge hand, and my breath hitched in a way that made him smile against my lips.

"Going to make you come so hard."

He was. There was no doubt about that. I was already on the edge, my body trembling as I panted beneath him.

"Move."

He lifted his head and complied, twisting his hips until he found that perfect spot inside me. I let out a yelp, and he watched my face carefully, a smirk appearing as he hit it again and again.

"There you go."

I began to pulse around him, and he removed his hand from my clit. "What—"

"Together this first time. I want to feel you clench

around me."

I couldn't argue with that. And I didn't want to since Nathaniel was cupping my hips, holding me still for him as he pounded into me.

My breath caught, every muscle in my body seized, and then I was crying out as pleasure danced through my body, my vision narrowing until all I could see was his face. His cheekbones were flushed, and he let out a groan of his own as he emptied himself inside me.

And suddenly, it was as if my mind had an extra compartment, one that belonged to him. I could feel his shocked pleasure, his possessive instincts, his *love.*

I trembled with the aftershocks of my climax while he rested his forehead against mine. I was out of breath, and Nathaniel looked just as dazed, although he shot me a smug smile. When he slowly drew out of me, I moaned.

"You have no idea how long I've wanted to do that."

"Pretty sure it matches up with the amount of time I've fantasized about your body."

"My body, huh?"

I just smirked at him. "You want me to tell you I fantasized about your mind?"

"I think you should tell me more about these fantasies. What exactly did we do in them?"

"Here's a hint—it ended just like that."

Nathaniel's contentment washed over me, and he pulled me into his arms until we were spooning, his chin resting on my shoulder.

He was already hard once more, and I angled my hips back. He just laughed, and I forced my eyes open.

When had I closed them?

"You're so tired."

"Mhmm."

"It's the full moon tonight. I'll shift soon and run with my pack."

"I want to come," I slurred, my eyes so heavy, it was as if they were glued together.

"You just did."

"Not funny."

His chest shook with laughter. "Next time," he promised.

EVIE

I stretched, opening my eyes. My body felt languid and used in the best kind of way. Pouting, I ran my hand over the cold spot where Nathaniel had slept. I knew he had a pack to run, but it would've been nice to—

I blinked. "One p.m.?"

I'd slept for approximately eighteen hours.

Okay, maybe I could forgive him for not being here when I woke up.

As if the thought had summoned him, Nathaniel opened the door. Our bond lit up, and I could feel his pleasure at the sight of me in his bed. I grinned at him.

"This is going to take some getting used to."

"Just don't leave."

And now I could feel his worry that all of it—the pack, the bond, and *him*—would be too much.

My chest clenched. "I won't. I promise."

I was the one who had a fear of abandonment, and I'd passed it on to my mate. Perfect.

"No," Nathaniel said, sitting next to me. "It was nothing you did."

"Are you reading my mind?"

A faint smile curved his lips, and I couldn't help myself. I leaned forward and kissed him.

Annnd, I definitely had morning breath. I leaned back, but his hand was in my hair, holding me still while he explored my mouth.

"Um, I should brush my teeth," I said when he slowly pulled away, his eyes dark.

"Evie, I could barely keep my hands off you when you were covered in blood and gore."

I grinned.

"To answer your question, no, I'm not reading your mind. It should settle in a few weeks."

There was something he wasn't telling me. I could feel it. I opened my mouth, but his expression had shut down, and I could no longer feel him in that little compartment in my mind.

It was clear he wanted privacy. Time for a change of subject.

"What day is it?" I asked. "I lost track."

"Wednesday."

"Shit. I'm meeting my uncle at my office."

I swung my legs over the side of the bed, grinning at Nathaniel when I felt his sudden interest.

"Later," I promised him. My body howled at me.

Nathaniel had warned me of the way we'd crave each other even more during the first few weeks of our mating. And all I wanted to do was roll him beneath me and...

He let out a groan and got to his feet. "Don't look at me like that unless you want me to tie you to that bed and fuck you until you can't walk."

My body heated. "You've threatened the bed-tying thing a few times now. When are you going to make it happen?"

"Just as soon as you give me the green light."

I leaned close. "Consider all my lights green."

He let out a rough growl. My toes curled, and he took a large step back. "I'll see you tonight."

"You're not going to kiss me goodbye?" I pouted.

"You little minx." His hand was buried in my hair before I'd realized he'd moved, and he pulled gently until I was staring up at him. His mouth crashed down on mine until all thought disappeared.

Then he was gone.

"Asshole," I called after him, hearing his rough laugh.

Tobias was bustling around the kitchen when I made it downstairs. He handed me a to-go cup of coffee, and I grinned at him. "Thank you." I surveyed the empty kitchen. "It's quieter than usual. Shouldn't everyone be in here, begging for lunch?"

"Naomi, Ryker, and Xander are doing a sweep along our borders. Nathaniel orders them every few weeks to make sure no one is getting through whom he hasn't approved. They'll be back for dinner."

"And Hunter?"

"He traveled to Frederik's pack."

"Alone?"

Tobias gave me a patient smile. "Nathaniel negotiated the visit this time. Frederik would never dare harm Hunter during an official visit."

"Why is he visiting?"

"To discuss what you and Nathaniel learned about the seelie king giving his people to HFE. And to make sure Frederik has no thought of doing the same."

"Will Hunter be able to tell if Frederik is lying?"

"Yes. That's why Nathaniel sent him. His wolf is incredibly sensitive to such things."

"What about the other packs in this country?"

"Nathaniel has notified any who are loyal to him that any Alphas found to have given their people to HFE will be killed and replaced."

I swallowed. "That's going to make them dangerous if they've already done it."

"Yes, but there will be pack members who realize Nathaniel will protect them. I have no doubt that some of them will find a way to alert Nathaniel if their Alphas have been committing such atrocities."

"It wouldn't surprise me if Frederik was doing something like that."

Tobias's expression darkened. "No. It wouldn't surprise me either."

I raised one eyebrow, and he gave me a gentle smile. "I was once a member of Frederik's pack."

I almost choked on my coffee. "You never said anything."

"It is difficult for me to talk about. I was younger. Scared. I imagined all Alphas were like Frederik. More interested in power than protection."

"How did you end up in Nathaniel's pack?"

He shook his head. "That's a story for another day. And you're late."

"Shit. I am. Thanks for the coffee."

"Promise you'll eat something."

"I will."

"Oh, Nathaniel told me to let you know Liam needed his car back." Tobias reached into his pocket and threw me a set of keys. "Take the car in the driveway."

"Thanks."

I beelined toward the car, my mind on Liam. We needed to talk. Soon.

"Evie? Can I talk to you?"

I turned and grinned at Levi. "Hey. It's good to see you."

I knew awkwardness when I saw it. It was also clear that the teenager had been waiting for me outside Nathaniel's. I leaned against the car. "Come here."

He wandered over, his shoulders hunched.

I stretched out my legs, turning my face into the sun to make it a little easier on him. "What's going on?"

"I just...I wanted to apologize to you. And to thank

you."

"For what?"

"For saving my life."

"You don't have to thank me for that, Levi. Fenrir wouldn't have been there if it weren't attracted to me."

"Because of the coin Albert's mage planted on you."

I glanced at him, and he smirked. "I hear things." Teenagers.

"Yeah. Because of the coin."

"So, it wasn't your fault either. I saw the way that giant wolf was looking at the book. It wanted it."

Something itched at the edges of my memory.

The thought flickered away as Levi took my hand. Surprised, I glanced at him. His cheeks had turned red.

"You looked after my brother when I hurt him."

"Levi. The book hurt him. That wasn't you."

"It wouldn't have been able to convince me to push you if that wasn't *in* me."

"We all have bad parts of ourselves. Parts we would rather ignore. We all suppress those instincts. The book just made it impossible for you to do that. And you never have to thank me for looking after Charlie. I would've done that, no matter what."

"Because you're the Alpha's mate?"

I winced. "No. I wasn't Nathaniel's mate then, remember? Or at least, I didn't know I was." I wrinkled my nose at the reminder, and as I'd hoped, Levi laughed. "I would've helped because I care about you guys. Because you're great kids, and you're fun to be around."

"Thanks, Evie. Um, you want to come hang?"

I grinned at him. "I have to go meet my uncle. But we'll hang out soon."

He nodded. "One more thing. Mom wants to know if you'll come for dinner?"

"Me and Nathaniel?"

He shrugged. "She'd never turn the Alpha away, but I think she wanted me to make sure you knew the invitation was for you."

Something warm and fuzzy took up residence in my chest. "I'd love that. See you soon, Levi."

He grinned at me and wandered back toward the forest. I got in the car Nathaniel had left me and headed to my office. The car drove like a dream. Which was good, 'cause I was running late.

Eachann was already waiting outside my office when I slid into my spot.

I pushed open the car door and wrestled with my seat belt. "I'm sorry I'm late."

"Never mind about that. You've been in the seelie realm."

I didn't ask him how he knew. My uncle was weird like that. By the time I'd gotten out of the car, he'd plucked the office keys out of my hand and unlocked the front door himself.

"Thanks. Yes, I've been in the seelie realm. In the castle, to be exact."

Eachann's eyes flared. "Now that's a story I want

to hear." He opened the door, gesturing for me to walk inside. We both went still as we took in the huge whiteboard Rose had placed next to the board I'd been working on.

She'd been busy over the past few days.

The whiteboard on the wall held the timeline I'd been working on, which covered everything I could associate with HFE.

Mom meets Lucifer's son. She has no idea the underking is his father.

Gets pregnant with Danica.

Learns Lucifer will kill Danica if he finds out about her.

Begins hunting Black Books to take Lucifer down.

Mom leaves Danica with friends. Lured to HFE lab by promise of Black Books. Kidnapped.

Gets pregnant with me. My father helps her escape.

Mom goes to Gemma's coven for safety.

Gemma's coven places a spell on me, tying me to their house.

Mom returns to Durham. Murdered.

Danica returns to hunt murderers.

Danica bonds with Samael.

Coven burned to the ground. Witches slaughtered.

Lab discovered, empty.

HFE on the run. Locations???

I shifted my gaze to the second whiteboard Rose had set up. She'd been working with Steve to find those locations, and she'd pinned a map to one side of the whiteboard. From what I could tell, a green dot meant she'd confirmed the lab was there. Yellow meant it was suspected. Red meant she'd been wrong.

I counted the green dots. "Twenty-six so far." My voice was hoarse.

Eachann placed his hand on my shoulder. "This is good work."

"Rose did it. She said someone owed her a favor. And I asked Steve to help as well."

"Steve?"

"He works for Samael."

Eachann didn't wince, but it was close. My uncle seemed a little befuddled by the ties my sister and I had to various paranormal factions. But those ties were going to help us shut down HFE. I knew it.

"I had a breakthrough of my own when you were gone," Eachann said.

I turned and studied him for the first time since I'd arrived. My uncle was unseelie, but today he looked… worn. Tired.

"Are you okay?"

He glanced at me, then turned his attention back to the whiteboards in front of us. "Fine."

I didn't know Eachann all that well, but he'd already wormed his way into my heart with his calm assurance, sly sense of humor, and determination to help.

"Eachann…"

"My research all led to one man," he said. He pulled out his phone, jabbing at it with his index finger as if there were a bug on the screen he was attempting to kill. I smiled, and he gave me a dark look.

"I spent most of my life in the unseelie realm, girl. Don't make fun of me."

My smile widened. "Sorry. Can't help it." My phone buzzed, and I took a look at the picture he'd sent me. "Who is this guy?"

"Lennox Rees. His father's name was Alistair, and he witnessed his mother's—Lennox's grandmother's—slaughter by a werewolf when the portals opened. Alistair made his money in pharmaceuticals, and within the next few years, he'd turned all of his scientists and labs toward understanding paranormals. Those first few years after the portals opened were chaos," he said. "So many died—both humans and paranormals—that no one would have noticed when Alistair began working with human bounty hunters to collect paranormals to use as his specimens. It's rumored that Lennox is half paranormal himself—the result of one of his father's many *indiscretions* with the prisoners."

I swallowed, my stomach churning. "What happened to him?"

"He was killed when an unseelie broke free."

"I hope it was agonizing."

Eachann smiled. "So do I. But as you can imagine, he raised his son to hate and fear paranormals. Once he took over, Lennox poured his inheritance back into HFE, expanding it throughout the country."

Determination warred with pity as I turned to pace. We'd found him at last. The man responsible for HFE's atrocities. After everything he'd done, and considering everything he *would* do if he had the chance, Lennox needed to die. But it was easy to see exactly how he'd become the monster he was now. Monsters were made, not born. And Lennox hadn't had a chance.

"This is good work," I said.

Eachann smiled. "Thank you. I also have a theory about the beast."

I'd sent Eachann the results from the blood test Nathaniel had run. I shouldn't be surprised that my uncle had found time to research the strange creature that had fought with Fenrir before it died.

"You said it acted almost...protectively," Eachann said.

"Yeah. It was weird."

"One of my people picked up chatter about a creature that escaped its handlers in Kentucky. From one of HFE's labs. I think it sensed you, Evie."

"You think that's why it came here. Was it hoping for...help?"

And I'd gotten it killed. My stomach knotted.

"I don't think it had the brain capacity for that."

I considered what else it could mean. "You think my DNA was close enough to that creature's that it considered me family?"

I turned to pace in the opposite direction, but Eachann was suddenly there. "We don't have time for you to question your humanity, Evie."

"I'm excellent at multitasking. Ask anyone."

The ghost of a smile crossed his lips. But he shook his head. "There are other theories. Someone at the lab could have sent it in your direction, hoping it would kill you."

"But it didn't. If you're right, it protected me."

"It would have been killed eventually, Evie. No one would have allowed it its freedom. But it's proof that HFE is creating all kinds of creatures and experimenting with them."

I went still. I couldn't even begin to imagine what else HFE was doing in those labs.

A knock sounded on the door, and my heart flipped when Nathaniel strolled in, nodding at my uncle.

Eachann's eyes narrowed as he glanced between us. "You've mated," he said softly. "I thought something was different when I saw you." He glanced at me, and I fought the urge to hunch my shoulders. Nathaniel was mine. Even if one of my two remaining family members didn't approve.

Nathaniel took a single step closer. "Are we going to have a problem?"

Eachann ignored him, which was impressive since my mate was currently radiating threat. My uncle studied my face.

"You chose him?"

"Yes. I'll always choose him."

Eachann sighed. "I'd planned to introduce you to a powerful unseelie boy I know. Royal line."

Nathaniel bared his teeth in a vicious snarl. I gave

him a look. He knew Eachann was no threat.

Turning my attention back to my uncle, I frowned. "Do you have to push him?"

Eachann grinned. "I must. It's my job. Your father would expect no less." His face sobered at the mention of his brother. "You'll protect her." He addressed Nathaniel this time, and it was my turn to scowl.

"With my life."

"I can protect myself," I muttered sullenly. Both men ignored me, and I ground my teeth.

"Fine." Eachann strolled toward the door. "I have work to do. Let me know when you're ready to hit the labs."

I sat on the sofa, rubbing at the back of my neck. It was strange, suddenly having more family. That reminded me…

"What's wrong?" Nathaniel sat next to me, wrapping his arm around my shoulders. I took a single moment to bury my head in his chest, soaking up his scent.

"Nothing. I just need to talk to my sister."

Kyla had told me she'd send a message to Danica when we got back, letting her know we were okay. I should've been the one to do that.

"I don't like the guilt you're feeling," Nathaniel said, and I pulled back, squinting at him.

"Butt out."

"I don't think so."

I wiggled out of his arms, my mood darkening at

the realization that I was only free because he'd allowed it.

"I've had quite enough posturing from the males in my life today." I scowled.

Surprisingly, Nathaniel grinned. "Forgive me, my love. I can't help it."

I rolled my eyes, but butterflies danced in my stomach at *my love*.

"I thought you had work to do."

He got to his feet. "I did. I was driving past, and the bond told me you needed me."

"How come I can't feel you like that?"

He just raised one eyebrow. "Perhaps you should ask yourself that question."

I studied him. "Are you pissed at me?"

"No."

Nathaniel didn't lie. But that didn't mean he wasn't…hurt.

Stepping closer, I ran one hand up his T-shirt and around to the back of his neck. "You're too tall," I complained.

A moment later, I was in his arms, my legs wrapped around his waist as he strode toward my desk.

12

EVIE

"Is this better?"

I opened my mouth, but Nathaniel was already kissing me. I couldn't help but laugh as he sat me on the edge of my desk. Tricky wolf.

He pulled away, and I blinked as my T-shirt was suddenly swept over my head. Nathaniel let out a sound like a rough purr, more cat than wolf, his gaze fixed on my breasts.

His mouth nibbled along the line where my bra met my skin, and I twined my hands in his hair, holding him to me. "God, you're sexy," he mumbled, and then he was undoing my bra, smiling in satisfaction as my breasts popped free.

He was still fully dressed, and I pushed his T-shirt up until he pulled it off. My jeans went next, and I squirmed as he just stood and stared at me.

Cool air teased my nipples, and I shifted on the

desk. Nathaniel groaned, stripping off his jeans.

And then he was kissing his way down my belly, one hand gently pushing against my chest and encouraging me to lie back. I shoved a folder aside, and Nathaniel chuckled as it fell to the floor.

He pressed his mouth against my hip, and I moaned. How had my hip suddenly become so sensitive? I blinked down at it, and Nathaniel peeled my underwear off with a grin.

"I love seeing you like this. Dazed, lost in pleasure. Because of *me*."

Possessive wolf. His mouth found my heat, and he pushed my thighs wider. He'd locked the office door, but it still felt taboo, lying naked on my desk in the middle of the day.

"Now, now, now," I chanted.

Thankfully, Nathaniel didn't tease me. Within a moment, he was pushing inside me, his gaze on the place where we were joined.

"You take me so perfectly. Look at how fucking sexy you are."

I almost came just from his rough growl and dirty talk alone. But he was pushing my legs wider, my knees higher, until I was splayed out beneath him and he was so deep, all I could do was moan.

He angled my hips until he was pressed right against my G-spot. I clenched around him, and he laughed.

"Right there, huh?"

He clasped my hand in hand, sliding it down to my clit. "Touch yourself for me."

My cheeks flamed. I wasn't a prude, but this was the middle of the day. The lighting in this office wasn't exactly flattering, and I hadn't had much time to work out...

"Evie."

Nathaniel stopped moving. His eyes hardened until he was staring down at me. "I've wanted you for so fucking long. You're the sexiest woman I've ever seen. Now, touch yourself for me."

I let one finger tease my clit. Nathaniel growled as I tightened around him, and my heart thrilled at it. Then he was thrusting into me, and the combination of the feel of him against my G-spot and the brush of my own fingers over my clit...

"That's it. Come around my cock, Evie."

I had no choice. My body ignited. Literally.

Flames poured from me. Terror flashed, even as my climax crested.

"Oh God, oh God, are you okay?"

Nathaniel was smiling down at me. And that was awe I saw in his eyes. "Your flames don't burn me, Evie. You could never hurt your mate."

He thrust into me again. He was still hard.

"You'll come just like that. Again. But this time, without fear."

I shook my head. I was far too sensitive for that. He just slammed his mouth down on mine, his tongue thrusting into my mouth as his cock plowed into my pussy.

I panted against his mouth, and he angled my hips even more, lifting my butt off the desk and holding me in place for him as he somehow drove deeper.

The sound I made was somewhere between a moan and a yelp.

Nathaniel smiled against my mouth. Then he was gazing down at me, his eyes dark.

"There you go."

He picked up his pace, his own breath turning unsteady, and it was seeing him losing control, seeing the way his gaze drifted over my body as if he were memorizing this moment...

I jolted as the flames burst from me again, but Nathaniel's smug grin let me know he wasn't being hurt. All I could do was shudder in his arms as my climax swept over me.

Nathaniel growled, his movements turning almost desperate. Then he was holding me close as he flooded me with heat.

I lay on the desk, staring up at the ceiling as I caught my breath. Nathaniel kissed along my neck, achingly gentle, and I slid my fingers into his hair, guiding him down to me so I could nibble on his lower lip.

Then he disappeared into the bathroom, returning with a cloth, which he used to clean me up, ignoring the way I blushed and squirmed.

Pulling on my clothes, I watched him as he pulled out his phone, frowning down at whatever he was reading.

I cleared my throat. "About the bond…"

"We'll discuss it later, when you're not so stressed," he said. "Tell Danica I say hi."

Prowling toward me, he pressed a kiss to my cheek and headed for the door. I just watched him go.

We weren't going to discuss the flames? Men.

I straightened up my desk, blushing at the way Nathaniel had made me moan for him.

Thankfully, my flames hadn't burned anything. I wasn't sure exactly what was going on with my magic, but I'd have to ask Selina about it.

Now *that* was going to be an awkward conversation.

I sighed. At least I'd stopped glowing at weird times. The flames were embarrassing, but Nathaniel was the only one who'd seen them.

Within a few minutes, I was locking my office door behind me and driving to the underworld portal.

Nerves rattled through me. A part of me was hoping to hit traffic. Maybe someone would call with an emergency that only I could handle. I glanced at my phone, which was sitting on the passenger seat. Of course, the moment I could actually use a calamity, nothing happened. Typical.

A demon I didn't recognize was guarding the portal. He must've recognized me, though, because he simply nodded and stepped aside. Seriously? If he were an asshole who gave me a hard time, I would've had an excuse to turn back around.

Blowing out a breath, I stepped through the portal. It wasn't like me to be this nonconfrontational. But not talking to Danica felt a lot like those long years when all I'd had was the coven.

"Hey," I greeted Sathanas, who was on his way to the portal himself. "You know where Danica is?"

"Hey, Evie. Last I heard, she was in the wyvern stable."

I grimaced and he laughed. "Yeah, my thoughts exactly."

"Thanks."

"No problem." From the curious look in his eyes, he knew all about my fight with my sister.

Demons gossiped worse than old ladies at bingo.

I slowly made my way down the stairs and into the wyvern stable. My sister was standing on the balcony, staring down at the wyverns below. She had that look she sometimes wore when she was attempting to figure out the answer to a difficult puzzle.

Danica flicked me a single glance as I approached. In her eyes, I saw a mixture of relief, sadness, and wariness. My throat tightened. She was expecting me to snarl at her again.

"Hi," I got out.

"Hi."

I gestured at the wyverns. "Any luck?"

"No. Whatever Lucifer did has kept them half feral. We've tried almost everything, but Samael is convinced we're only buying them time. This is no life for them."

I looked down, down, down, where the wyverns were chained, kept from flight. If given their freedom, they'd destroy anything and everything. It was how they were bred. My sister—who most people assumed was tough and unfeeling—was becoming almost desperate to find a way to let them take to the skies once more.

Clearing my throat, I watched the wyverns snarl and snap. "I've been thinking of a potential spell. I'm going to talk to Selina about it."

"Thanks."

"I think we need to talk," I said.

Danica glanced at me once more. Then she turned and leaned against the balcony railing.

"I owe you a better apology," she said. "One without any excuses. Lying to you was inexcusable. And you're right. You were lied to so many times over the years, and I hate that I—"

"No, listen to me," I said. "Please."

Danica clamped her mouth closed.

I took a deep breath. "I was so pissed at you. But I was more pissed at myself. For being someone who needed to be lied to."

"You're not."

I shrugged. "Everyone in my life agreed I would

run if I found out. And, honestly? I would have. I was a broken person after the attack on the coven. Losing Brooke… I don't think I'll ever fully recover. I was like a wild animal that would have chewed off its own leg to be free of a steel trap. And knowing I was Nathaniel's mate? Before I got a chance to really understand who he was and just how much he wants me to be happy? How much he loves me? I would have left Durham."

"You would've come back."

"Maybe. Maybe not." I took a deep breath. "I met a fae woman in the seelie king's dungeon. Her name is Hellaphine. She was half starved, filthy, dehydrated. We offered her a way out, and she refused. She told us she had to find her sister, even if it meant she was taken to the lab."

My eyes burned. "And I knew you'd make the same choice. If I were taken, you'd do whatever it took to get to me." My voice broke, and I brushed at the tears escaping my eyes.

"Of course I would," Danica murmured. "And you'd do the same for me."

"I would. I'd burn the fucking world down. Hearing how scared she was for her sister, it made me remember how short life is. How we all could've died not long ago. How you almost did. I'm still pissed at you for lying. But I should've taken a breath. Should've thought about what I really wanted to say to you, instead of screaming at you."

"You were pissed. You had a right to be. You have

no idea how many times I've wished Nathaniel didn't tell me you were his mate. But I think he was...shell-shocked by it all."

I nodded. "He never expected me. And I never expected *him*. I'm sorry for the things I said."

"I'm sorry for lying to you."

Danica wrapped her arms around me, and I breathed her in. My badass big sister.

When we were both finished blubbering, I pulled back.

Danica smirked at me. "You have sex hair."

"I have no idea what you're talking about."

"Uh-huh."

Time for a change of subject. "I have something to show you." I pulled Misty out of my knife sheath.

Danica gaped. "I left that with the Merqueen."

"I know. I don't know what it was doing in the seelie king's armory, but it's mine now." I preened.

"Be careful with that, Evie. It's more powerful than most people could imagine."

"I know. I remember that time it talked in my head." I shivered. "But I also know it can help us take down HFE. We've identified the leader now. His name is Lennox Rees. But we need the people he delegates to."

"Lennox Rees," Danica mused. "Your uncle has been busy."

"That's what I said."

"How are things with you and Nathaniel?"

I shrugged. "They're good… I think I pissed him off, though. He can feel what I'm feeling, and I can't seem to do the same."

"You want some advice?"

"Always."

"Don't try to shut him out. Tell him how you're feeling and let him in."

"That doesn't exactly come naturally."

She laughed. "Believe me, I know. You saw how hard Samael had to work. But if you're committed to Nathaniel, you need to be all in."

An image of him skewered with the metal bolt flashed in my mind, and I shuddered. That was the moment I'd made my choice, and I was just mad at myself that it had taken him being in that much pain for me to realize how much I loved him. If he'd died in that moment, he would have gone to his death thinking I'd never forgive him.

"What's wrong?"

I filled her in.

She winced. "Yeah, I understand. When Samael was turning to ash…" Pain filled her eyes, and some of the color drained from her face. "There's something about seeing the person you love suffer that makes you gain a whole lot of perspective real quick."

"It sure does. I better go. Thanks for the advice."

"Anytime. Evie?"

"Yeah?"

"You want to come stay for a few days when this

is over? You and Nathaniel?"

"For sure."

She grinned at me. Her hand came up to ruffle my hair, and I batted it away. "Don't even start with that shit."

She laughed, and I hauled myself up the stairs and back to the portal.

My mind raced as I drove back to wolf territory. HFE had continued to elude us. No matter what we did. They were always one step ahead of us. We couldn't afford to take them out one by one. We needed a plan that would take them all out at once.

I needed to turn right onto West Cornwallis Road to get back to wolf territory. At the last second, I changed my mind and drove straight toward Hope Valley.

Aubrey needed to know what the seelie king was doing to his people. And it was the kind of news I had to give him in person.

My gaze flicked up to my rearview mirror. The silver truck behind me had *also* turned at the last minute. It could be a coincidence. But I was betting it wasn't.

I made a mental note of the license plate. Then I took the next right. And the next.

The truck followed me. Sloppy.

Whoever was driving the silver truck was following me, and they weren't even being subtle about it.

There was no way I was leading them to Aubrey's. Or to the pack.

I ran through my options in my head as I drove.

These guys were morons. And if I could take one of them back to the pack, we could question them, and they could lead us to HFE.

I turned onto the next street. And another silver truck careened toward me.

"Fuck!"

I swerved just in time.

The truck drove past me and pulled into a driveway, using it to turn around. I flicked my gaze between the road in front of me and my rearview mirror as it joined the first silver truck behind me.

"That's cheating."

Two of them. There wasn't much chance I was going to be able to take down both drivers. Now, my plan needed to be all about escape.

I knew this neighborhood. Had spent enough time in both werewolf territory and fae territory to figure out a place where there would be few humans around to get caught in the cross fire.

The car I'd borrowed from the pack was loaded with safety features, and it would win if it came down to speed. But two against one weren't great odds.

My gaze shot to the rearview mirror. Several men were in the truck directly behind me, and I was betting the same for the other truck following it.

I slowed as we approached an intersection. The

truck directly behind me didn't slow.

It hit my bumper hard enough to give me a jolt. I crossed the white line and rolled into the intersection.

Thankfully, there were no other cars crossing. True fear slid into my stomach, thick and greasy. These guys didn't care who they killed, as long as they took me out. I couldn't create a ward around a moving vehicle and still concentrate on trying to lose them. I was good, but I only had so much focus. Especially with adrenaline pounding through my body.

I needed to make my way back toward wolf territory. At least there, I'd be close enough to call for help.

A third silver truck appeared on my right. It flicked its headlights at me, and my skin turned clammy. I was sandwiched.

I put my foot down. My heart pounded as I searched fruitlessly for an escape plan. Both sides of this street were wooded. But I'd take my chances.

Hauling the wheel to the right, I aimed for the grassy area next to the road.

The silver truck behind me clipped the back of my car.

I screamed as my car flew through the air.

EVIE

Stars danced in front of my eyes.

What had happened?

It came back in a flash. My head had hit the window when the car rolled. It had landed right-side up, but my brain felt scrambled.

I had to get out.

My seat belt had tightened until it was practically strangling me. I stabbed at the buckle, my hand shaking. My peripheral vision caught one of the trucks backing up, preparing to ram me again.

I opened the door and fell out of the car and onto the grass, my head spinning. My Beretta was in my hand automatically, and I aimed at the men pouring from the other two cars.

Where was the third truck?

To my left. Roaring toward me. I rolled down the shoulder of the road, and the truck rammed my car.

My ward was created with a thought, and I managed to stumble up to my feet, surveying the men who'd surrounded me on three sides.

"Give it up, witch. You're outnumbered."

I narrowed my eyes at the speaker—a weasel of a man with short legs and wide shoulders. "What exactly did you expect to happen from this rendezvous, gentlemen?"

"Come with us, and no one else needs to get hurt."

I smiled, taking in the empty street. "I don't see anyone else. Do you?"

He spat on the street, and my smile widened. My instincts had been spot-on when they'd urged me to get away from humans who could be used as leverage. Still, just because I wasn't in a busy area didn't mean someone wouldn't drive down this street in the next few minutes.

"We don't want to hurt you," another man called. He was wearing a suit for this little mission, and something told me he was more dangerous than Weasel. My gaze dropped to the syringe in his hand, and I laughed.

"Let me tell you where you can stick *that*."

One of the men fired, and his bullet ricocheted off my ward. I couldn't hold a ward this thick for long. I was still recovering from the power drain in the seelie realm. But hopefully they wouldn't know just how much it sapped my energy.

"Looking a little tired," Suit said. "That was a nasty bump to the head. Wonder how long you'll be able to keep us away from you."

Okay, so they definitely knew. Really, I shouldn't be surprised that HFE knew exactly how my power worked.

"More than long enough." I smiled.

I closed my eyes, ignoring their murmuring. Then I reached for my mate bond. I could almost picture it in my mind's eye, silver and twisted and *strong*.

I tugged.

"What's she look so happy for?" one of the men muttered to Weasel. He ignored him.

"Why exactly do you want me?" I asked, killing time.

The bond was the clearest it had ever been. I didn't know why—maybe because of my desperation? But I could feel Nathaniel's rage. Could feel his fear for me. He'd felt my terror, and he was on his way. Wherever he had been, he was moving toward me now.

Suit took another step closer. "You belong to HFE. Just like all the other lab brats. You've had your taste of freedom, and now it's time to return to your owners."

The thought made nausea swim through me.

Other lab brats.

I was going to free those kids, no matter what it took.

"It won't be that bad, darling," Weasel crooned, as if attempting to tame a wild animal. "You're powerful. HFE will give you more freedom than the others."

I mentally weighed which of them would know the most. Weasel was doing the talking, but the other men were flicking glances toward Suit. I'd paid enough attention to the werewolves' body language that I'd learned how to tell who was in charge.

If I fired on them—either with my power or my bullets—I'd have to drop my ward. One of these days, I was going to learn how to create a ward I could shoot out of but was still impenetrable from the outside.

I eyed the men, who'd spread out farther, likely hoping to rush me at some point. "Did you seriously think this would work?"

"You don't *have* to be alive," Weasel said. Suit just watched me out of those dead eyes.

That's what this was. They'd take me if they could, but if they couldn't, they figured they'd stop me from shutting them down. What they didn't know was that if they ever succeeded in killing me, my mate would rampage through their sick little group until they were all dead.

Nathaniel would never stop.

But he'd also never regain his humanity, and I couldn't let that happen.

I could feel my mate approaching from his territory. Given how close he was, he must have been driving. Good. We could put one of these guys in his trunk.

"This isn't going to end how you think it will," I warned.

One of the men positioned behind the truck fired again, and I barely kept my ward in place. The bullets thunked into my ward, then dropped to the ground.

"This is only a matter of time," Weasel called. "Be a good little girl and drop the ward. I'll tell my superiors you cooperated."

And then Nathaniel was there.

He wasn't driving like I'd thought. No, he was all wolf.

He must've run so fast, I wouldn't be surprised if his paws were bleeding.

The huge wolf launched himself at Weasel and ripped out his throat.

"Alive," I called. "We need at least one of them alive."

Nathaniel turned and snarled at me.

I sighed. "I'll stay behind my ward."

The HFE lackeys turned to run. Some of them disappeared into the woods on either side of the road, while others were launching themselves at the cars. Nathaniel took care of those first.

A car pulled up, and I ran toward Ryker, enveloping him in my ward.

"He's pissed." He nodded at Nathaniel.

"We need one of them alive. I nominate the guy in the suit. He seems to be relatively high up."

Ryker sighed. "Drop your ward."

I dropped it long enough for him to run toward Nathaniel. Naomi had gotten out the other side of the car, and she nodded at me. "You okay?"

"Fine." I automatically included her in my ward. She knocked on it, clearly annoyed, and I ignored her.

More cars were pulling up. Several wolves had already shifted, and they poured out of the vehicles, scouring the area for any other HFE members.

I had no idea where my phone was, so I turned back to Naomi. "Can you call Steve? Give him that plate number."

She nodded, turning away. Nathaniel had cornered Suit, who was deathly pale, pressed against his car. Ryker was talking to Nathaniel, and from the look on his face, he was attempting to calm him down.

I frowned. That was unlike Nathaniel. He had a temper, but he was usually able to control it when it came to the bigger picture.

I attempted to reach him with the bond, but now that I was out of immediate danger, the bond felt distant again.

He must have known I needed him, though, because he turned toward me, and within a moment he was human once more, stalking toward me.

He opened his mouth, and I shook my head at him, dropping my ward. "I don't have a lecture in me right now."

"Later, then." Hauling me into his arms, he held me tight, and I could hear his heart thumping beneath my ear. I'd worried him.

"Let's get you home," he murmured, steering me to one of the empty cars. One of his wolves threw him a pair of sweats, and he stopped just long enough to pull them on.

"What about—"

"Ryker and Naomi can handle it. Xander is on his way too." Nathaniel opened the passenger door and gently helped me sit. I would have protested him treating me like I was made of glass, but now that my adrenaline had worn off, *everything* hurt.

I was attempting to muffle my pain noises, but from the flash of the wolf in Nathaniel's eyes, I wasn't being as quiet as I thought I was. He closed my car door carefully enough that I suspected he was barely restraining himself from ripping it off and beating the closest HFE member with it.

He loped around the front of the car, slid inside, and closed his own door just as carefully. He was keeping his gaze away from Suit, who was currently surrounded by his wolves.

Nathaniel did a three-point turn, handling the car as expertly as he handled everything else. My cheek throbbed, and I poked at it. Pain exploded across my face.

"Don't touch," Nathaniel told me, and I glowered at him. He caught my hand in his and brought my palm to his mouth, laying a gentle kiss at the center.

It was hard to be mad at him when he was being so sweet. Unfortunately, I could also feel his wolf, simmering with fury.

"Sorry about the car."

He just shot me a look that said I was acting crazy. I sighed.

"Stay there," he told me, pulling up outside his house. I unbuckled myself but waited as he crossed around the car and opened my door. He held out his hand, and I moved as slowly as if I'd just turned ninety.

The house was quiet. Nathaniel escorted me inside and then took a deep breath, surveying my face.

"You have a fucking black eye."

I squinted at him. He was taking this worse than I'd expected.

"What's your deal?"

"What's my *deal?* Tell me, Evie, did you consider driving toward my territory? Toward your home?"

Okay, he was pissed. I angled my head, considering how I wanted to play this. Honesty was probably the best policy, which meant things were going to get worse before they got better.

I sighed. "Yeah, I considered it."

"And why did you decide not to?"

"There are kids here, Nathaniel."

He showed me his teeth. "Deep in our territory, tucked behind our sentries and several layers of security."

"Your pack has been dragged into enough of my shit." I pushed my hair off my face with a wince.

"And there it is."

"There *what* is?"

"They're your pack now too. They're your family."

I felt my lower lip stick out. "Doesn't feel like a family. Naomi still hates me, half the humans think I'm the worst thing to happen to this place…"

A flicker of humor appeared in those blue, blue eyes. "No one said that family was perfect. What is a family except a bunch of different people forced to get along and love one another even when they don't particularly *like* one another?"

I shrugged. His eyes turned cool again as his gaze got stuck on the bruise on my cheek. He'd seen me much worse off than this and hadn't lost his shit. Was it because I was his mate now?

"HFE followed you, blindsided you, and would've kidnapped you. And you were so close to my territory, my wolf could sense you. I could *feel* your fucking terror, Evie. But you were blocking me from finding you until you reached for the bond."

"I thought I had it handled."

"It's my job to handle it for you."

When cornered, go on the offensive. My sister had taught me that. "So, what? You're allowed to protect me, but I'm not allowed to protect you?"

It was the first time I'd seen Nathaniel speechless, and I enjoyed it. For about a microsecond.

"Need I remind you that I'm an Alpha werewolf?"

"Need *I* remind you that I'm a freak with plenty of magic at my disposal?"

"Call yourself a freak again," he said, his voice quiet.

Shivering at the threat in his tone, I cleared my throat. "We're getting off track. Look, we're both new to this. We need to find some kind of compromise."

"Here's my compromise. Next time you find

yourself being chased by our enemies—who would love to take you back to their lab so they can study your insides—you call me."

I winced at that visual. "That sounds more like an order than any kind of compromise."

He stared at me. I planted my hands on my hips and stared back. With a deep sigh, he closed his eyes, and when he opened them again, they were their usual dark blue. "I adore you."

I narrowed my eyes. What kind of tactic was this?

"Sweet-talking won't get you what you want either, buddy." Although it had a higher chance than his *orders*.

"And there's that cynical woman I fell in love with." He took a step closer until he could catch my chin in his hand. "I was worried for you."

"When I realized there was more than one of them, I was heading back toward wolf territory," I muttered. "I realized I was in deep shit, and I'd decided to..."

"Decided to allow me to help."

My traitorous lower lip was sticking out again. I sucked it back in. "Yeah," I admitted.

His eyes flashed. "I suppose I should be grateful for that, at least."

"Are you going to be like this all day? Just let me know so I can decide if I'll hang around."

"Fuck, you have a smart mouth. And you *will* be hanging around. You're going nowhere without me from now on."

I scowled at him. "Just try it, buddy."

"That look would work better if your face weren't bruised and swollen. You need some ice on it."

He wasn't wrong. I was feeling every bump and bruise. I followed Nathaniel into the kitchen. Tobias was nowhere to be seen. He'd likely fled when he heard us fighting. I couldn't blame him.

Nathaniel hunted through the freezer until he found an ice pack. I took it and held it up to my face with a wince.

He was watching me. "Where else are you hurt?"

"It's not a big deal."

"Evie."

"Fine. Just don't freak out." I turned and stalked out of the kitchen and up the stairs. Nathaniel prowled behind me, so close I could practically feel his warm breath on the back of my neck.

When we were finally in his bedroom, I dropped the ice pack on the bed and reached for my shirt.

My breath caught in my throat at the movement, and Nathaniel's gentle hands were suddenly there. "Let me."

I managed to keep most of my whimpers to myself, but from the way Nathaniel's wolf watched me, I wasn't fooling anyone.

"I'm okay," I said.

"I'll determine that," Nathaniel told me. "We should cut this."

I shrugged. I was wearing an old band T-shirt and leggings. I hadn't worn a pretty summer dress for a while.

Nathaniel's claws popped out, and my T-shirt fell away like it was nothing. I was wearing a sports bra underneath.

"Don't cut that."

"Evie."

"You know how hard it is to find a decent sports bra? And how expensive they are? Cut it and die, Nathaniel."

My threat removed the last of the wolf from his eyes, and his lips twitched.

"Let out your breath," he said.

I did, and his hands were gentle as he unhooked my bra.

A low growl sounded in his throat as he looked at me. I didn't take that growl to mean any sexy times were in my future.

"Seat belt," I said.

I was going to have one hell of a bruise. It started above my left shoulder and tracked diagonally across my body.

"You'll see a healer," Nathaniel said.

Since I wanted to be able to function over the next few days and I could already feel myself stiffening up, I agreed.

What I didn't agree with was his tone.

I narrowed my eyes, and Nathaniel stared back, unamused.

"You're seeing a healer. Period."

I sniffed. "Try again."

I watched as he considered me. Finally, he smiled.

"Evie Amana, love of my life," he purred, and my thighs clenched. "I would like for you to see a healer, so you're not in pain when I fuck the sass right out of you."

I grinned at him. "Good luck with that. My sass happens to be permanent. Besides, it just so happens I *want* to see a healer."

He leaned forward and nuzzled me, achingly gentle. Then he turned and stalked into the bathroom. I attempted to peel off my leggings while he was in there, but bending over hurt like a bitch. Nathaniel prowled back out of the bathroom, his wolf in his eyes.

He dropped to his knees in front of me, gently encouraging me to step out of the leggings so I wouldn't need to lean over. He pressed a kiss to one of my knees, then the other.

"Go get into the bath. I'll have the healer come here. And then you'll rest."

I didn't bother arguing. Honestly, after the day I'd had, I could use some doting. And if the healer managed to do something with this bruising, I could probably seduce my mate.

My toes curled at the thought, and Nathaniel glanced back up at me, raising one eyebrow. "What exactly are you thinking?"

I smirked down at him. "Never you mind."

When I was completely naked, Nathaniel took me by the hand and led me into the bathroom. I blinked at the frothy bubbles. Whatever he'd dumped in the bath was filling the room with the scent of jasmine.

He'd taken the time to light a candle, and it was sitting on the side of the tub next to more of my shampoo and conditioner.

I knew damn well Nathaniel hadn't had candles or bubble bath before I'd appeared in his life. I'd scared the crap out of him, and he'd still taken the time to attempt to spoil me.

"Evie?"

"I love you."

Surprise flickered across his face. But the smile he gave me was so sweetly open, I couldn't help but nestle closer and lift onto my tiptoes for a kiss.

Just that amount of movement hurt. I tried to cover it up, but I ended up gasping against his mouth.

Nathaniel growled. "Get in the bath."

This time, I didn't bother attempting to stifle my pain noises as he helped me into the tub. When I was finally settled, Nathaniel's wolf was staring back at me. He leaned over, placed a kiss on my head, and strode out.

This was difficult for him.

This whole mating thing was new to both of us, but *I* didn't have an entirely different creature inside me to negotiate with.

A while later, Nathaniel knocked on the door, immediately striding into the bathroom. "Healer is here."

Getting out of the tub was worse than getting in.

When Nathaniel had bundled me into a robe, he led me into our room and gestured for me to sit on the bed. Several ice packs were waiting next to the bed, and he managed to position them right at all my worst aches and pains.

When I was settled, he let Neana in. She'd healed Charlie's arm, and, according to Tobias, Nathaniel was in negotiations with her to move in to wolf territory so the pack would always have a healer close by. Nathaniel's other healer often traveled with the dominants, which kept them safe. But he wanted someone close by as well.

"Hi, Evie. Wow, you really did a number on yourself, huh?"

"Hi. It's not that bad. Really."

She tutted as she took in the bruising, pulling a hair tie off her wrist and tying her hair back. "Seat belt definitely saved you from much, much worse injuries."

I swallowed at the thought, my mouth suddenly dry. If I'd been trapped in that car, in too much pain to get out or create my ward, I likely wouldn't be here.

Nathaniel was pacing, and I held out my hand. He knelt by the bed and pressed a gentle kiss to my knuckles. Glancing at the healer, he raised one eyebrow. "What's the prognosis?"

"I can take care of the bruising now, but you'll still be a little sore for a few days," she told me. "Likely a bit stiff."

Not ideal, but it wasn't like I could do *anything* in

my current condition.

"Okay. Thanks."

She got to work. Nathaniel sat next to me and took my hand. My eyes grew heavy. One of the main side effects of healing was a long, deep sleep. It was as if the body had to catch up to the unnatural speed of recovery.

My eyes closed entirely against my will. "Don't leave yet," I murmured.

Nathaniel pressed several gentle kisses across my face. "I won't. Go to sleep."

"More orders."

But this one, I wanted to follow. I curled up next to my mate and drifted off.

NATHANIEL

I sat on the edge of my bed and watched my mate. She was sleeping peacefully now, most of the bruising gone, but the healer had focused on the deeper injuries.

I knew it would take time for Evie to truly feel like the pack was her family. And yet her commitment to protecting the kids proved that she was already a part of the pack. The thought of her alone and scared in that car...

My claws shot out, and it took a long moment before I could tuck them back where they belonged.

She'd done everything right.

I wouldn't have brought them back to my pack either. It was difficult to admit, because the thought of my mate alone and in danger made me want to turn back time and rip all of the HFE members apart.

There was still one alive. The fact that he was breathing was an insult, but we needed to get any information from him that we could. My people would be going through their phones, but for now...

My phone buzzed, and I dug it out of my pocket. Xander had the one Evie had nicknamed "Suit" in our cell.

Rolling to my feet, I leaned over and placed a kiss on Evie's cheek. I would find out exactly what they wanted with her. And I would make them regret ever targeting my mate.

Naomi was waiting downstairs. "Evie asked me to message Steve with the license plate number. He's still checking, but he said it's registered to a family in New York."

"Not difficult to mess with license plates if you know what you're doing."

Good thing we had one of the HFE members alive.

Five minutes later, I was smiling down at "Suit." Ryker stood next to him, while Kyla leaned against the wall. She'd come as soon as she'd heard Evie had been attacked.

"Do you know who I am?"

He strained against the ropes holding him. Then

he spat on the floor. "Alpha werewolf."

"That's exactly right. And the woman you attempted to kill is my mate."

A dark stain spread along his pants, and Kyla chuckled as the scent of urine filled the air.

"Yeah," Ryker growled. "You fucked up."

"We weren't going to kill her. We were just going to—"

"Deliver her to a life of torture and misery?"

He clamped his mouth shut. I took a step closer, and he began to shudder. My wolf was pleased by his terror.

"You have one chance to live," I said. "Tell us everything you know. You lie, you die."

"They'll kill me."

"I'll kill you worse," I promised. "We let you go, and you have a chance to run. Or you die here. Decide."

His eyes darted. Satisfaction slid through my veins. This man had terrorized my mate. Now he would feel exactly what she had felt.

"What do you want to know?"

In the end, we didn't get much out of him. Someone had said Lennox Rees's name when Suit first began working for him. But we already had that information.

Suit's orders were to take Evie to an abandoned warehouse in Raleigh, where another group of HFE members would pick her up. Ryker had snapped Suit's fingers one by one. Either he didn't know where they'd planned to take Evie after that, or he was tougher than we'd thought. And the stain on his pants proved he wasn't exactly resilient.

Smart of HFE to make sure none of the men they'd sent to capture Evie could lead back to them. I glanced at Ryker, and he nodded.

"On it."

He'd take a group of wolves to the abandoned warehouse, but I had no doubt HFE would have fled the moment they learned their little friends weren't returning.

My claws slid out before I was aware they were free.

Suit's gaze dropped, and he swallowed. "You said—"

I lashed out, my claws slicing through his throat. Blood sprayed and I smiled. "I lied."

14

EVIE

I woke up feeling more refreshed than I had in weeks. Unfortunately, the sun was streaming through the gaps in the dark curtains, and Nathaniel was nowhere to be seen.

I'd overslept. Again. If I wasn't careful, I was going to get a reputation as a sloth.

My body felt better, though. The pain had shifted from an all-encompassing agony to a dull throb.

Clearly, I was winning at life.

I picked up my phone and checked my messages.

Enjoy your rest, sleeping beauty. Message me when you wake up.

Nathaniel. I flicked him a quick message asking where he was, and I wasn't surprised when he didn't immediately respond. He was probably out doing Alpha stuff.

My phone buzzed again.

Come see me when you wake up. We need to talk. Kyla. That sounded concerning.

I gave my body a stern talking-to and made it to my feet with a groan. My gaze landed on the end of the bed, and I was lifting the clothes before I realized I'd moved.

"Is he crazy? Cashmere? I'll ruin this within an hour," I muttered. A piece of paper fell to the floor, and I picked it up.

Stay comfortable today.

PS: I don't care if you ruin it.

He knew me too well. I raised the soft-as-butter sweater to my face and snuggled into it.

Two minutes later, I was dressed in the gray sweatpants and sweater. Although calling them sweats seemed ridiculous. Nathaniel even included a tank with a surprisingly supportive built-in bra, so I didn't need to wrestle with a real bra.

"He's a keeper," I murmured, scooping my hair into a ponytail. I made my way downstairs, but Tobias stepped out of the kitchen, blocking my path to the front door.

"Nope," he said. "Come with me."

I sighed but followed him back into the kitchen.

"I need two minutes." He handed me a coffee, and I sat at the huge island while he bustled around the kitchen.

Exactly two minutes later, he handed me a Tupperware container with two breakfast sandwiches, complete with egg, sausage, and cheese.

"How'd you know I was up?"

"Nathaniel messaged me."

That sneaky wolf. "These look great. Thanks."

"Tell Kyla I say hello."

"Is there anything you *don't* know?"

"Very little. Nathaniel said to tell you that if you need to use the black SUV in the driveway, you can. But he would prefer you rested."

"Mm-hm. And he thought it would go better for him if you communicated that little preference to me, huh?"

Tobias grinned. "That's right."

"Thanks for these. I better go."

Kyla had her own cabin and she'd sent me directions, so I moseyed toward it. She was lounging on her porch swing when I arrived, a cup of coffee in her hand. Virtus was sprawled out on the porch next to her. He opened one eye and greeted me with a nod of his head. I leaned over and scratched his ear, handing the box to Kyla.

"Tobias thought you might be hungry."

"I love that man."

"I'll fight you for his affections."

She grinned at me and tapped her breakfast sandwich to mine.

I stroked the griffin's silky ear some more. "Sorry, Virtus, I didn't know you were here."

He opened his other eye, and the fact that he'd

already eaten appeared in my mind. Communicating with him could be strange.

"You look comfy," Kyla said.

Taking a seat on the swing, I took a giant bite, careful not to drip on my pants.

"How did he get his hands on these so quickly?" I asked.

Kyla shrugged. "Wolves are tactile. We like soft fabrics and things that feel good against our skin. I wouldn't be surprised if he had an entire closet of stuff for you, but he's holding back 'cause he knows you'd freak out."

Butterflies rampaged through my stomach. Sometimes, I still struggled to believe Nathaniel was *mine*. He was running his pack, we were throwing all our resources at finding HFE, and he'd still taken the time to make sure I was comfortable today.

"I don't like the thought of him holding back."

She shrugged one shoulder. "It's smart to keep men like Nathaniel on their toes."

That summed up Kyla's usual theory when it came to men. God help the man she eventually chose to be hers. At least he'd never be bored.

We chomped on our sandwiches.

"How have I never seen your place before?" I asked Kyla when I was done.

She glanced at me. "I don't spend a ton of time at home anymore. Plus, I insisted on taking one of these cabins as far away from everyone as I could get. For obvious reasons, Nathaniel needed to be convinced that I could move home again after the whole almost going feral thing. I'd only moved back in a few days before he hired you to look into the kids." Kyla slid off the swing, stepped around Virtus, and gestured for me to follow her inside.

I gaped. Kyla's front door opened straight into her living room. One whole wall held built-in bookshelves, with so many books on them, she'd been forced to place books on top of the careful stacks.

"Wow, you really like books, huh?"

"Yeah. I don't get as much time to read these days either. More coffee?"

"Please."

The gray sofa in front of the bookshelves looked worn-in and comfortable. Across from the sofa, a single armchair sat near the TV console, which had more books stacked on top of it.

I wandered over to Kyla's shelves, pulling a few books at random, scanning the backs.

"Romance?"

Kyla sniffed as she walked back in, carrying two cups. She placed them on the coffee table and curled up on the sofa.

"Men are trash. Except in fiction."

I grinned, picking up my coffee. I felt incapable of sitting, so I carried it to the window, sipping as I gazed out at the forest. "Great view." I waited for Kyla to get to whatever she needed to talk about.

"Can't complain." Kyla sighed. "Okay. I'm a little concerned."

"About what?"

"Nathaniel. He…interrogated the HFE member. I can't explain it, but there was something off with him. He seemed to *enjoy* killing him, which I've never seen from him before. I don't know if he's just stressed or what's going on, but…" She shrugged.

"He *has* been acting a little weird," I admitted. I immediately winced. Talking about Nathaniel behind his back felt like a betrayal, even though I knew Kyla only had the best intentions. "I think maybe I need to talk to him about it. Alone."

Kyla nodded. "I was going to suggest just that."

"Did you guys get anything out of Suit?"

"He gave up Lennox Rees. But we already had that name, thanks to your uncle. They were planning to hand you off at a warehouse in Raleigh. But the moment they didn't show, HFE would've known we had them."

"We need to hit them soon." I turned back to the window. "I've been thinking…"

"Oh yeah?"

"Gabriel. He keeps demanding a meeting with Nathaniel. And obviously, he's hoping to make him pay for killing Albert. But I never understood one thing. Keigan."

She frowned. "What do you mean?"

"Well, he said HFE put him in place to keep an eye

on the Mage Council, right?"

"Yeah."

"What if he was put in there to keep an eye on the mages? To make sure those mages didn't betray HFE?"

"You think the Mage Council has been working with HFE this entire time?"

I had no proof. Just a hunch. But it was a hunch I couldn't ignore.

"The Mage Council has always wanted one thing—to ensure humans were protected from paranormals. They formed the council, hired bounty hunters, trained their people—all to keep humans safe. It's not a huge leap to think maybe they learned about HFE and decided their way was better. HFE may be bigots and murderers, but they do it under the guise of evening the playing field between humans and paranormals."

"If that's the case, maybe we have an opportunity here."

"Exactly. Gabriel knows exactly who killed Albert, and he's hoping to take Nathaniel out. We need to take *him* out instead."

Kyla made a strangled sound. "You have any idea how powerful he is?"

I turned to face her. "Well…no. Do you?"

She shrugged. "No. But he's an unknown threat. We fail to take him, and we're in deep shit."

"Hmmm."

"You're already planning it, aren't you?"

"I sure am."

We strolled out of her door. I leaned down to say bye to Virtus, and he got to his feet, staring me dead in the eyes.

He was ready to be healed. But he wanted Danica to be there too. Along with me and Kyla. And Meredith, if she could make it.

"Not a problem." I smiled at him. "I'll get it sorted."

I glanced at Kyla, and she scratched Virtus's fluffy head. Of course she would know what Virtus was up to. When she was home, they were practically joined at the hip.

She jerked her head. "Someone's here to see you."

I turned, and my breath left my lungs in a rush.

"Liam. Hi."

"Hi."

"I haven't seen you since…"

"Since I gave you my car, and you used it to drive to the seelie portal."

I winced. "I guess Nathaniel wasn't too happy about that, huh?"

He shrugged. "He knows you. If you hadn't used my car, you would've gotten there some other way."

"True. Ah, you want to walk?"

He nodded, and I waved a hand at Kyla, still studying Liam. "How've you been?"

"You know, I'm okay. It's been strange having Nathaniel look at me like I'm a threat to him. He's stopped doing it so much now that you've finally mated." Liam glanced over his shoulder as if checking Nathaniel wasn't about to stalk out of the forest.

The forest seemed to have gone quiet around us as we walked back toward the road. "Did you know I was his mate? Before I found out?"

Liam sighed. "No. But when I heard you were his mate, it made perfect sense. I think my wolf knew, and I refused to see it. Afterward, when I was thinking about it... It was strange. One day, all I could think of was getting you naked, and the next, it was almost like you were a cousin or something."

I stared at him. "Excuse me?"

That lopsided grin flashed. "Yeah. I think my wolf recognized you were my Alpha's mate and would never be mine. It helped numb that part of me until my emotions caught up."

"Um..." I didn't know what to say to that, and he just patted me on the shoulder.

"You don't need to worry about me, Evie. I'm even dating again."

Interest sparked, and I grinned at him. "Tell me everything."

His cheeks flushed, and I couldn't help my smirk.

"It's new," he muttered, shifting on his feet. "You can meet her in a few weeks."

"How did you meet?"

"On Portal. She's a witch."

Portal was the paranormal dating app— responsible for more cross-faction cooperation than any treaty or deal ever created. I angled my head. "Do I know her?"

He shrugged. "I doubt it. She just moved here from Tennessee. She's looking for a new coven."

"Well, if she wants any advice about the Durham covens, tell her she can come to me."

Liam grinned. "Thanks, Evie."

NATHANIEL

Evie was standing with Liam.

He said something that had obviously amused her, because she burst out laughing, then punched him in the chest.

"Not flirting," I muttered to myself. I knew Evie. She didn't play games like that with people. Especially not with people she already thought she had hurt.

The boy thinks to take what is yours, a voice said in my head. *Kill him quickly, painlessly, and Evie will forgive you.*

I frowned. No, she wouldn't. Evie would never forgive anyone for killing someone she considered innocent.

My hands came up to my temples. I had a vicious headache.

"Nathaniel?"

I turned, finding Naomi watching me. After a

long moment, she finally spoke. "Hunter said to tell you he's on the way back. No sign that Frederik has been sending his wolves to HFE, although he's been approaching other wolves in an attempt to form an alliance and take you out."

A growl left my throat. "I should've killed him all those years ago."

Naomi just shrugged. "The power vacuum would've been a pain in the ass. Is everything okay?"

"Fine." I glanced at Evie again. Liam had left, and she was walking toward me.

"I have work to do," I said. Turning, I attempted to ignore the hurt flickering over Evie's face as I stalked back toward my car.

EVIE

I swallowed down my hurt as Nathaniel walked away from me. Beneath the hurt was confusion. He *knew* there was nothing between Liam and me. He likely even already knew Liam was dating someone else, thanks to his compulsive need to know *everything* that was happening in his pack.

Annoyance battled with concern. As much as I wanted to fight it out with Nathaniel, he'd made it clear he didn't want to talk. If he needed his space, I'd give it to him. To be honest, after that reaction, *I* needed a few hours of space.

Changing course, I headed back toward the road. I had work to do anyway. We needed to find the remaining labs—not to mention, we also needed to come up with a plan that would allow us to hit them all at the same time.

Rose was in my office when I arrived.

"You look glum," she said, and I sighed.

"Relationship stuff."

"I heard about the mating. Congrats."

"Thanks. What have you got?"

She nodded at the board. "Your uncle got in touch. He decided to follow the thread Keigan left when he spilled everything to Danica." Her face twisted, and I couldn't blame her. Keigan had been a Discipulus mage and my sister's mentor. Rose had worked with him too. And when Danica was held in the underworld, she learned he'd worked at the very lab that had kidnapped and imprisoned our mom.

"What did Eachann say?"

Rose's mouth twisted. "He's obviously the mysterious type. He said to tell you he found something, and that Keigan is just the start."

Well, that was cryptic. Thankfully, I was due to meet my uncle here tomorrow. I'd pick his brain then.

Rose planted herself at Kyla's desk, and we worked quietly for a few hours. The biggest issue with narrowing down the labs was digging through the various shell companies. If we were going to take

HFE down, we had to make sure they could never reorganize again.

Pulling the lapis lazuli out of my pocket, I studied it. I'd been compulsively checking it every day, but so far, Hellaphine was still in the seelie realm. As much as I hated how she was being treated, the longer she stayed there, the more time it would give us to find all the labs.

Eventually, Rose left to meet with Steve. "I'll keep you updated," she said as she strolled toward the door.

Nodding absently, I dove into my research. Excitement shot through me. I was seeing the patterns now. HFE thought they were untouchable. Sure, they'd buried their labs in those shell companies, but they used the exact same pattern each time. As soon as I dug deeper, their cover fell apart.

"Evie."

I jolted. Hunter was standing in the doorway. "Jeez, make some noise. How was your trip?"

"Fine. But what the hell is going on here?"

Frowning, I clicked into the next link. "What are you talking about?"

"Evie. Something's wrong with Nathaniel."

I looked up, my attention narrowing on his face. Hunter's expression was livid, and my heart thudded harder in my chest. "What do you mean?"

"I mean, he's acting strangely. In a way he's never acted before."

I told you, a little voice inside my head said. *You*

knew something was wrong.

A chill ripped through me as I watched Hunter. As I took in the concern in his eyes. He was one of Nathaniel's most trusted people. He knew him better than almost anyone.

"Strangely how?"

Hunter turned and paced, his lanky legs taking him from one side of my office to the other within a few paces. "Nathaniel has always been Alpha, but he's never wanted a pack that would do everything he said without question."

I knew that too. It was one of the reasons he'd asked me to help with the kids.

"But I just had a meeting with him, Ryker, Naomi, and Xander. Nathaniel is refusing to listen to anyone who disagrees with him, or even hear any suggestions. It's not like him. It's as if he's becoming..."

"A despot," I muttered, my head spinning. How had I missed it? How the *hell* had I missed it?

The way Nathaniel had spoken to Ryker that first night back. The shock in Ryker's eyes, and the way Tobias had stared. It was completely unlike Nathaniel not to be open to discussion with his people.

He'd overreacted with my uncle too. The Nathaniel I knew should've given Eachann a languid smile and assured him he loved me. Instead, he'd snarled.

Kyla had specifically told me how out of character it was for him to enjoy killing a prisoner.

Not to mention the look he'd given me a few

hours ago when he'd seen me talking to Liam. It had been as if he was a stranger.

Because part of him was.

I could feel the blood draining from my face, and I shakily made it to my feet. "That fucking book. He said he was giving it back, and I completely forgot about it. I handed him the backpack and never thought to check in with him. Oh God."

Hunter frowned. "What book?"

My lips had turned numb. I grabbed my keys and my purse.

I'd fix this. I could fix it. I knew I could.

"Evie. Stop. Explain."

Hunter stepped in front of me, and I met his gaze, guilt spearing into my gut.

"The book the kids took. The one that was making them invisible. Finvarra let Nathaniel borrow it so he could use it to get into the castle. But he was never supposed to keep it. We all forgot about it. I should've taken it back to Finvarra when Kyla and I gave him the sword. There's a reason Finvarra kept it in one of his random estates where no one could find it. It turns the owner into someone obsessed with power. Shit, it already has him."

Not only did it have him, but the book would turn him into someone he wouldn't recognize, until the only solution would be to kill him.

"Evie. Evie." Hunter's hands were on my upper arms. "It's going to be okay."

"It is." I attempted to sound confident, but my voice was high and thready. "I won't let it keep him. I won't."

"Shh." Hunter wrapped me in his arms. He smelled like Nathaniel in a way I knew was the mating bond telling me he was safe because he was pack. I took comfort in him as his low voice rumbled in my ear. "Tell me what you need."

"I need to talk to Finvarra. He should have expected this, the son of a bitch."

"Okay. Let's go." Hunter gave me a look. "You didn't think I was going to let my Alpha's mate go to the unseelie realm alone, did you? We all heard about how HFE came for you."

Nathaniel had told me I wouldn't be going anywhere alone. I eyed Hunter. "There are wolves following me around, aren't there?"

"Of course."

I didn't have time to protest. I'd talk to Nathaniel about having me guarded another time. For now, I just hauled ass out of my office, locked the door behind me, and unlocked my car.

"I'll steal the book off him if I have to," I said. "He's not in his right mind. Oh God, how did I forget about it?"

He would never have forgotten about something like that when it came to me. We were a few days into this mating business, and already, I sucked at it. Sucked so badly that my inattention could cost him his life.

"Hey."

Hunter leaned down until we were seeing eye-to-eye. He had to stoop. "Something tells me that if this book could enspell an entire kingdom, it was likely working on those closest to Nathaniel first. My guess is you've been fighting the book's power this whole time."

"Maybe." I shook off my guilt. I could wallow in it later, when Nathaniel was fixed. "Let's go talk to Finvarra."

EVIE

Finvarra kept us waiting. I wasn't sure if it was a power play or if he was truly in a meeting, but I paced in the sitting room we'd been directed to. An unseelie guard stood outside the door, his gaze watchful.

"It'll be okay, Evie." Hunter said.

I shrugged. Now that I knew something was seriously wrong, I felt like I'd crawl out of my skin if it wasn't fixed.

"Explain to me how it works," he said. I had a pretty good feeling he was attempting to distract me, but I took a deep breath anyway.

"The book has been in Finvarra's family for centuries. The seelie gave it to his ancestors, and it turned the king insane, until his son returned to the kingdom and killed him. Finvarra kept it in one of his estates where it couldn't affect him, but his cousin took it and attempted to sell it with the other artifacts." My throat ached as I ruthlessly suppressed the urge to burst into tears. "I should've known."

"The book dampens the intuition. Within days, the people closest to you begin to overlook your personality changes. That's what makes it so insidious," Finvarra said.

I whirled. The Dark Fae King Finvarra stood outside the door, dressed in black. A black crown was perched on his head, the jewels glinting in the lights from the chandeliers above us. But it was the man who commanded all attention.

From his formal dress, we *had* interrupted him.

"You knew this would happen."

He shook his head. "I hoped it wouldn't. Your wolf held out longer than most."

I curled my hands into fists. Finvarra dropped his gaze, and he moved into the room, his stride long, relaxed, a panther's prowl.

"Why didn't you do something?"

He waved one hand. "Do what? I warned him. I told him he needed to return it immediately. I didn't anticipate your wolf would be so easily affected. Usually, it takes weeks before the book manages to change a ruler's personality."

"He was injured," I ground out. "Badly. Multiple times."

Finvarra angled his head. The black jewels along the top of his crown gleamed in the light. "Ah. That changes things. If the book sensed the Alpha was injured, it would have struck when he was at his weakest."

"Well, are you going to take it from him?"

He gave me a faint smile. "That's not how it works. If it were, the book would not be so dangerous. Do you remember the story I told you of my ancestor?"

I swallowed, my mouth suddenly dry. "You said his entire kingdom was affected by the book."

"Yes."

"How come Hunter and I are not?"

"What is the pack hierarchy?" Finvarra asked.

Hunter growled.

"It's relevant," the unseelie king said.

"Technically, I'm number two in the pack. Now with Evie, I guess I become number three." He grinned at me. I shifted on my feet at that. I'd figure out pack politics later.

"That is why. Those closest to the holder of the book are typically the first to be affected. Evie spent more time with both Nathaniel *and* the book. The book would have been working constantly on her mind, ensuring she forgot about it."

"It succeeded," I said.

Finvarra studied me. "If it had, you wouldn't be here."

"Hunter noticed."

"I just got back from out of town," Hunter said, reaching out to squeeze my shoulder. "The book hasn't had a chance to work on me."

Finvarra leaned against the wall. "If the book had taken you completely, you wouldn't have believed this wolf. You would have gone to Nathaniel and told him Hunter was no longer loyal to him. Then you would have happily watched as Nathaniel put him to death."

Nausea swept through me at the thought. Hunter wrapped his arm around my shoulders. "Unnecessary," he gritted out, narrowing his eyes at Finvarra.

Finvarra just raised an eyebrow. "It's important for you to understand just how dangerous the book is. There's a reason I would never hold it for more than a day or two before sending it away. Tell me what you remember of my ancestor," he instructed.

Hunter growled, his wolf obviously disliking the order, but I elbowed him and took a deep breath.

"You said the king's son killed him. He'd been away and was unaffected by the book."

"Yes."

Terror thundered through me. "I'm not killing Nathaniel. Ever."

"Not even to save your realm from an Alpha wolf who's insane with a lust for power?"

My face was numb. I stared at Finvarra, who stared straight back, his dark eyebrow still cocked.

"I'll save him," I vowed.

"And there it is," he said with a faint smile.

"There *what* is?" Hunter ground out.

"The difference between my ancestor's queen

and the Alpha's mate. The queen didn't love the king. There was nothing in her that urged her to fight for him. No instinct that told her he was losing himself. There are two ways to save someone from the book," Finvarra said. "The first is to kill them."

"Not an option," I hissed.

He ignored me. "The second is to convince them to give you the book. Once it is out of their possession, their mind will clear. But be warned. The book has its own defenses, and it hasn't tasted power like Nathaniel's for centuries. It will fight to keep him."

My fear grew claws, slashing into my mind. "It can't have him." I took a deep, shuddering breath. I would do whatever it took. Just as Nathaniel would for me. "You've been very helpful." I narrowed my eyes. "Why?"

"I have no desire to deal with a rabid Alpha wolf."

I studied him. The fae couldn't lie, but something told me that wasn't all it was.

"How come you didn't ask for the book back when we returned the sword?"

A muscle ticked in Finvarra's jaw. "Once out of my reach, the book did as it usually does. It can impact even my memory. I need to get back to my meetings," Finvarra said.

I nodded. "What's with the crown?"

A flicker of amusement crossed his face. "Occasionally, my advisers must be reminded of who their ruler is." The amusement disappeared, and

Finvarra's eyes were suddenly so cold, I shivered.

He nodded at us and sauntered out.

Hunter was quiet as we made our way back toward the portal.

"We need a plan," I said. It felt almost like a betrayal to be talking about Nathaniel this way. But he wasn't himself. And when he realized just how the book had struck while he was at his weakest, his rage...

"Evie?"

"Sorry. I just... This feels like my fault. Mine and Kyla's. If we hadn't gone after the sword without a real plan, Nathaniel wouldn't have—"

"Don't do that. He wouldn't want you to do that. Let's just focus on fixing the problem."

The portal came into view, and he gestured for me to go first. Millions of tiny needles stung my skin, and then I was through.

"I think it's best if you make sure Nathaniel and I are alone," I said. "Keep everyone away from his house until I message you."

"I don't like it. I think I should stay. The book could turn on you, Evie. Could convince him to hurt you. And if that happens, Nathaniel is lost."

I shook my head. "He'd never hurt me."

"Usually, I'd agree. A wolf would never hurt their mate. But we don't know how much of him is himself and how much is the book. If he comes back to himself and realizes he hurt you, he'll make the Decade of Despair look like a cocktail party."

"I hear what you're saying, but I need you to trust me."

Hunter was quiet. "He can't lose you, Evie. You don't understand what it's been like for him."

"I do. He's been alone. In charge of the pack. With no one to fight for him. But I'm here now. And *I'm* fighting for him. That fucking book won't win."

I wouldn't let it.

NATHANIEL

Evie returned, and my wolf howled a welcome. She grinned at me as she got out of the car, and I smiled back.

Until I scented it.

"You've been with Hunter."

"We had something to take care of."

I didn't like it. I leaned down, scenting her skin, ensuring he hadn't been too close. But it was just her clothes. And her hand. I let out a low growl.

"Nathaniel?"

"He touched you."

"Hunter is a pack member. The pack is all about touch. You taught me that."

Her voice was too patient. I stepped back and narrowed my eyes.

She's lying to you, a little voice hissed. *Ask her where she's been with your second. And if they've been planning for him to take your place.*

A snarl ripped from my throat. Evie's eyes widened, but her hand—her traitorous hand that had touched another man—came up to pat my chest.

I grabbed that hand, wanting nothing more than to crush it.

My wolf pushed me aside. It happened without warning. Evie gazed up at me. I could hear and see her, but my wolf had taken over.

I needed to kill that part of me. That part that refused to fall in line. I knew it could be done. Somehow.

"Hi," Evie whispered.

"Something is wrong," my wolf said.

Colluding. They were colluding together. All of them. I fought against the wolf, slamming it into the walls of my mind over and over again.

"I know," Evie said. "I'm going to fix it."

Finally, I shoved the wolf aside. It took more effort than it ever had.

"Don't talk to him," I bit out. "Talk to me."

"Of course." Evie smiled up at me. "What do you want to talk about?"

"I want to know where you went with my second. Lie," I warned her, "and I'll kill him in front of you."

The blood drained from her face. "Oh, Nathaniel. I'm sorry. I'm so sorry I didn't see it."

"Didn't see what?"

"Can we talk inside?"

"Yes." I wanted her inside, where that part of me was kept, where I could influence her. Where I could teach her that, just like everyone else, she was created to obey me.

I stepped inside and frowned. The house was quiet. Too quiet.

"Where are my people?"

"Tobias had something to do, and the wolves are busy working on the HFE stuff," she said without hesitation.

Liar. Sweet, beautiful liar.

"Nathaniel?"

I was quiet as I led her upstairs. As I led her closer to my power. I opened the bedroom door and gestured to the bed.

"Sit, Evelyn. Sit and tell me what it is you want me to know."

Her eyes fired, but she controlled her reaction.

"Will you sit next to me?"

I sat and waited for the lies to begin.

"Do you remember Finvarra warning you about the book you took?"

Don't listen to her, that low, silky voice urged. *She wants your power. Wants you dead so she can rule with your second.*

The thought jolted something within me.

"Something is wrong," I growled. "Evie, you need to get out of here. Now."

"No," she said calmly. "I need you to listen to me.

The book started working on you when you were injured. When that b-bolt went through your chest."

Her voice hitched, and the silky voice receded until my mind felt clear once more, my wolf torn to pieces by her pain.

"Get out," I said, and my voice was coated in desperation. "Please, sweetheart. I need you to leave."

"Never," she told me. "I'll *never* leave you."

We'll make her leave.

"Then *I'll* leave."

She caught my hand. "Can you listen? Please? For me?"

My wolf wouldn't allow me to move. But that foreign *something* raged inside me. "Spill your lies, and then get out," it hissed.

She flinched, but then her expression turned hard. Determined. The strange force planted deep inside me didn't like that expression. Knew it was dangerous for us.

"The book is making you act this way. It took advantage of you when you were weakened, and by the time we made it back, it had been working on all of us. Hunter was away, so he wasn't affected by it. When he came back, he was able to remind me that you still had the book." Her beautiful blue-green eyes gleamed with tears. "You have to give it back."

I wanted to pluck out those eyes. Wanted to use my claws to—

"Leave," I ground out. I attempted to get to my feet,

but that voice, that *book,* had taken control of my body. My wolf paced within me, waiting for its chance.

"Give me the book," Evie said. Her gaze darted toward the bedside table, and I slowly got to my feet.

"Take it," I dared her. "Take it and see what happens, witch."

Evie smiled a slow, feline smile. "Oh, Nathaniel," she purred, eyes glittering. "You know I'm more than just a witch."

I launched at her, my fist striking out at her face. My wolf howled a mourning song inside me.

My fist hit a hard pocket of air, and then I was pressed against the wall, that air holding me still.

I could've killed her. My throat closed tight, pain stabbing into my gut at the thought. I could've fucking killed her.

"Get out." My voice was more wolf than man.

"It's okay," she said. "Let your wolf out."

I would. And together, we'd rip out her lying throat.

The bands around my arms loosened, and then I was launching myself at her once more. Her gaze met mine, open and sad.

And the world went black.

EVIE

I saw the moment the wolf completely took over. Nathaniel shifted in midair, his clothes tearing apart. His wolf changed his trajectory, landing on the bed, away from me.

Nathaniel's words ran through my head. *My wolf adores you. He'd do anything you asked.*

It had been a risk, coaxing out his wolf. But I'd known that the moment Nathaniel attempted to hurt me, his wolf would push him aside. And the wolf couldn't be impacted by the book. The wolf was all instinct, and he would *never* hurt his mate.

"Hi," I whispered.

The wolf snarled at me, and despite my confidence that he wouldn't hurt me, my heart thumped faster. Not only was he *pissed*, but he'd been dealing with the insidious book as well. I dropped my gaze, and he prowled toward me.

His nose was suddenly pressed to me, and I shivered. His teeth caressed my throat, and I angled my head for him. It was one of the most difficult things I'd ever done.

His teeth bit down lightly. So lightly, he didn't even break the skin. But the threat was there. Then he was backing away.

I slowly raised my gaze. "I need you in human form. Please."

A moment later, I was staring at the wolf in Nathaniel's body. He stalked toward me. "This was dangerous, mate."

"I know."

I remembered the other words Nathaniel had said, what felt like months ago now.

"If I ever turn, and you meet my wolf for real, you need to kill me, Evie."

"I could never kill you."

"If it meant protecting everyone you loved, you could. If you ever look into my eyes and see nothing but wolf, you need to do the world a favor and put me down."

I had more faith in Nathaniel's wolf than he did.

"I need you to give me the book," I said.

"No. The book is powerful. It will hurt you."

My heart twisted. Even now, Nathaniel's wolf was determined to protect me.

"It can't hurt me. It needs a few weeks before it can get into my head. We're going to give it back to Finvarra."

The wolf watched me. I lowered my gaze, but he seemed more in control now.

"I will do this, mate. But you should prepare yourself and keep your ward in place. The fae object will fight me."

"I know."

Nathaniel walked toward the bedside table. As

much as I wanted to do it myself, I knew he had to physically hand it over. I couldn't be involved until he'd given it up himself.

His eyes flashed darker, and he went still. Then his eyes were wolf again.

Another step. Another.

I choked out a sob, wishing I could do anything to help.

"I love you," he ground out, and it was Nathaniel. The book took hold once more, and he bared his teeth at me, his eyes filled with malice. "Kill you."

Those pale, pale blue eyes gleamed at me, and I could feel his wolf, reaching for the bond between us. I poured everything I could into the bond, until dizziness swept over me.

He was leaning down now, opening the drawer.

"Be ready, mate," the wolf said, and I took a step closer. Nathaniel lashed out, but his wolf caught his hand before it could even get close to making contact with me.

"We give you this book," Nathaniel's wolf said, his eyes steady on mine. "To take and to hide. We reject it and everything it stands for."

I could sense the book now—could feel it waiting, sly and ready.

I would need to drop the ward to take the book. And the book knew it.

Blood began to drip from Nathaniel's nose. His wolf was gone. And then it was just him. "It's okay," he told me. "It's going to be okay."

I dropped the ward. He held out the book.

His claws popped out, hand slashing toward me. I ducked, but I didn't need to. His claws were buried in his own stomach.

"Take it and run," he gasped out.

It took everything in me to leave him like that, but I knew I only had moments.

He flew at me, and I flinched as he slammed face first into my ward. He roared, smashing into it again and again. Hurtling down the stairs, I aimed for the front door, hoping, hoping Kyla had gotten my message.

And then she was there.

"Go," I sobbed. "Go, go, go."

Her expression was grim, but she didn't hesitate. Snatching the book from me, she sprinted away. She'd get it to Finvarra.

My heart raced. I made my way back up the stairs, hoping, begging the universe that it was okay. That he'd be okay now.

I found him in wolf form, blood still pouring from his wound. Icy eyes met mine.

"Shit," I said. "I'll get a healer."

"*No, mate,*" his wolf said in my head, and I jumped. "*We just need you.*"

I sat on the bed. Slowly, he made his way toward me. I caught the barest shadow of his pain as he jumped onto the bed, but then it was gone as he hid it away from me once more.

Leaning my head against the headboard, I let the tears come. Nathaniel rested his head on my thighs, and I stroked his soft ears before burying my head against him.

"I'm sorry," I said. "I'm so sorry."

FINVARRA

The summoning was like an itch beneath my bones. I let out a growl. How had I forgotten the wolf still had the ability to summon *me*? I'd given her the blood stone when I helped remove Fenrir from this realm. And the sly little wolf had kept it.

I would ensure she never used that ability again.

With a thought, I was standing in wolf territory. Howls sounded from every direction as they realized I'd appeared out of thin air—regardless of their wards, their sentries, and their Alpha.

The idea of the expression on the Alpha's face when he learned of my little visit was enough to dull the fine edge of my rage. Infuriating him was pleasing.

"Hi," Kyla said.

She was barefoot, wearing thin sweatpants and a tank top. She was also holding the book.

I ignored the urge to tear that book from her hands and throw it in the nearest river. My ancestors had attempted to burn it, bury it, even crush it. Spells had been created, power had been sacrificed, but it always returned.

Kyla cleared her throat. "Evie managed to get Nathaniel to hand this over." She curled her lip at me. "No thanks to you."

I ground my teeth. "You forget yourself, wolf."

Her eyes flashed, and I had the sudden urge to fist her hair, to pull her to me and make her apologize for her sharp tongue.

Appalled, I almost took a step back. Something about this woman, this *wolf,* brought out the worst in me. From the malice in her eyes, the feeling was mutual.

I held out one hand, forcing *her* to come to me. Wolves understood dominance games more than most creatures. But *this* wolf sauntered toward me slowly, her hips rolling in a way that made me clench my teeth.

She likely walked toward her lovers just like that.

The book was in my hand a moment later. I watched her. "And the stone."

Surprise flashed through her eyes as she clutched the stone tighter in her hand. I'd given it to her for one purpose and one purpose only. The fact that she had used it once more could be forgiven, considering how dangerous the book was. But no more.

Kyla took a single step back. And then she was a wolf, the stone falling as she transformed. I crouched, sweeping the stone toward me, but she was already there, the stone in her mouth.

"Don't make me come find you," I warned.

She scampered away, almost like a puppy. Her eyes shone as she took off toward the forest.

At the edge of the clearing, she turned to watch me. I refused to chase her like a human chasing a wayward pet. Using my powers in Nathaniel's territory—particularly on one of his wolves—was a declaration of war.

The wolf turned, and her white fur seemed to glow beneath the light of the moon. She canted her head to the side as I took one step toward her.

The wolf opened her mouth, revealing the stone. Her tail wagged in a blatant challenge. The look she gave me was all stubborn female arrogance, even in her wolf form.

And then she *winked.*

Right before she turned and disappeared into the forest.

EVIE

Butterfly wings on my cheek. And my nose. And my chin.

I sighed, opening my eyes.

I was lying on Nathaniel's bed, the sun streaming in. I glanced at my phone. Six a.m. We'd missed dinner and fallen asleep. Nathaniel had refused to allow a healer into our home last night. I'd argued for it, but the wolf was just as stubborn as the man. His territory had been invaded by the book, and he'd allow no one else near me.

Thankfully, his claws had missed most of the important stuff when he'd buried them in his stomach. He'd bled like a stuck pig onto the towels I'd placed beneath him, but he'd been content to curl up next to me.

I'd monitored him for most of the night, ensuring the bleeding stopped. If it hadn't, I would've gotten a healer myself and dealt with Nathaniel's ire.

He'd almost gutted himself to protect me.

He was back in his human form, completely naked against me. And I saw no sign of either his wolf or the book in his eyes.

His lips brushed my forehead gently, so gently. "My brave mate."

I let out a tiny, broken sound, and then I was burrowing into his chest, burying my head against the curve of his neck as I sobbed.

He stroked my back as I let it all out.

"I'm sorry," I sniffled. "I was so scared."

"Never apologize for that. I'm so angry with you, but so proud too."

"Seems about right."

His chest shook beneath my head as he laughed. "Next time I tell you to run, you run."

"Never. I'll never leave you."

He stiffened, and I lifted my head. "Partnership, remember? You have to let me be there for you too."

"That was dangerous."

"Your wolf would never hurt me. I knew that. The book knew that, too."

He stroked my hair, and I squeezed him tighter.

"Thank you for the sweats," I murmured. "I love them."

Nathaniel ran his hand down my butt. "They're very...soft." He slid his hands inside the sweats and beneath my underwear until he was stroking my skin.

"But this is softer."

"You scared me," I admitted.

"I'm sorry." Something that looked a lot like shame darted across his face.

"Not *you*," I clarified. "You could *never* scare me. It was the thought of the book taking over. Of losing you so soon after I found you."

"It never would have happened." Nathaniel leaned down and gently scraped his teeth along the side of my neck, making me shiver. "My mate is too powerful, and far too stubborn." His tone was smug, and I laughed.

"Much of last night is a blur," he said. "But I'll remember one part until the day I die."

"Oh yeah?" I shifted until I was on my back. "What part?"

Leaning over me, Nathaniel nuzzled at my cheek. "The part where your eyes turned to aqua-colored flames and a silent breeze ruffled your hair, and you informed me that you weren't *just* a witch."

I swallowed. "Sounds creepy."

"Oh, it was. And sexy as hell."

"You didn't think so at the time."

"I was out of my mind. But I'm not now."

"I could turn dangerous one day, Nathaniel. We know nothing about my powers. Sometimes when I use them, I can feel different parts of them just lying in wait."

"You'd never hurt me. Just like I'd never hurt you."

"But what if I hurt the pack?"

"If I ever thought you'd come close, I'd take you far from here."

I stared up at him. "You can't leave the pack."

"I can do whatever it takes to keep you safe. You want to go, you just tell me, and we're gone."

"Nathaniel—"

"The pack is mine, but you're mine too. The difference is, I could survive without the pack—as long as I knew they were happy and healthy. I couldn't survive without you. I wouldn't want to."

Tears flooded my eyes, and his gaze turned tender.

I didn't understand how he'd become so important to me so fast. I'd crushed on the Alpha wolf and fantasized about him from afar, but as soon as I'd gotten to know him like this, I hadn't stood a chance. It was a little embarrassing just how quickly I'd fallen in love with him.

I shifted, and Nathaniel allowed me to roll him onto his back. His eyes were heavy-lidded as I kissed my way down his chest.

All that remained of his injury was a light pink scar. And it would likely turn white in the next few days. Wolf healing was incredible.

I pressed a gentle kiss to his scar, and he let out a rumbling growl. Smiling against his skin, I brushed my lips against the bump of one of his abs.

God, I loved exploring his body.

I turned my attention to the spot where his obliques cut into his torso and the V cut pointed down at his erect cock. My mouth watered, and I nuzzled along the line, my tongue darting out.

He immediately twined his fingers in my hair, holding my head hostage. I gazed up at him from beneath my lashes, and he cursed.

"You're going to tease me?"

"Revenge is sweet."

He grinned, letting me go, and he folded his hands beneath his head, all those glorious muscles flexing as he raised one eyebrow at me.

I smiled back at him. I was going to make this man lose his goddamn mind.

Nathaniel had a beautiful cock. That was a weird thing to say, but it was true. It jutted up, hard and velvet smooth, with a slight curve to the right. Darting my tongue down his abs, I kissed around his cock, ignoring it while he groaned.

Scraping my teeth along his thighs, I smiled as he arched, impatient already.

My hand found him, and he went still. He was so thick my fingers couldn't touch. I leaned down and licked the tip, glancing up to find him staring at me, his gaze enraptured.

I blew a stream of air over him, and he shifted beneath me.

"Feel good?"

He let out a low growl, and I smiled.

My teasing was driving *me* crazy too. I slowly lowered my head, watching Nathaniel the whole time.

His gaze burned into me, and I licked the underside of his cock before taking the head into my mouth.

His thighs tensed, and everything in me thrilled at the knowledge that this powerful Alpha was at my mercy.

"Enjoying yourself?" he rumbled.

I lifted my mouth off him with a *pop*. "Of course."

Swirling my tongue around the head, I took him deeper this time, until my mouth was so full of him and I had to breathe through my nose. He cupped my cheek, and I looked up to find him staring at me, still captivated.

Get a guy's dick in your mouth, and you suddenly have his full attention.

I smirked, and he groaned as the edge of my teeth scraped him.

"Again," he said.

Why wasn't I surprised that he could take a little pain with his pleasure?

I lowered my head again, but the impatient wolf was already lifting me.

"I'm not done."

"Oh yes, you are."

Then I was on all fours, and he was leaning over me, his cock sliding inside until I let out a squeak. He was even bigger in this position.

"You can take me." I could hear the smile in his voice, and I turned my head. He was staring at me, his eyes wild as he took me in. One of his hands slid to my breast, the other finding my clit, and he tweaked my nipple, stroked my clit, and thrust inside me, all at the same time until I was moaning incoherently.

"There you go." His voice was lit with humor, but I could hear the strain in it.

"Harder," I got out, on the edge of a climax that might just kill me.

Nathaniel complied, pounding into me, his cock hitting my G-spot in the most delightful way. Every muscle in my body tensed, and I shuddered as my orgasm tore through me. Nathaniel leaned forward and bit my shoulder, just hard enough to make me gasp as he came inside me.

I collapsed. He landed next to me and nuzzled my hair. I wanted to sleep some more. My body needed it. But my mind refused.

I knew if I needed to talk, Nathaniel would listen. If I needed to brainstorm, he'd help me with that too. I was learning that the best parts of having him as my mate didn't just involve our incredible sex. It was the continual support. The knowledge that no matter what happened, we really were a team.

"Question," I got out, my voice rough.

"Answer." Nathaniel pressed a kiss to my sweaty head, and I rolled until I was facing him once more.

"When are you planning to meet with Gabriel?"

Surprise flashed through his eyes. "I'm not sure yet. Why?"

"Okay, hear me out. I think the Mage Council is

in bed with HFE and has been for years. Think about it—they both have a common goal."

He considered it. "Just a couple of years ago, I wouldn't have thought it possible, but the more we learn about the Mage Council, the more we see just how morally bankrupt most of them are. On the surface, they're all about protecting humans from paranormals. But no one knows exactly where the mages are getting their power—and how they're distributing it. Gabriel is a mystery. And I don't like mysteries."

Nathaniel frowned, and I could see him calculating his next move.

"What if he's trying to meet with you so he can take you out *for* HFE?"

"The enemy of my enemy is my friend," Nathaniel said. "Taraghlan, Gabriel, and Lennox all working together. All of them would be planning to use the others while they needed them, and then eventually turn on them."

I nodded. "Even if we're wrong and Gabriel isn't a part of it, we need to be careful."

Nathaniel nodded, pressing another kiss to my forehead. "You hungry?"

My stomach rumbled in response, and he laughed. But I rolled out of bed. "I need to go talk to Aubrey. I'll grab something later."

He glanced at the door. "You're lucky that door is closed. Tobias knows we both skipped dinner last night."

We showered together. Of course, that resulted in another shuddering climax, my legs wrapped around him as he plowed into me. Finally, I pulled on a summer dress, watching as Nathaniel's eyes darkened. I didn't *think* anyone would try to kill me today, and I missed feeling pretty.

Nathaniel prowled toward me. I knew that look. I bolted for the bedroom door, only escaping because he let me. He followed me down the stairs and into the kitchen, stroking one of his fingers along my bare shoulder.

"Waffles," Tobias announced, and my stomach started up again.

"Yum. Thank you," I said as he served us both. "What are you doing up this early?"

"I figured you two would wake early."

"We could've managed," I said, and he just waved that off.

"I should have noticed you weren't yourself," he said to Nathaniel.

Nathaniel shook his head. "That's not how the book works."

He explained the magic to Tobias while I helped myself to fresh berries and maple syrup, attempting to ignore the way Nathaniel's eyes darkened when I licked syrup from my thumb.

"You little tease," he whispered in my ear, and I grinned at him.

I carried my plate to the sink and rinsed it,

ignoring Tobias's protests. "I need to get going."

"I'm coming with you," Nathaniel said.

"To Aubrey's? Why?"

"I want to spend more time with you."

"Mm-hm," I said as we walked out of the house and got into the car. "A likely story."

Nathaniel turned the key and leaned over, nipping at my neck. I squeaked and batted him away. He just winked at me. Then his face turned serious.

"The last time you were planning to travel to Aubrey's, you nearly died."

"That's an exaggeration."

"Tell it to my wolf."

I just sighed. My phone buzzed, and I pulled it out of my pocket.

Eachann. *Left something for you in your office.*

My uncle couldn't seem to help himself. He simply had to be mysterious.

I messaged Vas with the update and my thoughts about Gabriel. He spent more time in the underworld than I did, and he would let Samael and Danica know what I was thinking. By the time I tucked my phone away, Nathaniel was pulling into Aubrey's drive. He navigated around the roundabout and parked next to the fountain.

Aubrey answered his door himself. It was one of the things I liked about him. Considering he was fae royalty, he never put on airs. And his staff seemed to love him for it too.

"Evie." He greeted me with a kiss on the cheek. "I didn't know you were bringing your mate."

"Word gets around, I see."

"The incomparable Evie Amana mated to the werewolf Alpha? This is the most exciting thing to happen in Durham since your sister decided to blow up the Mage Council."

My expression got stuck between a scowl and a wince. Nathaniel just threw his arm around me and steered me inside.

"Now, what has you looking so serious?" Aubrey asked, leading us into his huge sitting room.

I plopped onto one of his plush sofas, pulling Nathaniel down next to me. He didn't look happy about it, and I knew he'd prefer to stand—he'd told me it wasn't comfortable for his wolf to have people standing while he was seated—particularly if they were a threat.

Thankfully, Aubrey gave me a wink and sat.

He missed nothing.

I took a deep breath. "I feel bad coming to you yet again. You've given us so much help. But your king has been doing something unforgivable."

He briefly closed his eyes. "What is it?"

I filled him in about the prisoners Taraghlan was giving to HFE.

The color slowly drained from Aubrey's face. For a wild moment, I thought he might pass out.

"He wouldn't. Even *he* couldn't... His own people?"

"It gets worse." I told him about Hellaphine.

He stared at me. "You left her there?"

Guilt twisted in my gut. Nathaniel let out a warning growl, and I squeezed his hand. "She insisted, Aubrey. They've got her sister."

Aubrey cursed, closing his eyes.

This was the kind of king the seelie needed. A man who wouldn't sleep tonight because he knew his people were in danger.

"I need to know if you'll help us. There are so many of these labs, Aubrey, and our only chance is to hit them all together. That means all of us cooperating and going in at the same time, so we can completely wipe them out. HFE are like cockroaches, and unless we eradicate them, they'll come crawling back to ruin more lives."

"Tell me what you've got so far."

"We've managed to locate most of the labs, and we won't hit HFE until we find them all. My uncle found the leader of HFE. His name is Lennox. That makes him the most important target. But if we leave his underlings alive, we risk them rebuilding. I want them wiped out."

"I want the same." Aubrey's voice was hoarse. "My people will help. Depending on how soon we need to move, I can gather anywhere from a few hundred to a few thousand seelie."

"Thank you. We'll keep you updated."

"Hellaphine... Do you think she'll survive?"

"Yes. She's determined and she's angry. And most importantly, she believes she has to live so she can get to her sister. She's powerful, which means they'll transport her to the main lab—where they put her sister. As soon as we know where she is, we'll know where Lennox is."

And the man who'd arranged for my mom to be kidnapped, who'd sent his minions after me, who'd ordered my coven to be slaughtered and beheaded my best friend...

I'd finally kill him myself.

EVIE

That afternoon, I strolled into my office, pausing at the sight of a pink bakery box. I opened it to reveal a chocolate donut with sprinkles.

"Well, thanks, Uncle Eachann." It was a little strange, considering he was supposed to meet me in a few hours, but obviously my weakness for baked goods had gotten around.

Kyla stalked in behind me half an hour later and raised her eyebrow at the bakery box. "Nathaniel already knows about your sweet tooth, huh?"

"This was from Eachann."

She leaned closer, clearly scenting the box. "Nope. That has Nathaniel's paw prints all over it. Soooo, are you going to become one of those annoying loved-up people who never has time for their friends anymore?"

Offense raged through me. I scowled at her, and she smirked.

"You're so easy."

I sniffed, messaged Nathaniel thanks for the treat, and got to work. Kyla started up her computer. An hour later, I lifted my head to find her sitting back, legs crossed at the ankles as she rested them on the desk.

Her thinking pose.

"What is it?"

"I just feel like there's something big that we're missing." She glanced at me. "Anything from the stone?"

I wiggled the lapis lazuli from my pocket. "Nope."

"How you gonna know if it's in your pocket?"

"It'll heat up."

"Cool." Swinging her legs off the desk, she got to her feet. "I have a meeting with Selina."

I raised one eyebrow. "You want me to come?"

"Nah. Now that I've returned the sword to His Majesty," she sneered, "I wanted to check in with Selina to see if anything has changed."

Selina wasn't a seer. But she occasionally had visions. And those visions hadn't exactly been filled with joy when it came to Kyla.

You will trust someone who will betray their word. But you will find allies in the places you will least expect. You must return the sword to its rightful owner.

The bargain has been struck. But you must return the sword to its true sheath or the realms will burn. You will have a choice to make. Choose wrongly, and you will be chained to a throne. Choose correctly, and you will sit on one.

"Any ideas about the true sheath?" I asked.

"Nothing. I've been poring over every historical account I can find, reading magical scrolls until my eyes cross, and making list after list of possibilities. I just can't figure it out."

"We'll get to the bottom of it. I promise."

"You're—"

"Not invited for the dirty work, which is rude as hell, considering all the fun things I've dragged *you* into." I gestured at the board. "Case in point. But I can still help with the research part of things."

"You have more than enough on your plate. And I *am* investigating anyone with ties to HFE. I just need to—"

"Find out if your future is looking a teeny bit brighter. Get gone."

She grinned at me and prowled out the door.

A few hours later, I was pacing. Eachann hadn't turned up for our meeting. Sure, he could have forgotten about it, but that wasn't like him.

A dull, insidious panic wormed its way into my chest.

Something had gone wrong. I knew it had.

I'd give him another fifteen minutes, and then I'd

stop by the house he was renting.

I gave him ten, and then I was striding out my office door.

"Evie."

I jolted. "Jesus, Nate, you scared the shit out of me."

He gave me a slow smile, and despite my worry, my body heated.

"I like when you call me Nate," he purred. He leaned closer, sniffing at me. "What's wrong? I felt your panic."

I frowned at him as I locked the door. "What are you doing here?"

"I was driving past, and my wolf told me something was wrong."

"Well, that's creepy."

"Evie. What's wrong?"

"Eachann didn't show up for our meeting."

Nathaniel studied my face. "You think he's in trouble."

"Oh yeah. Please don't tell me I'm overreacting."

"You have good instincts. Let's go by his house."

I wrapped my arms around him.

"I love you."

"Hey." He tipped my chin up, his eyes dark. "We'll find him. I promise."

His side of the bond radiated calm confidence. In Nathaniel's arms, I felt safe, protected. I knew I wasn't in this alone. Knew that, whatever happened, we would face it together.

"I really, *really* love you."

He smiled. "I love you too. Now get in the car."

I was lost in thought as we made our way to Eachann's temporary home. He'd gone for the outskirts of Hope Valley, close enough to the fae to rendezvous with them whenever he pleased—which, from what I knew of my uncle so far, wouldn't be often—but also an easy drive downtown. Nathaniel turned onto the quiet street and parked.

Sliding out of the car, I studied the house. Unlike most fae, my uncle hadn't chosen a house with more space than he needed. The house was white—so white it had either been recently painted or someone had used some kind of dirt-resistant spell.

The house had been designed to mimic a French château. From where we were standing, I could see a balcony covered in flowers. It looked like a peaceful spot to sit and curl up with a book, although something told me Eachann hadn't done much of that.

Striding toward the house, I reached for the wards. From what I could tell, Eachann's wards hadn't been disturbed. I didn't want to break them and give him a migraine, so I took a deep breath and used my new trick.

Nathaniel raised an eyebrow as I held my hand to the ward and allowed my power to imitate it. Within a few seconds, it was gone.

"Impressive."

"It's a good thing I have a moral compass, because this little skill would set me up well for a life of crime."

Nathaniel grinned. I slid my tools from my pocket and picked Eachann's lock. His grin widened. "A life of crime, indeed."

In a move I hadn't seen coming, he pulled me out of the way and pushed the door open, blocking the entry with his huge body.

"You shithead," I hissed.

"Save the dirty talk, darling."

I was going to make him eat those words. I pushed in behind him, but Eachann's house felt empty.

"I'm the one with the magic," I snarled.

"Stay here."

I scowled at the order, but he was already stripping off his clothes, leaving them in a pile by the front door. Obviously, he was planning on doing a sniff test.

He shifted and padded out of the room. I wandered over to the spider plant on Eachann's kitchen counter. The dirt was bone dry, and the leaves were turning brown at the ends. I watered it and then opened his fridge.

I hadn't exactly expected Eachann to cook for himself, and I wasn't wrong. There was no expired milk, old takeout, or anything else that could give me a hint as to the last time he'd been here.

Nathaniel stepped back into the room.

"Anything?" I asked.

He shifted back to human and picked up his

clothes. "If he was taken, it wasn't from here. No new scents."

I wandered through the house anyway, checking the towel hung next to the shower—dry as dust. His bed was neatly made. And while one knife was missing from his weapons, it was the knife I'd never seen him without.

"Whatever happened, it happened outside of this house," I said. "I told him to be careful." My voice cracked, and then I was wrapped in Nathaniel's arms, inhaling his masculine scent.

"I just found him," I managed to choke out before my throat tightened completely.

"I know. What was he working on, Evie? Where was he keeping his notes?"

I took a deep breath and glanced around. We'd checked his office...

Cursing, I slid my phone from my pocket. His message.

Left something for you in your office.

I'd thought it had been the donut. When Kyla told me it was from Nathaniel, I'd completely forgotten about my uncle's message.

"I need to search my desk."

NATHANIEL

My wolf attempted to rise to the surface when I parked outside Evie's office. Ever since the book had tried to make me kill my mate, my wolf had been restless, untrusting of my ability to protect Evie.

I would have been irritated if I didn't feel the same way.

"Enough," Evie said, and I glanced at her.

She got out of the car, and I stalked to her side, sliding my hand into hers. "What do you mean?"

"I can feel your guilt."

Contentment radiated through me. Our bond wasn't fully open yet. I'd told myself it would take time. But if Evie had felt that…

"I'm sorry," she said.

I scowled down at her. "What for?"

"Whatever I'm doing wrong. You seem to be able

to feel my emotions, but I usually can't feel yours."

"It takes time."

"It didn't for you."

I just squeezed her hand. "We'll figure it out."

Frustration came from her end of the bond. That was clear. I knew my mate well enough to know she was disappointed in herself. That she was beating herself up. And that was unacceptable.

"Hey." I caught her chin in my hand and waited until she met my eyes. "I never dared to even imagine that I could have you. That you'd be my mate. That I'd be this happy. The bond will sort itself out. Or it won't. Either way, you're mine, and I'm yours."

She took a deep breath. "Okay."

I couldn't resist lowering my head and taking her mouth. She immediately responded, curling her body into mine.

Her hand pushed at my chest, and I smiled against her lips. I knew what she'd say now.

"Why exactly were you feeling guilty, mister?"

"I almost killed you the other day."

"Oh please. Did you forget the part where my ward met your face?" She smirked. "'Cause that was pretty funny."

I nipped at her ear, and she burst out laughing. Within a moment, she'd sobered. Standing on tiptoe, she twined her arms around my neck. "I talked to Finvarra about the book," she said, and I barely suppressed a snarl. Her lips curved. "He told me all about his ancestor—the one who fell to the book. Apparently, the reason he was able to go so cray-cray for so long was because his queen didn't love him. She didn't fight for him."

My heart twisted at that. But Evie's hand was cupping my face. "So instead of beating yourself up because the book struck when you were *impaled by a goddamned metal bolt,* maybe you should be appreciating that you have Hunter, who knows you so well, he immediately knew something was wrong. That you have Kyla, who got the book to Finvarra. And, of course, that you have such a smart, powerful mate who managed to kick the book's ass," she preened.

I leaned my head back and laughed. No one amused me the way this woman did. My life was gray before I met her, and when Evie waltzed into my house that day, it was suddenly full of color.

"Well, my smart, powerful, *beautiful* mate, let's go figure out what your uncle left behind."

Evie slid her hand back down to mine and led me into her office. My wolf finally rested, content to follow our mate. I smiled. I was arguably the most powerful Alpha in this country, and I would trail after this woman like a puppy.

Amusement curled in my chest. But it died away as I felt Evie's worry for Eachann. I hadn't particularly liked the unseelie—although now, part of me wondered how much of that was the book—but I'd do whatever it took to make sure she got her uncle back alive and well.

"Can you scent where he would've hidden whatever he left for me?" Evie asked.

Stepping close to the desk, I inhaled, catching his scent. "He sat here for a few minutes. But I also have him on that sofa and in almost every inch of this office."

She closed her eyes. "He's been here multiple times."

"Let's check all the drawers first."

We found it in the bottom drawer, beneath a stack of unopened mail. I raised my eyebrow, and Evie scowled at me. It was obvious she'd cleared her desk by opening a drawer and dumping the mail into it.

"Not all of us have multiple pack members they can delegate to." Her chin jutted out, and I couldn't help but grin.

"Those pack members are yours, too. Why don't you take one of the older kids on as an intern?"

Those pillowy lips pursed, and my mind immediately cast me back to the last time we were at this desk. I forced myself to focus.

"Not a bad idea. Let's talk about it after we take out HFE." She opened the envelope Eachann had left for her.

"I don't understand why he didn't message…"

"I get the sense he's paranoid as hell. Happens to most paranormals with age. You live long enough, and you learn just how easily you can be betrayed."

She fluttered her eyelashes. "You'd know."

"Smartass. I'm not *that* old."

She just grinned, plopping onto her desk chair. "Okay, let's see what we have here."

We both studied the pictures. "Who are these people?"

I frowned. "I know him. He's the mage equivalent of Albert—only on the West Coast." Pulling out my phone, I messaged Ryker.

On my way. Give me ten.

"We need to talk to Ryker. He's the most up-to-date on the inner workings of the Mage Council."

Evie nodded absently. "There's a USB in here too." Turning, she slid it into her laptop. "More pictures. And...wow."

I leaned over her shoulder. "This is impressive."

Eachann clearly had people of his own whom he trusted enough to spy for him. Each of the labs we'd identified were numbered, and he'd been working on the guards responsible for securing the entrance of each lab. Not only had he listed the names of those guards, but...

"Those are kids."

"Your uncle is a smart man."

She just looked at me, and I shrugged. "We have zero chance of turning every guard we need. Some of them could be paid off or threatened, but if they're on the front gates, it's because HFE considers them loyal. It would take too much time to try to convince them to work with us. Your uncle clearly had the same thought. If we can't turn the guards, we need to force them to work with us. And that means letting them think we would hurt their families."

"But we won't."

"They don't know that. They just see us as vicious, dangerous paranormals."

Evie was watching me, her eyes dark. "What are you thinking?"

Picking up the stack of pictures, I flipped through them. Each picture was of a man, taken from a distance. Some of them looked familiar enough that if they were who I thought they were…it would explain many, many things.

"Let me check with Ryker before I start making allegations."

Evie didn't look happy, but I glanced at my phone. "He won't be long. Besides, I have a few ideas about how we could spend the time."

She smirked. "What kinds of ideas?"

EVIE

It turned out Nathaniel's ideas involved long, deep kisses and whispering filthy suggestions in my ear. By the time he stepped away from me, I was a horny wreck.

Ryker strolled into the office and made a face. "Gross."

I didn't blush, but it was close. Nathaniel just gave him a warning look. But he winked at me when Ryker wasn't looking. As far as distractions went, he definitely knew what he was doing.

"Before we get started, I wanted to apologize," Nathaniel said.

Ryker met Nathaniel's gaze, but he canted his head in that wolfy way that seemed to demonstrate that he wasn't attempting to challenge his Alpha.

"You have nothing to apologize for."

Nathaniel just shook his head, a faint smile on his face. "It costs me nothing to apologize when I have behaved in a way that hurt my pack. That impacted the stability of that pack."

Ryker just grinned. "You think our foundation's that shaky? We just thought you were finding your new status as a mate a little…difficult." He slid me a sly look, and I couldn't help but grin. "Look, it was the book. The pack understands exactly what that disgusting fae object did. And thankfully, our Alpha's mate was strong enough to save you and, by extension, the rest of us."

I flipped my hair over my shoulder. "Yeah, yeah, say it with chocolate."

He laughed. Since Nathaniel seemed to need it, Ryker bowed his head. "I accept your unnecessary apology."

Nathaniel sighed. I took that moment to gesture to the pictures. "This is sweet and all, but can you please tell me who these men are?"

Ryker ambled over to the desk. All the amusement left his face. "You were right," he told Nathaniel. "This is one of the ten."

"The ten mages under Gabriel?"

Ryker nodded, pulling out another picture of a dark-haired Latino guy. "Our spies already pinpointed this guy as the replacement for Albert." He glanced at my whiteboards. "You got any spare room?"

Kyla and Rose had brought in a few more whiteboards to account for all of our notes. The closest board had wheels, and I turned it, waving my hand at the empty space. Ryker got to work, taping up each photo, along with the names and cities. He glanced at his phone a few times, nodding when he checked his work against whatever notes he was keeping. Finally, he stepped back.

"Jay Bolton. Donovan Downs. Maxton Gardner. Bruno Stafford." He continued listing the names, his expression tight.

"All of them are Mage Council members, aren't they?" I murmured.

"Yes."

I could feel the blood draining from my face. Could feel my hands shaking, could feel ice-cold sweat gathering at the nape of my neck. But everything else was numb.

"Eachann found out they're all working with HFE. He came here to warn me, and when I wasn't here, he dumped the file." I took a deep breath. "We need to check the recordings from any cameras in the area. He got too close, and they either took him or killed him."

"Evie. *Evie.*"

I met Nathaniel's eyes. They were dark with concern. But the concern was for me. He was still radiating that calm confidence.

"We'll find him," I said. It sounded like a question, and Nathaniel nodded.

"I think we need to pull in our allies and discuss our plan." He gestured to the board. "No more labs have been added since the last time I checked. This might be all of them."

I sucked in a breath. "Okay. When we raid the main lab, we'll have access to their systems. We'll also keep as many HFE members alive as we can, so they can be questioned. As soon as they transport Hellaphine, we'll know which lab is the most important head of our hydra. But we need to be prepared to move. If they don't take her through a portal in the next few days, we need to go with what we've got so far. I'm not leaving Eachann to be tortured."

Nathaniel rubbed his hands up and down my arms, warming skin that had become chilled. "If we have to break in to Taraghlan's castle to rescue Hellaphine, we will. It'll be a date."

"Okay. But then I want dinner, a movie, and an

awkward kiss at the door."

Ryker winked at me and stepped away from the board. "Time to gather our people."

EVIE

We worked late into the night, until Nathaniel finally hauled me upstairs. I was asleep before he laid me down on our bed.

The next morning, I was up with the sun while all our allies negotiated a time and place to meet.

We had a lot of people to gather. And many of them were currently in various other realms, which meant we couldn't exactly call them. Maybe I just needed to think outside the box...

In the meantime, since we had time to kill while we waited, we were going to try to heal Virtus.

"Evie?"

I turned.

Danica was wearing jeans and a blue tank top. Her hair was tied up in a ponytail. She looked as tired as I felt. "Samael had business in the tower, so he's already there. He suggested we use one of the larger conference rooms when everyone agrees to meet."

Sliding my phone from my back pocket, I messaged Nathaniel.

"Nate says it's okay."

"Morning."

We both turned to find Kyla leaning against a tree, one arm clamped over her mouth as she yawned. Danica strode over, and they hugged it out.

"Let's find Virtus," I said.

He chose that moment to stroll out of the forest, and we all studied his twisted wing. The loyal griffin had been wounded when unseelie creatures attacked his pack. He'd leaped in front of his pack's leader—saving his life—and the creature had almost ripped his wing from his body. That pack abandoned him while they fled to a safer spot, and he'd been left half dead. Somehow, he'd survived, recovering from his wounds and tracking his pack, only to find them about to leave once more. Danica had told me this was how he'd lived, always following them on the ground, while they ignored him, flying to each new location. Not once had they made any allowances for his exhaustion. If I could make his pack pay for how they'd treated him, I'd do it in a heartbeat.

Danica dropped to her knees and wrapped her arms around his neck. "If this doesn't work, we'll keep trying until it does," she promised.

The griffin nuzzled her in response.

"The healer is here." Nathaniel's deep voice sent a thrill through me, and I turned, meeting his eyes. He stepped closer to me, and for a moment, we were in our own little world.

"Hi," he said, leaning down to brush my lips with

his.

"Hi." I smiled against his mouth.

"Let's go," Danica said, clearly antsy. I couldn't blame her. I wanted this for Virtus. He deserved to be able to fly once more.

We gathered in Nathaniel's living room. Samael had brought his own healer—likely at Danica's insistence. Eldan radiated peace and calm, and being in his presence made you feel like everything was going to be okay. It was a little similar to the confidence Nathaniel projected, only with Eldan, you knew it would be okay because the universe would ensure it. With Nathaniel, you knew it would be okay because he would kill anyone who risked the peace.

"Hello, Evie." Eldan smiled at me, and I couldn't help but smile back. The seelie was almost delicate, in that fine-boned, light fae way. His long blond hair had been braided back from his face, the rest of it left to fall down his back.

The door opened, and Meredith walked in. Her eyes met Virtus's.

"I know you wanted me to rest, but too bad."

The griffin sighed, and faint smiles appeared on a few faces. Mere hugged Danica and me.

"Why does he want you to rest?" I asked.

Mere made a face. "Morning sickness. I'm *fine*, but all the males in my life are being impossible."

"You're barely keeping anything down," Vas growled, walking in behind her.

"We'll talk about this later," she hissed, and Vas just shook his head, giving me a pleading look.

"Isn't there something you can do?"

"Morning sickness is a hard thing to treat. But I have a few ideas."

Hope flared in his eyes, and I gave him a one-armed hug. "It'll be okay."

Eldan was laying out his tools. Lots of metal. Lots of blades. I sucked in a breath.

"What are the chances of this working?" I asked.

"High. But it's not without pain." Eldan knelt down and spoke to Virtus directly. "The bones will need to be rebroken, the twisted cartilage reshaped. I'll then direct my healing once the bones have been adjusted into their correct places."

"It sounds agonizing," Danica bit out.

I knelt next to Eldan and met Virtus's eyes. "Are you sure you want to do this?"

Virtus's gold eyes seemed to look into my soul. He was sure. He was tired of not having a purpose. He wanted to be useful.

A lump formed in my throat. I opened my mouth, but Nathaniel was already leaning down to talk to Virtus. "The pack loves you without your needing to be *useful*," he said. "You don't need to do this for us."

Virtus lifted his head and looked at all of us, one by one. He was doing it for himself as well. He missed the sky with a wild sorrow that tugged at him day and night. He was willing to experience the agony if it meant he would be whole again.

He'd made his choice. I wouldn't argue. But…

"Can't you do it while he's unconscious?" I asked.

Eldan shook his head, his expression sorrowful. "Griffins are creatures of magic. He wouldn't stay unconscious through so much agony, and it would be dangerous if he woke in such pain."

Virtus looked at me. He would be fine. He was ready.

"Okay." I leaned down and pressed a kiss to his furry head. "Let's get it done."

EVIE

Nathaniel had four wolves hold Virtus down. But first, he patiently explained the necessity of each step, waiting for Virtus to give permission. My heart stuttered in my chest. I'd never loved him more.

Virtus looked at all of us, making it clear he knew such a thing was necessary. My heart thudded in my chest until I could hear each beat in my ears. Since Virtus was a pack member, Nathaniel stayed next to him, murmuring encouragement in his ear. Hopefully, being able to scent his Alpha would help Virtus through the worst of it.

And then Ryker began to break bones and cartilage, carefully following each of Eldan's instructions. His face was grim, mouth a thin line. Everyone loved the griffin, but Ryker and Virtus often ran together in the forest. This was hurting him, too.

Nathaniel kept his arm around Virtus's neck. The griffin had his lips pulled back in a silent snarl. But he didn't make a single sound.

Kyla padded back into the room in her wolf form and wiggled under Nathaniel and close to Virtus's chest. She let out a low whine, obviously attempting to let Virtus know it was okay to cry out.

He refused. And part of me knew it was because he was trying to protect us, even now. He didn't want us to know how much pain this caused him.

Danica, who'd been sent to kill the griffin, who'd refused to hurt him, even if it meant losing one of the few leads she had to save Samael's life, who'd let Virtus follow her home and introduced him to our pack…

She sat next to me, as close as we could be without getting in the way. Her shoulders shook with silent sobs.

Eldan worked quickly, still radiating that serene energy. His eyes narrowed, and he moved without hesitation, slowly shifting Virtus's twisted wing into the correct place.

My face was wet, and I wiped at it. There were few things worse than watching a friend go through this kind of agony. Even if it was their choice. Virtus met my eyes.

It would be okay.

I just shook my head. "You don't have to be strong for us. You can let it out."

And then, Virtus had no choice. Because Eldan

did something that broke even the bravest griffin in all the realms. He pulled out a piece of bone and dropped it next to him. Then another.

Virtus let out a roar, twisting in place, an instinctive reaction as his body attempted to remove him from the pain. Nathaniel held him tight, letting out a sound that was almost like a purr. Virtus went still, but he panted, and his eyes were mournful.

"What are you doing?" I croaked out.

Eldan didn't spare a glance. "The damage was worse than I thought. He's going to have to regrow these."

"He can do that?" Danica asked.

"Yes. It'll be painful, but it's the only way to ensure he regains full function of his wing. He's been in pain every second since the accident, his bones grinding against one another with each movement. That ends now."

Everyone went quiet at the thought of Virtus in that much pain. Danica leaned close to him as Eldan gathered his tools, giving the griffin a small reprieve.

"You've been in that much pain?" she whispered.

He looked at her. She just shook her head. "Oh, Virtus. It doesn't matter if we couldn't do anything to help. We're your family. We would have made things easier for you."

I slid closer and gently petted his silky ear, careful to stay away from his wing. He nuzzled my hand. Eldan looked up.

"This will be the worst part, but it won't last long."

"You've got this," I murmured in Virtus's ear. To my left, Kyla nuzzled into the griffin. Danica held his gaze, while Nathaniel began a low hum that caused more than one wolf in the room to turn heavy-lidded.

Ryker and Hunter held Virtus still.

I couldn't look. All I could do was close my eyes and shudder as he let out a roar.

"Almost done." Eldan's voice was tight. "Beginning the healing now."

I felt Virtus go limp and opened my eyes as he was guided down. His wing was bloody in places, and I could see several parts where he was missing bone—particularly near the joint connecting it to his back. But it was straight.

"I'll need to see him first thing in the morning, for more healing and to check that the bone has begun to regrow," Eldan said.

"Stay the night," Nathaniel offered. "We have more than enough room, and you must be exhausted."

Eldan hesitated, but Tobias stepped closer from where he'd been leaning against the wall. "It's Mexican night," he told him. "I'll show you to your room."

There were very few people who could argue successfully with Tobias—especially when he mentioned his food. Eldan caved, and a few minutes later, Nathaniel had placed a blanket over the griffin, who'd fallen into a healing sleep.

"Do you have another healer here?" Vas asked

Nathaniel.

"Yes." Nathaniel glanced at him. "You need to see her?"

"Meredith does."

Mere pinned him with a look from where she'd been gently running her hand over Virtus's head. "Vassago," she said warningly, and I couldn't help but grin.

"You're losing weight, baby. Please."

Nathaniel angled his head. "Is something wrong?"

"Morning sickness," I said.

Tobias beamed at Mere. "Congratulations. We have something that could help."

Surprise flickered across her face. "You do?"

"Our people distrusted magic for a long time. It is only recently that Nathaniel has begun using fae healers. But we are creatures of the forest, and the forest has long provided."

"Uh, what does that mean?"

"He means we have a tea that suppresses nausea. Totally safe for pregnancy." Naomi had stepped into the room, and she gave Virtus a guilty, pitying look. She'd disappeared once he started roaring. I didn't judge her for it. I had a feeling she'd done it so she wouldn't slit Eldan's throat when he caused Virtus that much pain. "The human mates have all used it for decades."

Hope danced in Mere's eyes. "I'd love to try it."

"The meeting is officially happening. We need to get to the tower," Danica said, glancing up from her phone. "Why don't you guys meet us there?"

Within a few minutes, we were all piling into separate cars. Kyla and Danica rode with us. "It's cute seeing Vas fuss over Mere," Danica said. "I haven't been here enough. I hadn't even known she was struggling with the morning sickness."

"Neither had I, and I live here." Guilt twisted in my stomach, and Nathaniel took one hand off the steering wheel and reached for mine, bringing my palm to his mouth.

"You've been a little busy," he reminded me. "Do you think our kids would get your curls?"

I momentarily lost the ability to speak. Behind us, Danica chortled. "Way to distract her from feeling guilty."

"Uh..."

Nathaniel glanced at me. "You don't want kids?"

"I hadn't really thought about it."

He shrugged. "We have plenty of time."

We were all quiet for the rest of the drive to the tower. Nathaniel was lost in his own thoughts, while Danica was busy ensuring everyone knew where we were meeting. Kyla hadn't said a word since she'd shifted back to human.

Meanwhile, I was busy picturing kids with blond curls and Nathaniel's eyes. Kids had always been a *maybe* for some time far off in the distant future. I'd never been overly concerned about whether I had them, and I'd figured I'd decide at some point in the next ten or fifteen years.

Nathaniel would be a great father.

Except, if we thought Vas was overprotective, I couldn't even fucking imagine my Alpha mate if I let him knock me up.

"You're thinking too hard," he murmured, squeezing my hand. "Relax, Evie. I don't need to impregnate you tomorrow."

My cheeks flamed. Behind us, Danica and Kyla sniggered, whispering back and forth. I shot Nathaniel a dirty look. He smirked, unconcerned.

Samael had apparently instructed us to park in the underground garage, so Danica directed us, waving at several of the demons who dropped into low bows. It was my turn to snigger.

"Guess the whole *no bowing and scraping* message hasn't yet made it to this realm, huh?"

Danica just sighed, nodding to the demons as we drove into the garage. Once there, we took the elevator up to one of the conference floors. Twenty or thirty of Samael's top demons were already gathered. Danica wandered away to her mate, who was deep in discussion with Bael. Samael immediately grabbed her hand, pulled her to him, and kissed her, long and deep. From the pained look on Bael's face, this was a common occurrence. I stifled a smirk.

"The seelie are on their way," Kyla told me.

I glanced at her. "Are you okay?"

Clearly, she wasn't. She'd been quiet since she'd

met us in the forest. I had a feeling her talk with Selina hadn't gone all that well.

Kyla sighed, opening her mouth. Then she let out a strangled sound. "What the hell is *he* doing here?"

I knew that tone. Which meant I knew who had just walked in before I turned.

Finvarra stood in the doorway, dressed—as usual—in black. On one hip, the hilt of the golden sword gleamed, tantalizingly close.

"I have absolutely no idea," I said.

The room went quiet. Finvarra met Samael's eyes, and the demon king nodded at him, clearly not at all surprised to be hosting the unseelie king. Behind me, Nathaniel had gone very still, in the way of wolves on the hunt.

This much testosterone in one room? I'd be surprised if it *didn't* end in bloodshed.

Nathaniel leaned over and murmured something in Kyla's ear. Her chin jutted out, but she nodded, stalking over to talk to Aubrey as he walked in.

Across the room, Lilith began walking toward us, her hips rolling in that way of hers. Within the blink of an eye, she was standing close. *Too close.*

Lilith flipped her long, glossy red hair over one shoulder. Her lush lips curled as she smiled at Nathaniel.

"Well, hi," she purred.

He flicked her a distracted glance and then dropped his gaze to his phone. "Hello."

Lilith's eyes lit up at the challenge. My teeth clenched, and I glanced away. Across the room, Bael sent me a grin. As Lilith's mate, he knew exactly what was happening.

Nathaniel lifted his head, his gaze finding mine.

"What's wrong?"

"Nothing."

He went still, and his eyes lightened several shades. His large body crowded mine, until he'd backed me a few feet away, ignoring Lilith completely. "We agreed, no lies between us," he murmured in my ear.

We had. "It's not important now. We'll talk about it later."

Nathaniel shoved his phone into his pocket, captured my wrist in his hand, and pulled me toward the door.

"Hey!"

"We need a moment," he announced to the room at large.

My face burned. He led me out of the conference room, past Danica and Samael, who were having a hissed discussion of their own—likely about Finvarra's presence. Nathaniel ushered me into one of the soundproof meeting rooms.

Nathaniel released my hand and strolled over to the window, closing the blinds with a snap of his wrist.

Then he folded his arms. "What's going on, Evie?"

Mortification slid through me. I covered my face with one hand.

And then he was tugging my hand away from my face and pressing a kiss to my palm. "You can tell me anything," he said. "*Anything*. Just don't hide from me. Ever."

"It's embarrassing. I know you're my mate. And I know it's for life. I just..." I attempted to back away, but he followed me, caging me in against the wall with his huge body. I narrowed my eyes at him, and he merely grinned, pulling one of my curls free from my messy bun so he could play with it.

I dropped my gaze to his chest. "I got jealous, okay?"

"I know. I could feel it. But I don't understand why."

Was he trying to be obtuse? Or did he just not see it?

My mind helpfully provided me with images of Nathaniel's distraction and disinterest in Lilith's obvious flirting.

He *didn't* see it.

"Evie?"

"Hold on. I'm having a realization."

He raised one eyebrow but waited patiently, as if we had all the time in the world.

"I was jealous of Lilith. Because she's incredibly beautiful. And immortal. She never has to worry about leaving her mate behind. But one day, when I'm gone..."

Fury. That was fury in Nathaniel's eyes now. All

calm and patience had left the building.

"One day when you're gone? Where exactly are you planning to go?"

I sighed. "When I'm dead, Nathaniel. You'll move on, eventually. Wolves are pack animals, and they're not meant to be alone. And it'll likely be with someone like Lilith. The next sixty years are a blink of an eye to her. But I'll age, and you won't w-want me anymore."

My throat had tightened. Nathaniel looked torn between hopeless amusement, annoyance, and fury.

I'd known this when I mated with him. I wouldn't let my insecurities ruin our relationship. Even if it meant aging while he stayed young and gorgeous. "Don't get me wrong, I plan to age as disgracefully as possible. It'll be a fun ride. But one day, I'll—"

"Evie. Stop. I would never move on from you. If something happened, I'd follow you."

"Don't say that." Panic dug between my ribs and stayed there. "Nathaniel—"

"You haven't been paying attention to the human mates, have you? Have you seen any elderly women?"

I went still. No. All of them were relatively young and healthy. But if some of them had been mated since shortly after the portals opened, that was impossible. Duh.

"How does it work?"

"Mating extends a human life-span. I believe you would have lived longer than most anyway, thanks to your unseelie father and whatever other DNA...

Anyway, you won't grow old. Not the way you think you will. It will take a few centuries before I even get to see how you'd look with a touch of gray in this beautiful hair."

Well, that was…a lot.

His expression hardened. "But more importantly, we need to address this certainty that I'd ever choose another woman. Or that my wolf would tolerate such a thing."

"Nathaniel…"

"It's tiring justifying my feelings to the woman who holds my heart in the palm of her hand. If you don't understand how much I love you by now, then I've done something wrong. I've messed up somehow. Because I don't know how to make you see, make you *feel,* how much I need you."

Tears pricked my eyes. "I'm sorry. You haven't done anything wrong. I don't want to be this way. I'm *not* this way. I don't know what's happening to me."

His eyes softened. "It's the initial stages of the mating. There are a lot of…emotions to deal with. Most mated pairs will go somewhere to be alone for the first few months. We haven't had that chance. I should've explained it to you, so the normal jealousy and possessiveness wouldn't have made you feel like you were going crazy. As soon as this is over, we'll take some time. We'll go away for a while."

"I'd like that," I whispered, and he cupped my cheek.

"I already know where I'm taking you." He smiled. But it wasn't a full smile. He was still...sad.

I didn't know how to fix what I'd broken.

"What do I do, Nate?"

"Open your side of the bond to me, Evie. You don't have to keep it open. Just let me in."

I frowned at that. "What do you mean?"

"You don't know." He shoved his hand through his hair. "Of course you don't. It would be natural for you to shut it down."

"Explain. Please."

"Do you remember how you tugged on our bond? When you were being chased by the HFE members?" His eyes flickered light blue at the memory, and I took his hand in mine. "And how you could feel my guilt the other day outside your office?"

"Yes. Of course."

"Those were examples of you using the bond. Of you opening your side." He brushed his hand down my cheek. "Close your eyes."

I complied. He leaned closer, and I inhaled the masculine scent of him, so familiar by now. He smelled like home.

"Good. Now go to that place you went to when you needed me. Picture the bond in your head. What does it look like?"

"Um..." I strained, but I couldn't see it. Why couldn't I see it?

"You're trying too hard. When you reached for

me after the car accident, how did it feel?"

I rolled my shoulders and thought back to the moment I realized I was heavily outnumbered. I embraced the terror, but beneath it all was the knowledge that, no matter what happened, Nathaniel would come for me.

He would never leave me. If those men took me, Nathaniel would hunt them to the ends of the earth. And he would find me.

A blistering ache slid up the back of my throat. My breath stuttered, and then hot tears were sliding down my cheeks.

Nathaniel watched me with calm eyes.

"I...I knew I just had to hold on. I didn't have to fight them alone. You would come."

"And what did you do?"

"I just reached for you."

I closed my eyes and let in that calm certainty. I breathed in the knowledge that, unlike so many people in my life, Nathaniel would never abandon me.

He'd come to the seelie realm for me. He'd dropped everything and *run* to the scene of the accident for me. No matter how much I pissed him off—and during our long lives, there was bound to be plenty of that—Nathaniel would always be there.

I hiccupped out a sob and pulled the bond toward me. It was shiny and strong, but Nathaniel seemed so far away at the other end of it.

Nathaniel's lips brushed my forehead. "You're still

blocking it."

I shuddered and looked deeper. Looked into the heart of myself, where my greatest fears lived.

Looked at my own insecurities and the deep-seated belief that, one day, I'd drive Nathaniel away. The way I drove everyone away.

Nathaniel was right. It wasn't fair to him. Either I believed he would stay with me no matter what, or I didn't.

Sucking in a deep, trembling breath, I understood what the problem was. The bond was there, but it was too…long. Each foot of extra length between Nathaniel and me represented an insecurity. A belief that I wasn't good enough, that I was dangerous to be around, that I would ultimately end up alone.

Fuck that.

I yanked on the bond.

Opening my eyes, I saw the flicker of pain on Nathaniel's face before he hid it away.

A dark, cold fury took up residence in my gut. I closed my eyes again and pictured all that extra length. All those miles of insecurities. I created a ball of fire in one hand as I surveyed the rope. God, I hoped this worked.

Channeling all my fear and rage into the flames, I aimed the fireball at our bond.

EVIE

My head spun dizzily. Nathaniel hissed. I had to stop burning the bond at the right time. "Evie?" Nathaniel's voice was worried, but beneath the worry, I heard something that sounded a lot like joy.

My gaze met bright blue, and our bond slammed into me. My fire disappeared.

I gasped as I felt everything Nathaniel felt for me. His love was so deep, so pure, the thought of him paying attention to any other woman was ludicrous. When I was in the room, all he saw was me.

He could see all of me. All my hidden insecurities and my secret beliefs that no one would ever truly love me enough to stay.

And I could see him. His belief that he was a monster. But that he'd been changed for a reason— to save his pack. His certainty that he would never be good enough for me, but he would never let me go. His unwavering determination to make sure I had the best life possible by his side.

"Wow." I stumbled a little, feeling drunk. "That's… interesting."

He threw back his head and laughed, and I could feel his joy, radiating toward me. The fact that *I* was the one who caused him such joy gave me a warm, fluttery feeling in my chest.

Nathaniel held me steady, and then his hand was buried in my curls. He pressed me against the wall, his mouth finding mine. I lost myself in the feel of him against me.

"Are you two going to stay in here and make out all day?"

Nathaniel slowly lifted his head, and I smirked as Danica planted her hands on her hips. "Let's get this done before Kyla and Finvarra kill each other," she said.

"Yeah, whose idea was that anyway?"

"Finvarra's. But he cleared it with Samael first. Someone obviously has a big mouth since no one *invited* Finvarra to this little party."

That explained Danica and Samael's hissed conversation. My sister was intensely loyal, and if she'd known Finvarra was coming, she would've warned Kyla.

"You have two minutes." Danica eyed us both. "Don't make me come back in here."

She left the door open, clearly in an attempt to

dissuade us from getting distracted once more. Danica stalked in the direction of the conference room, and an arm shot out of the next meeting room she passed, hauling her inside.

Samael.

Nathaniel's amusement radiated down the bond. I leaned against the wall.

"Is it always going to be like this? Not that I don't love feeling your emotions, but…"

"You're worried there would be no room left for your own."

"Well, yeah."

"Don't worry. It'll settle down in a few days. And then we'll only be able to feel each other when we reach for the bond."

He leaned down and nuzzled me. "I love you."

"I know." I could feel that love, and there was no end to it. The bond made all of my previous insecurities irrelevant. I knew Nathaniel would never betray me. Would never leave me. He simply loved me too much.

"It'll take me some getting used to…"

I wasn't just talking about the bond. I could list my best attributes, and I was one hell of a catch. But knowing just how much Nathaniel loved me was both mind-boggling and a little difficult to believe.

He dropped a kiss to my nose and took my hand. "Let's get this over with."

Within a few minutes, we were all gathered in the conference room once more. Mere and Vas had joined us, and Mere already looked better. She was stuffing a burger into her mouth, Vas practically radiating contentment as he watched her.

Rose stood next to Kyla, and I smiled at her. Rose was the only human here—Steve was still working on the tech side of things—but she'd been instrumental in our research so far.

Finvarra lounged in a seat at the table. I took the empty seat next to him, Nathaniel sitting next to me. It seemed like a smart move to have someone between them.

Kyla leaned against the wall on the opposite side of the room, ignoring the unseelie with a studied nonchalance that told me she was imagining ripping out his throat.

"Why are you here?" I muttered to him.

"Your uncle is unseelie," Finvarra said. "That makes him one of mine. Not to mention, my greatest enemy has colluded with your little human hate group for years. That makes it entirely too likely that many of *my* missing people will be found in these labs."

His face had turned so cold, I wouldn't be surprised to find it was ice if I were dumb enough to reach out and poke his cheek.

I sighed. Those were pretty good reasons. I shot Kyla an apologetic look, and she shrugged, clearly hearing our discussion over the conversations continuing around us.

"Okay," Danica said. I'd asked her to run this

meeting. "Everyone knows why we're here, so I won't rehash it. But let's go over what we know so far."

She nodded at Bael, who dimmed the lights. Everyone went quiet as a picture of the map we'd created appeared on the wall in front of us.

"These are the labs. There could be more, but we need to move soon. Evie's uncle has been taken by HFE. That means our timeline has sped up."

"How are we going to get in?" Mere asked.

"Good question." Danica nodded to me.

I took a deep breath. HFE had taken Eachann. He could be suffering through torture at this very moment. Nathaniel reached for my hand, and I sent him a grateful look.

"Eachann had been working on the guards at each lab," I said. "We know where their families are, including the children's schools, spouses' workplaces, et cetera."

Mere dropped her gaze, clearly uncomfortable with our line of reasoning. I couldn't blame her. Samael just smiled, but no one was expecting the demon king to have second thoughts about threatening humans with their loved ones.

"It's our only choice," I said. "We have to hit all the labs at the same time, or we risk them disappearing. No humans will be harmed, but the guards don't need to know that."

Did threatening their loved ones mean we were dipping our toes into bad-guy territory? Maybe. Would

I do it anyway? Without a moment's hesitation.

"We need people on the ground, finding these guards and ensuring they fall in line," Samael said. "My demons can cover half of them." He looked at Nathaniel and Finvarra, then flicked his glance to Aubrey.

"My people will take longer to travel," Nathaniel said. "Not all of them can use portals. We'll cover anyone in the Carolinas, the East Coast, Nashville, and Alabama."

Aubrey nodded. "We have a portal that will allow us to head to Texas, Louisiana, Mississippi, and Arkansas. I can't promise more than that, I'm afraid. While I have many loyal to me, Taraghlan has been successful with his reign of terror. Most won't risk getting involved."

Finvarra met his eyes. "We will take whatever is left, providing there are portals close by."

Look at us all cooperating. Long may it last.

"We still need more numbers," I said. "If every lab is as large as the one we found in Tennessee, then we'll be hopelessly outnumbered when we attack."

"The witches refused to help," Danica said. She glanced at me, and I sighed. I knew that look.

"You think *I* can convince them? Wasn't it Samael who made Gemma fall in line last time? And don't think I haven't wondered how the hell he did *that*." I raised an eyebrow at him, and he just gave me a faint smile.

"Worth a try." Nathaniel squeezed my hand. "I'll come with you."

I just shook my head at him. Nothing was less

likely to make Gemma cooperate than showing up with the werewolf Alpha.

"I'll try the witches," I said. "But I have another idea. I think we need to contact Nelson."

Nelson was a detective who was in charge of the newly formed paranormal task force. He paid me a small retainer each month to be on call for any paranormal shenanigans that involved murdered humans.

That went over about as well as I expected. I waited patiently for the outrage to die down.

Nathaniel didn't. He let out a low, rumbling growl that seemed to crawl into every inch of the room.

"Let my mate speak."

Aubrey winked at me. He knew where I was going with this. And he seemed to be the only one who was open to working with humans.

"It's out of his jurisdiction, so he'll be forced to cooperate with the FBI," I said. "We'll negotiate with them. We go in first, and they can come in for cleanup."

"What's the point?" Bael asked.

"There are humans in those labs. Not just the guards. Those humans are likely being experimented on too. After all, the whole point of HFE is to ensure humans have access to the same powers we have. The FBI will have medical staff on standby for the humans. That allows us to focus on finding the paranormals."

There was grumbling, but eventually, most people nodded. I blew out a breath. Good.

"Before we get to work, there's something you

should know. Taraghlan knows the sword was taken," Finvarra said. "He has already attempted to sneak several of his best people into my realm through the Middleground."

"And how did you respond to that?" Kyla asked.

He flashed his teeth at her. "I sent him back their heads."

That was approval I could see written all over Kyla's face.

"Does he know who took the sword?" Nathaniel asked.

"Yes. My spies tell me he's particularly unhappy about the hydra."

I smirked. So did Kyla.

Beside me, Nathaniel frowned. I knew that look. He was already planning how he'd remove the seelie king as a threat when this was all over.

From the cold look on Finvarra's face and the determination on Aubrey's, he'd have to get in line.

"We also need to take out Gabriel," Nathaniel said.

"He's planning to kill you," Samael mused. "In retaliation for Albert."

From the look on Samael's face, he was wishing he'd been the one to end Albert.

I stiffened at the thought of Gabriel succeeding.

"I'm harder to kill than he thinks," Nathaniel murmured in my ear. It didn't make me feel any better. I'd back my mate against anything that required strength and speed. But all evidence was pointing to

Gabriel being insanely powerful.

"The mages are in this up to their necks," Danica said. "This is a good thing, though."

Vas leaned back in his chair. "Why is it a good thing?"

"Because we've previously treated them like the good guys with a few bad eggs. In reality, they're rotten at the core. Now, the gloves are coming off."

"How many clichés can you spout in one sentence?" Vas winked at her.

"Danica's right," Mere said. "Now that we know what Gabriel and the other mages are up to, we all need to be careful. But at the same time, it frees us up to take them out."

I raised an eyebrow, unused to hearing Mere talking about taking anyone out. Although, I'd recently discovered she had a ruthless side when she needed it.

"Okay," Danica said. "Let's talk teams. We want a good mix of paranormals on each team, covering for any weaknesses."

The meeting wrapped up quickly after that. I jerked my head toward the door and waved at the others.

"And where do you think you're going?" Nathaniel asked.

"To talk to the witches."

"I'll take you."

EVIE

I called Nelson on our way to Gemma's. He took the news of our plans about as well as I'd expected.

"We're inviting you to our party, Nelson."

"A last-minute invitation, halfway through that party. And only so we can help you clean up the paper plates and stale pizza."

"Do you want to be involved or not?"

"Of course I do. But we're going to talk about this, Evie. Our agreement—"

"Our agreement involved me helping you with paranormal crimes. There was nothing in there about calling you in every time we were going to play."

He let out a growl, and I matched it with one of my own. Nathaniel quirked a brow at me.

"My uncle is in one of those labs, Nelson. You think I'm going to risk the FBI finding out about this and trying to go in before we're ready?"

He sighed. "I see your point. I'll contact everyone who needs to be involved at our end."

"Thank you."

He hung up. Clearly, he was still pissed.

Nathaniel pulled up outside Gemma's, and we both got out.

"You take the car," he said.

"Are you sure?"

He smiled, tucking the keys into the pocket of my blue sundress. "Have I told you how pretty you look today?"

My heart fluttered. "You have now." Sliding my hand to the back of his neck, I pulled him down for a kiss.

"I have business on Main Street," Nathaniel said. "There will be a pack member in the neighborhood when I need to go home."

"Keep an eye on Kyla, will you?"

"Of course."

Kyla had disappeared as soon as the meeting was finished. I wanted to ask her about her talk with Selina, but it was clear she needed some space.

I studied the house in front of me. Several other cars were parked outside, which meant some of the coven was already gathered here. This would be awkward.

"Are you okay?" Nathaniel asked.

"I'll be fine. Go about your business."

Nathaniel pressed a kiss to my forehead, pulled out his phone, and strolled down the street.

Knocking on the door, I fought not to shift on my feet. I had no doubt they knew I was here. They'd be watching to see just how nervous I was. At their hearts, witches were like any other paranormal. Weakness was to be eradicated.

They kept me waiting. I pasted a placid expression on my face and peered down at my nails, picking idly at my cuticle. Finally, the door swung open.

"Evie." Freya looked drawn and tired. She was still pregnant, her bump visible beneath her sweater.

"Hi. How are you?"

"Fine. Yourself?"

Empty small talk. This was going about as well as I'd expected.

"Fine. I need to talk to Gemma."

"She's busy."

The dagger on my hip glowed red for the first time. Misty was working. I didn't know if it'd been asleep, or if this was the first time I'd been lied to. But either way, Freya's gaze dropped to the dagger, her cheeks reddening.

"I thought that was Danica's."

"Mine now. You want to tell me the truth?"

"She's not well."

It glowed once more. "Fine," Freya snapped. "She's dying."

Misty went dark. And so did the edges of my

vision. "And you weren't going to tell me?"

A flicker of what might've been regret darted across her face. Then she sighed and stepped back, opening the door. "You know what she's like. She didn't want anyone to know. It was Gail who got in touch with us, against Gemma's wishes. We all arrived today. Healing spells are no longer working. It's only a matter of time."

I stepped into the house. The air was heavy, and farther inside, I could hear someone weeping. They were immediately hushed.

The curtains had all been drawn, candles and lamps used in place of the sun. Freya jerked her head, and I followed her into the living room.

Gemma lay on the sofa, piled with blankets. I spotted a crocheted blanket—identical to the blanket that had been draped over the sofa in our last house. I couldn't remember who'd made it, but they'd obviously replaced it. Seeing it pushed me back to the many times I'd curled up under the original blanket, watching TV and listening to the sounds of the coven around me.

Gemma's eyes met mine. She was pale, and her hand trembled when she pushed one of the blankets off her. "Evie."

"Gemma." I nodded. I wasn't entirely sure what to say, but if there was one thing I knew about her, it was that she would loathe anything she considered pity.

There were powerful witches in this coven. A few of them had good contacts within other paranormal factions. If Gemma had wanted to live, she could've. The fact that she was dying simply meant she was ready to go.

I wouldn't ignore that informed choice by weeping at her side. Even if a lump was forming in my throat at the thought of the world without the cynical, sharp-tongued witch in it.

She'd raised me after my mom had taken Danica and fled. Sure, Gemma had had the coven to help, but all final decisions regarding my upbringing had been hers. And for a kid who'd continually felt abandoned, I'd still had an almost idyllic upbringing.

However, I couldn't help but ask… "Are you sure about this?"

I'd expected her to scowl. Surprisingly, a smile lit up her face. "I've never been more sure. Extending my life is a waste of good power. I'm old and tired. My bones hurt." She eyed me. "Why did you come?"

"It doesn't matter."

Marie snorted. "If Evie is here, it's because she wants something."

I didn't flinch, but it was close. No, I hadn't visited much since the coven was attacked. Since Brooke and the others were murdered. Since Gemma told me I could no longer be a member of the coven. The people hunting me were too much of a threat.

Slowly turning, I met Marie's gaze. "And how many times have you guys called me? When have I been invited back? You chose to kick me out of the coven. I haven't exactly felt welcome."

She planted her hands on her hips, opening her mouth. But Freya shot her a look.

"She's right," she said. "We don't get to pretend like Evie doesn't care. We're the ones who told her to leave."

From Marie's sneer, she didn't agree. I ignored her and sat on the floor next to Gemma. She'd closed her eyes when we were sniping at each other, but now she opened them once more.

"You have a new family now," she said. She didn't say it in a mean way, but I hunched my shoulders just the same. Gemma shook her head at me. "The wolves will keep you safe. And you will keep them safe. As it should be."

The breath left my lungs as I watched her. Gemma regretted kicking me out. Oh, she'd still justify it until the moment her heart stopped, but that was coven business. It wasn't often that I could separate the coven leader from the woman who'd bandaged my scraped knees, but in this, I could see it.

But she was right about the wolves. They would face any threats together. And I'd be right there with them, fighting for all I was worth.

"Tell me why you came," Gemma said. I sighed but didn't bother arguing.

"We've found HFE's labs. We're going to take them all out. At the same time."

I didn't worry about one of the witches opening

her mouth to someone she shouldn't. Everyone here hated HFE for what they'd done.

"Who is *we?*" Noelle asked from where she was sitting next to Gail on the other sofa.

"The unseelie, the wolves, the demons, and some of the seelie who are loyal to Aubrey. We'll also be including the FBI for cleanup."

Interest sparked in Noelle's eyes. The witches had joined us in the battle against Lucifer—the covens allying for the first time. I saw longing on enough faces that I knew at least half of them wanted to join the fight.

But it wouldn't happen. With Gemma on her deathbed, no decisions would be made. And once she died…

I sucked in a breath.

Technically, Gail was next in line to be coven leader. But that would never happen. She was frail, lost in grief over Caroline and now Gemma, and wanted nothing more than to be left alone.

Prickles of dread danced along my nerve endings. While it would be nice to imagine that Gemma had prepared for this, it was more likely that she'd accepted the power vacuum that would occur when she died. She had always been extremely pragmatic when it came to infighting in the coven. Growing up during the Decade of Despair had hardened her, and I wouldn't be surprised if she'd chosen to die without an obvious replacement to ensure the most powerful witch rose to the top.

After all, she wasn't going to be around to see the fallout.

No, the witches wouldn't be helping us. They'd be too busy with the internal drama and power struggles that would happen in the next few weeks.

"I will speak to each of you separately," Gemma mumbled, her eyes closed. It was clear that so much talking had exhausted her. "Then I will die alone."

She held up a shaking hand at the instant denial from every corner of the room. I kept my mouth shut. No part of me was surprised by her choice. Gemma had once told me that death was a solitary experience. No matter how many people were at your side, you took that final trip alone.

I could feel the amount of power that was pouring into the coven leader. The moment that flow of power stopped…

She would be gone.

I took a deep breath and added my own power. Gemma's eyes popped open. A gurgle of a laugh left her throat. "Well, that will help me get through the next few hours. Thank you."

"You're welcome."

We all filed out. Since Gail was clearly not up to the task, Marie took over. "We'll visit her alphabetically," she said. "From Z to A."

I rolled my eyes. Several people frowned at her, but no one protested. Fine.

"Text me when it's my turn," I said.

Opening the front door, I strolled down the steps and toward our old home.

I messaged Danica while I was on the way. No one had bothered to tell her either. She was pissed at Gemma for many things, but Gemma had still helped us when it counted, ensuring Lucifer was defeated and Samael regained his throne. She deserved the option.

I'll be there soon.

Sliding my phone back into my pocket, I turned the final corner, preparing for my heart to feel as if it had been ripped from my chest.

There was a reason I stayed away from this part of Durham.

No one had built on the lot. It remained a collection of overgrown weeds. I hoped no one ever did. I couldn't imagine most people would want to live in a place that had seen so much death.

The lot seemed too small to have contained our home. My memory of the house itself was already fading. Funny how it happened so quickly.

I stared at the weeds, and for a moment, I could've sworn I felt the rest of our coven around me. My eyes burned. "I'm sorry," I got out. "I know it's not my fault—at least, I know that now. But I'm still sorry. You lost your lives because HFE targeted me. But I swear to you, no matter what it takes, I'll make them pay."

Brooke's face flashed in my mind. I knew she wouldn't want me to mourn forever. But every time

I thought of her, all I could think was how scared she must have been. And how much she'd had to offer the world. She'd had so many plans…

Many of them had involved partying until the sun came up, but they were *her* plans all the same.

"I miss you so fucking much, Brooke. I'd do anything to turn back time. Anything."

"She knows that."

I jumped about a foot in the air. Danica landed beside me, her wings disappearing. She grinned at my reaction, but the grin fell when she gazed past me at the lot.

"How'd you get here so fast?" I asked.

"Nathaniel heard Freya tell you Gemma was dying. He messaged me. Are you okay?"

I shrugged. "It's hard to imagine the coven without Gemma at the head. Gail's not going to take over."

"Not our circus…"

"Not our monkeys. I know. But that doesn't stop me from wishing I could help in some way. Gemma's talking to us one by one. But I'm last, which means you can come with me."

Danica just nodded, frowning at the weeds in front of us. "Maybe I'll buy the land."

I gaped at her. "*This* land?"

"Yeah. Samael asked me what I wanted for my birthday. His suggestions were ludicrous. This is a little more reasonable."

If land in one of the most sought-after areas for

witches in the country was reasonable, I couldn't even imagine what Samael had attempted to convince Danica she needed. The thought brought a smile to my face.

"What would you do with it?"

"Turn it into a garden. Something simple to remember them all. A few benches. Maybe a gazebo for shade. You could come here to talk to Brooke."

Tears pricked my eyes. Most of the coven had turned their backs on Danica the moment they learned she was involved with Samael, and yet I knew she'd think of each of them when she planned that garden.

"I won't tell them I'm responsible." She smiled. "Then they'll use it."

"I love you."

She flung her arm around my shoulders. "I love you too. Let's go see Gemma."

By the time we got back to the house, most of the coven had already taken their turns with Gemma. A few smiled at Danica, but most of them ignored her. While I was used to it now myself, seeing the way they treated Danica made me want to set something on fire.

"Ignore it." She smiled serenely as we sat on the staircase, waiting for our turn.

"Since when are you a live-and-let-live kind of person?" I slitted my eyes at her, and she just shrugged.

"Turns out, running a realm keeps me so busy, I don't have time or energy for petty bullshit. Unless I'm the one starting it."

Freya walked toward us. Her face was wet with tears. "Your turn."

"Thank you," Danica said.

We stepped into the living room. Surprise flickered across Gemma's face when she spotted Danica.

"You don't look like you're dying," Danica mused.

Gemma nodded at me. "A nice little influx of power from your sister."

"Want some of mine, too?"

Gemma let out a chortle. "I want to die, not live for the next few weeks."

"Fair enough." Danica sat cross-legged on the rug next to the sofa.

I concentrated on the power and frowned. I was the only one left...

She'd made the others stop the flow of their magic. My power was the only thing keeping her alive.

"I never would have expected both of you to be at my side during my final moments," Gemma said. "But I find it oddly fitting. Your mother... If she could see you both now..."

I readied myself to hear about how ashamed my mother would be of us. Danica's face had turned blank. The reason she'd fought Samael for so long was because Mom had made her promise to stay away from the demons. With just a few words, Gemma could break my sister.

"She would be proud," Gemma finished, and I

frowned. "Oh, she wouldn't have wanted you to end up where you have. At her heart, she was as insular as the rest of us, even if she stumbled when it came to your father." She nodded at Danica. "But she would be pleased to see both of her daughters powerful, with the kind of allies that ensure they will never have to run for their lives like she did."

"Thank you," Danica said gravely. The lump in my throat was too large to speak.

Gemma shifted her attention to me. "It's time."

Hot tears spilled from my eyes. I opened my mouth.

"I—"

Gemma shook her head. "I know. Now, let me go."

Danica grabbed my hand and squeezed. I took a deep breath, memorizing Gemma's face. And then I pulled my power away.

Gemma let out her last breath and closed her eyes.

She didn't open them again.

NATHANIEL

Evie's emotions were a tangled web when I picked her up from Gemma's. She walked out of the house and stopped, staring at me.

"What are you doing here?"

"I thought you could use a ride home." I gave her

a smile.

Her eyes filled with tears. A dull panic took up residence in my gut. There were surely *some* things I hated more than seeing Evie cry. But it was an incredibly short list.

Danica followed Evie out. Her face was pale, eyes red-rimmed, but she smiled at me. "Oh hey, werewolf king. You come to pick up my sister?"

Evie was silent. That, more than anything, made the panic spread.

Her eyes met mine. "I'm fine."

Danica rolled her eyes behind Evie's back, and Evie waved one hand, setting Danica's shoes on fire.

Danica put the fire out and slung her arm around Evie's shoulder.

"What do you usually do when you're feeling like this?" I asked them both.

"Go to the bar," they muttered in unison. Despite her sadness, a flicker of amusement danced in Evie's eyes.

"While that seems like an excellent and not-at-all-unhealthy coping mechanism..."

The sisters glared at me. Evie's hands lit up in warning, and I grinned.

"The bar is closed," Danica said mournfully. "It's Monday."

"You know, Tobias makes a mean martini," I said, hoping desperately for a smile.

Evie's eyes met mine, and her face softened as she

strolled toward me. "You don't need to worry," she murmured.

"It's my job to worry about you."

"Cute," Danica said. "As is the idea that Evie would drink anything as highbrow as a martini. Can Tobias make something with enough sugar to hide the taste of alcohol? That's more Evie's speed."

Evie sighed but didn't argue. I grinned at her. She would usually go to Meredith's when she was feeling like this. Instead, she would be coming home to me. To my pack. My wolf was absurdly pleased.

"Let's go, then."

Evie handed me the keys back, turning to face Danica as we got into the car. "You don't have to get back to the underworld?"

"I told Samael I was hanging with you. We haven't had nearly enough time together since the whole underqueen thing."

I glanced at her in the rearview mirror. "You mean that time you became queen of an entire realm?"

Danica just waved her hand. "Potato, potahto."

"When did you tell Samael what you were doing?" Evie asked.

Danica tapped her head.

"Ohh. Must be weird."

I couldn't help it. I focused on my mate.

"Weird like this?"

Her shriek stabbed into my sensitive ears in the confined space of the car, and I scowled at her.

Behind us, Danica cracked up. "I'd heard mated wolves could communicate that way," she murmured.

Evie just gaped. "Why didn't you tell me?"

"We only just solidified the bond," I said. I didn't tell Evie that before she fully opened her end, the thought of reaching for her in such an intimate way, only for her not to be able to hear me...

It had been intolerable.

"We'll talk later," I said. Evie glanced at Danica, who was frowning into space, likely having a conversation of her own.

"Okay."

I parked outside my house. Tobias opened the door and grinned at Danica and Evie. "I made snacks," he said.

Danica glanced at me. "You told him we were on the way?"

I nodded, and she stepped inside, inhaling the scent of his famous crack dip.

"Maybe Bael was right about stealing Tobias," she muttered.

Evie bared her teeth at her sister. "Ours," she growled, and it was the cutest fucking thing I'd ever seen.

I couldn't help but drag her to me for a deep kiss. She smiled against my mouth.

"I'm going to let you spend some time with your sister," I murmured, forcing myself to pull away.

Evie frowned, but a glance at Danica had her

nodding. They hadn't spent nearly enough time together, and I knew Evie missed her.

"Nope." Danica moved toward the living room. "I need to get to know my new brother-in-law. Have a drink with us, Nathaniel."

Tobias had disappeared into the kitchen.

"One drink," I said.

"I want to check on Virtus first," Evie said.

Virtus was still resting on the sofa. "Hey, buddy," Danica murmured, leaning down while Evie stroked his ears. "How are you feeling?"

Virtus opened his eyes and yawned, flashing his teeth.

"He says he's feeling better," Danica relayed. "And he'd like us to drink in here so he can hang out with us."

Evie frowned down at the griffin. "Are you sure? I think you're supposed to be sleeping."

The griffin gave her the side-eye, and she grinned. "Fine."

EVIE

Danica choked, tequila dripping from her nose. I cracked up. Beside me, Nathaniel let out a low rumble of amusement.

I hadn't had this much fun in a long time.

Tobias had made frozen margaritas and served nachos, crack dip, and chocolate brownies—which we had demolished. I'd invited him to come drink with us, but he'd insisted he had things to do.

The wolves were giving us a wide berth. Except for Kyla, who'd just strutted in, a huge grin on her face.

"Well, well, well," she said. "Look what—" Tobias appeared with a margarita in his hand, holding it out for her.

She took it with a grin, pressing a kiss to his cheek. "Don't mind if I do. Hey, Virtus. How are you doing?"

They had a private conversation, and he must've said something amusing, because she cracked up.

Nathaniel scooted over so she could sit on the floor next to him. We were seated around the coffee table, cards from a drinking game spread out in piles. Danica had insisted on tequila shots for the drinking game, and Nathaniel had put away more tequila than both of us combined. But he didn't seem to have even the slightest buzz.

"What's your secret?" I slurred.

"His Alphaness immediately burns off anything his body considers poison," Kyla informed me, taking a healthy slug of her margarita. "Part of the gig. He can't protect the pack if he's stumbling all over the place."

I pouted. "So I'll never get to see drunk Nathaniel?"

He leaned over and nuzzled me. Kyla pounded three shots in quick succession.

I gaped at her, and she shrugged. "What? I need

to catch up."

Danica grinned, and her wings appeared. "Oops." She frowned at them, and they disappeared. Then reappeared.

"If I drank down three bottles of tequila, you'd see drunk Nathaniel," my mate murmured. "But you'd very quickly have a hungover Alpha on your hands, and no one wants that."

I wanted that. I wanted Nathaniel at his best *and* at his worst. All of him. Forever.

"I feel the same," he told me, and I realized I'd spoken aloud. Kyla winced, looking embarrassed for me. I just stuck my tongue out at her.

A knock sounded on the door. Tobias strode out from the kitchen before any of us could get up. A few moments later, Samael's low voice carried into the living room.

"Drink?" Tobias offered.

"No. But thank you." Samael stepped into the room, took one look at Danica, and his usual I-want-to-kill-someone expression transformed into a grin.

Danica blinked blearily at him from where she was lounging on the floor. One of her wings fluttered in his direction. "What are you doing here?"

"Something told me you were a little impaired." He tapped his head. "I thought I'd make sure you could get home safely."

"Shot, shot, shot," Kyla began chanting. Danica joined her.

Samael had a pained expression on his face. Danica just arched an eyebrow.

"All who enter must pay the toll," I informed him. Although a hiccup ruined the seriousness I was attempting.

Nathaniel leaned over and kissed the tip of my nose.

Samael sighed, leaned down, and took the shot Danica had just poured from her hand. He tossed it back like it was water.

"Well," she muttered. "That was anticlimactic."

Samael leaned down. "You know what's *not* anticlimactic?"

"Ewwww," I gagged.

Danica gave him a lewd wink, and he scooped her up.

"Booo," I said, but he just shook his head at me. Danica was already closing her eyes and nuzzling into his chest.

"Lightweight," I taunted. She opened one eye, held up her middle finger, and then twined her arms around her mate.

"Meeting tomorrow," Nathaniel said. "Gabriel gave us an address for the meeting."

Samael nodded. "Send me the details."

This was weird. I mean, it was great that Samael and Nathaniel could work together, but it was still weird.

Nathaniel walked them to the door. When he

walked back in, my eyes got stuck on the way his T-shirt clung to that chest of his.

"So..." I fluttered my eyelashes at him. "Come here often?"

"Annnnd I'm out," Kyla announced. "I'll see you guys tomorrow."

I opened my mouth to protest, but Nathaniel was already scooping me up.

"So, about that tying me up thing..." I said.

"Good God, wait until I've left the house." Kyla slammed her hands over her ears, but the movement made her stumble on her feet.

"Are you okay to get home?"

"Werewolf. I'm fine."

Nathaniel grinned at her. "Goodnight."

Then he was walking up the stairs, his clean, masculine scent teasing my nostrils. I leaned close to his neck and inhaled.

"You're sniffing me?"

"Can't help it," I mumbled. "You smell so good."

"Something's on your mind," he said.

"I can't stop thinking about Eachann. How can I have fun when he's likely stuck in a cell—or worse."

He went still, pausing at the top of the stairs. "You've put everything into HFE. Not only that, but because of you and Danica, paranormals are working together, and we're going to shut all the labs down. There is literally nothing left for you to do tonight. You needed to relax a little. Do you think your uncle would judge you for that?"

"No." But my eyes had filled. Nathaniel looked like I'd gutted him. "I just… I don't want to lose him."

"You won't. He's kept himself alive all these years. Give him some credit."

I nodded, and Nathaniel stalked into our room, placing me gently on the bed.

I reached for him. "Need you."

"You've got me. Always."

21

EVIE

Sunlight stabbed into my eyes.

I groaned. Everything hurt. "So bright."

My nose caught the scent of a freshly showered Nathaniel. I kept my eyes closed, but I inhaled as he leaned close.

"Water and painkillers," he said, dropping a kiss to my forehead. I opened my eyes to find the bedroom door open. Clearly, Nathaniel had already been downstairs, likely being productive.

I groaned again. Nathaniel smiled. "Tobias said to tell you he's cooking you a large, greasy breakfast with sausage, bacon, hash browns… His eggs are a little runny, though. Especially the white part."

I shot out of bed and stumbled into the bathroom, where I emptied my stomach.

"I hate you," I croaked, flushing the toilet.

Nathaniel handed me the water and meds,

watching as I took them. He leaned over and flicked on the shower.

"I thought you were all about doting on me," I pouted.

"Tough love, baby. And the alcohol was better out than in."

I scowled and stripped down, getting into the shower. I could feel Nathaniel's immediate interest, and I glowered at him. "Don't even think about it."

He just laughed and prowled out of the room.

I had a vague recollection of wanting to jump his bones last night. Instead, I'd passed out and likely snored in his ear all night.

It was a good thing the man was already mated to me. No escape for him.

I visited Virtus. He seemed to be doing better. At least he'd moved from the sofa to the floor and stretched out more at some point in the night. That had to mean he was in less pain.

"How's the healing going?"

Gold eyes met mine. He was feeling much better and was looking forward to coming with us to attack the labs.

"Uh, let's see what the healers say."

He ignored that, closing his eyes. I left him to sleep and wandered into the kitchen.

Thankfully, Tobias hadn't made runny eggs. In fact, from the offended sniff he gave Nathaniel, he'd heard his threat and hadn't been amused.

He slid a plate of food in front of me, along with a smoothie. "To replace some of the nutrients," he told me. "Drink the whole thing."

Since I was now ravenous, I complied.

"Where is everyone?" I asked.

Nathaniel grabbed a piece of toast and began buttering it. When he handed it to me, I decided I could potentially forgive him for making me puke.

"Anyone without a job to do in the next couple of days has been deployed to the labs. They're approaching the guards."

To threaten their families. I pushed my food away. Tobias turned and raised his eyebrow at me. Sighing, I picked up the smoothie and gulped at it. Strawberries, mango, banana, and likely a variety of vegetables Tobias had smuggled into it. Either way, it was delicious.

"The demons and fae have been working all night as well. We're close to having all the guards in our pocket. There's still the chance that one of them will turn on us, but I find it difficult to believe that HFE has generated that kind of loyalty."

I nodded, my mind already returning to today's meeting with Gabriel. Nathaniel picked up his coffee, studying my face.

"We have to take him out, Evie."

"I know. I just have a bad feeling about this."

Nathaniel watched me for a long moment. Then he reached for his phone, typing out a quick message.

"What are you doing?"

"Telling Hunter I want more wolves with us for our little meeting."

I must've looked surprised, because he reached out and took my hand. "If your intuition is sparking, we need to listen to it. Besides, my wolf agrees with you."

"What time is the meeting?"

"Two p.m."

I glanced at my phone. I had more than enough time.

"I need to run a couple of errands."

Nathaniel gave me a look that said he knew damn well I didn't give a shit about errands. But he didn't bother asking what I was up to. If it worked, I'd let him know. If it didn't... Well, I'd figure out Plan B after that.

"I don't want you going alone."

I took a deep breath, and he just looked at me.

"Fine. I'll take Kyla if she's not busy."

Kyla looked fresh as a daisy when she strolled in a few minutes later.

"I hate you," I muttered.

"Hey, werewolf metabolism. My hangover hit right after I left, and I slept through the worst of it. You going to tell me where we're going?"

"No."

She studied Nathaniel. His eyes had gone wolfy, and I knew it was because he couldn't contain his curiosity.

"Good work," she told me. "All wolves want a woman of mystery."

I smirked at that. Every werewolf I knew was insatiably curious.

Nathaniel gave Kyla a mock growl, and she strolled out. "I'm going to check on Virtus."

Stuffing the last of the toast into my mouth, I got to my feet.

"Be careful," Nathaniel told me.

I didn't dignify that with a response. Just chased my toast down with the last of my smoothie. Leaning over, I pressed a light kiss to Nathaniel's lips.

He had slid his hand to my neck before I realized he'd moved. And he held me in place as he kissed me. Languidly. Thoroughly. His tongue danced along my own, and I shivered, suddenly wanting nothing more than to drag him back upstairs.

"Laters," he told me as he slowly pulled away.

My mind had gone blank. I just nodded and stalked toward the door, ignoring his low chuckle.

"Virtus is coming with us," Kyla announced.

I narrowed my eyes at the griffin, who'd gotten to his feet. He moved slowly, and it was clear he was still in pain.

"Are you sure?"

He blinked at me. Not only was he sure, but if we didn't stop babying him, he was going to roar.

I'd been there.

"Fine. Let's go."

We took Kyla's car. Unfortunately, our first stop was a bust.

"She's not home. Did you message her?"

Kyla narrowed her eyes at Selina's house. "I messaged her this morning. Do you think we need to worry?"

"That's not like her. Let's poke around."

I checked the mailbox as Kyla shifted, hunting for any scents she didn't recognize. Virtus strolled up the steps to her porch and peered in the window. He liked Selina.

The lock on Selina's mailbox was warded. From what I could see when I peered into it, it was also nearly full. Two copies of Durham Denizens had also piled up outside her front door.

"She might've gone out of town suddenly," I said when Kyla reappeared. Virtus turned and padded down the stairs.

"I'll ask Aubrey if he knows anything," Kyla said once she'd shifted. She pulled on her sweats and a T-shirt and frowned at Selina's house. "In the meantime, we should keep an eye on this place. Now what?" she asked me.

I sighed. "You're not going to like it."

EVIE

"Are you serious?" Kyla groaned as I gave her the address.

I was right. She didn't like it.

Neither did Virtus. He laid his head on my shoulder and sighed.

"You can stay in the car if you want," I told him, giving him a scratch.

He ignored that, readjusting his body in the back. Kyla had folded the seats down, but the griffin barely fit. Usually, he liked shoving his head out the window and terrifying any humans in the vicinity. But today, he was staying still, likely because the stubborn creature was still in immense pain as he continued to regrow his bones.

Kyla was driving in a slow, careful, and distinctly un-Kyla-like way, ensuring Virtus wasn't jostled too much. Her hands tightened on the wheel as she scowled at me.

"Look, we don't have much choice. Gemma's dead." My voice cracked, and Kyla softened enough to send me a sympathetic look. "The coven will be too busy replacing her to help, and half of them want nothing to do with other paranormals anyway. Selina's gone. Hannah's our only shot."

"She'll probably demand your firstborn child as payment," Kyla muttered.

"She prefers Venmo."

Kyla showed me her teeth, and I smirked as she parked outside Hannah's.

"You can stay in the car, too," I told her.

She got out, opening the door for Virtus.

Hannah's mint-green bungalow looked freshly painted. I wasn't surprised. She'd earned enough helping us take down Lucifer to upgrade to a bigger house entirely. I had a feeling she enjoyed living on the edge of witch territory, though.

She took a while to come to the door. She may have been busy in the kitchen. Or it may have been a power play. With Hannah, it could go either way.

Finally, she opened the door. She was wearing an apron, and the house stank of black magic. My mind helpfully offered me a variety of spells she could be cooking up in her kitchen at this very moment. None of them was good.

"Evelyn," she said, nodding at me. "Kyla. And your pet griffin."

Virtus ignored her. She knew he wasn't a pet. Hannah sighed, obviously put out that she hadn't gotten a rise out of him.

"You're injured," she said to the griffin.

Kyla bared her teeth warningly at the black witch. "That doesn't make him vulnerable. Not with us here."

Hannah just rolled her eyes and turned, hobbling

into her kitchen. The witch was looking older, her curly white hair a little sparse on top, while the lines next to her eyes had deepened. This was a good sign since it meant she wasn't sacrificing any humans to keep her youth.

Although that didn't mean she wasn't sacrificing them for other spells. With Hannah, it was best to prepare for the worst.

Virtus padded directly after her, clearly unconcerned. Kyla prowled after him, and I followed them, a headache beginning to pound behind my eyes.

From the sick look on Kyla's face, whatever was bubbling away in Hannah's huge pot smelled even worse with her werewolf senses. Virtus merely let out a sigh and lay in a patch of sunlight near the window.

Danica was the one who'd first begun talking to Hannah. She'd needed Hannah's help so she could steal from Samael's dragon.

When I was a kid, black witches were the outcasts of our world. They crossed lines that white and gray wouldn't go near, like sacrificing animals, and—for some of the worst of them—children. Then I grew up and realized that while witches were considered black or white, life was rarely that simple.

Hannah might be a lot of things, but she'd fought with us in the underworld. In fact, she'd saved hundreds—if not thousands—of lives. Sure, she charged out the nose for her services, but it was dangerous for any witch to live alone these days. She needed to keep herself safe, and that meant expensive spell ingredients.

Regardless, we all understood each other. Danica, Kyla, and I were all willing to look the other way for some of her more worrisome activities, and we put up with her sucking down our negative emotions if we happened to come to her feeling angry or upset. But she knew if she ever turned to human sacrifice, either Danica or I would strike her down. If Nathaniel or Kyla didn't get there first.

Kyla had always been wary around Hannah, but that wariness had turned into loathing after the last time Hannah had decided to give her a few words of wisdom. I hadn't been there, but Kyla had quoted Hannah's words to me over a drink at Meredith's.

"You will lose everything one day," she'd told her. *"When you are ready, you will come here and allow me to feed on your misery, and I will give you the advice you will need. Eventually, if you're not an idiot, you may find happiness in the place you least expected it."*

To say Kyla had been unimpressed had been an understatement. I couldn't blame her. Not many people wanted to think about losing everything and hitting rock bottom.

Hannah waved a hand at the stools next to the wide island in the middle of her kitchen. Kyla and I took our seats, and Hannah prodded at whatever it was she was cooking in that pot.

"You want me to help you with the human hate

group," Hannah said.

Poke, poke, poke. Noxious steam poured from the pot. Kyla gagged.

I wasn't surprised that Hannah knew what was going on. She'd always been good at keeping one ear to the ground.

"Yes," I said.

"What about your little coven of white witches?" Hannah gave me a sly look that told me she knew Gemma was dead. I narrowed my eyes, and she sniffed.

"So, I'm your last resort."

"Do you want the job or not?" Kyla grumbled.

Hannah gave her the beady eye. "What's the plan?"

I knew exactly what she wanted to hear. "We'll go in as a team. The lab we will hit is the one where some of the worst experiments have happened, on some of the most powerful paranormals. There will be humans, witches, fae, and likely demons in the lab, all contained, all having survived torture."

Kyla got up and walked out.

I couldn't blame her. Entering the labs would be horrific, and the people who had been unfortunate enough to have ended up there would likely have wished for death a hundred times over. And I had to sell the place to Hannah. Had to lure her in with the pain and suffering, which she would suck down and use for her own spells.

"Vicious, that one," Hannah said, as Kyla slammed the front door behind her.

Virtus opened his eyes and pinned her with a look. He let out a hint of a growl, and that was enough for Hannah to go still.

"You dare threaten me in my own home?"

Virtus just kept his gaze on her face.

My heart rate tripled.

Hannah was the first to look away. She scowled.

"It just so happens I could use a good meal. But my services won't come cheap."

"They never do."

By the time I left Hannah's, I had a bad taste in my mouth. And it wasn't entirely due to whatever she'd been cooking in that pot. Virtus shoved his head beneath my hand in an effort to steady me as I walked down the stairs.

"Thanks. How are you feeling?"

He was feeling better, he told me. His wing hurt, but he knew one day he would fly again, so it was all worth it.

My heart twisted. After everything his last pack had done to him, they hadn't damaged his spirit. It would've been easy for Virtus to turn cold, vengeful, and bitter. Instead, he continued to think positively, soaking up every drop of joy he could from life.

"Let's go find Kyla, huh?"

She was leaning against her car, her long legs crossed at the ankles as she gazed down at her phone.

"What are you doing?"

"The usual. Swiping on fuckboys."

My phone buzzed. Nathaniel was calling.

"Hey."

"Hey yourself." His low, rough voice made my toes curl.

"What's going on?"

"We've agreed to meet Gabriel. It's going to be a trap, but hopefully that trap helps lead us to him."

My muscles seized up. "I'm coming too."

Kyla looked up from her swiping. "Me too."

"Wouldn't have it any other way," Nathaniel said easily. I narrowed my eyes. Kyla nodded. This was suspicious.

"We'll need all the power we can get if we're going up against the mage," Nathaniel said, clearly well aware of our suspicions. "While our wolves could rip out his throat faster than he could blink, we're outgunned when it comes to magic. That's where you come in."

"Good. Give me the address."

"Sending it now."

We hung up, and I opened our message thread.

The address Nathaniel had sent was on the outskirts of redcap territory. I shivered. Danica had once described the creatures to me, calling them "vicious little fuckers," and both my sister and Meredith had once almost been killed by them.

The fact that Gabriel was sending us so close to their territory could be a taunt or a coincidence. It was hard to know.

"You want me to drop you back home?" I asked

Virtus. He shook his head, but I didn't miss how slowly he moved when he got back into the car.

Males. Stubborn, no matter their species.

Most of redcap territory was encompassed by Cheek, Junction, Ferrell, and Carpenter Roads. Still, only an idiot would go poking around on the outskirts of their territory if they didn't absolutely have to.

Gabriel had directed us to an address on Clayton Road, which ran off Cheek Road. Kyla drove, and by the time we arrived, Nathaniel and at least twenty of his wolves had gathered outside, along with Neana. Seeing the fae healer soothed the worst of my nerves.

Unsurprisingly, Aubrey had turned up as well. Since it was likely the seelie king was working with Gabriel, Aubrey probably wanted to try to convince Gabriel to see the error of his ways.

Good luck with *that*. Still, the fact that Aubrey would try such a tactic was further proof of how much better of a ruler he would be.

I got out of the car. Virtus placed one paw on the back window, and I opened the door.

He stayed in the car but stretched out, using the additional space.

Kyla stood next to me, and both of us surveyed the house.

"It doesn't exactly look like the kind of place the most powerful mage in existence would be hanging out," Kyla said.

"No," Nathaniel said, walking up to us and

pressing a kiss to my cheek. "It doesn't. But that's likely the point. We enter in teams."

My mate turned away and began ordering everyone to fall in line. Thankfully, Hunter was there to relay those orders, and by the time everyone knew what they were doing, it was time to send the first group of wolves close enough to have a good sniff.

"No sign of life," Hunter growled when he returned. "There's definitely something dead in there, though. It's a trap, boss."

"Not unexpected." Aubrey strolled over to us. "But it seems like a strange tack for him to take. He's smart enough to know you wouldn't blindly walk into the building."

I watched as Nathaniel thought through our options. If we went in, we risked setting off whatever trap Gabriel had arranged. But there was a chance we could find a clue that would lead us to wherever he *was* hiding.

"Did you scent explosives?" Nathaniel asked.

"Nothing over the scent of the body. Likely one of the reasons it was left behind."

I wanted to know who that body was. Panic was fluttering in my belly at the thought that it could be someone I knew. A nice little "fuck you" from Gabriel.

"It's going to explode," Nathaniel said. "Either it's on a timer, or he's got someone planted here, waiting until we go in. Send a team to check out the neighborhood. Let's see if anyone knows anything."

I was biting my nails before I realized I'd lifted my hand. Nathaniel caught that hand in his.

"What's wrong?"

"Redcaps," I muttered.

He just smiled. "You know why they mostly keep to their territory, and they're not terrorizing the city and stealing small children?"

"Why?"

"Because when the portals opened, and I finally gained control of the werewolves in my territory, I knew they needed to learn how to work as a pack. I was tired of seeing the redcaps run wild. So, we hunted them, rounding them up until they agreed to take this territory as their own. And if they step out of line, I send a few wolves out to kill the offenders."

Pride and a savage kind of satisfaction roared through me. Nathaniel smiled, obviously feeling it through the bond.

The building exploded.

White-hot flames roared toward us.

Then I was on the ground, attempting to suck in a breath. The air was scorching, ash floating above my head.

"Evie." Nathaniel's voice was shaky. I'd never heard him sound so scared before.

I blinked. His hard body was over mine, one arm thrown over Kyla in an attempt to save her too.

"I'm fine," I got out. "But you're squashing me."

Relief roared down the bond. Along with a healthy

dose of retribution. Good. I was feeling the same.

Nathaniel helped me to my feet.

Kyla had a cut on her forehead and vengeance in her eyes. She stood next to us, and then we were all sprinting toward the building. Wolves were down. Several of them covered in rubble. However Gabriel had set his trap, he'd ensured that the building exploded in an unnatural way so anyone outside it would be hurt.

Sick son of a bitch.

The pack members who'd spread out to check the surrounding area were suddenly lifting steel beams, digging through rubble, and dragging out their pack mates.

I dropped to my knees next to Xander. His thigh had a steel pole sticking out of it.

"Hey." He took my hand. "It's okay."

"I'm supposed to be telling you that."

His chest shook, and he grimaced. "Don't make me laugh."

Water dropped onto his face, and he reached up, wiping my tears away. I hadn't even realized I was crying. "Sorry," I choked out.

"Don't be sorry. Just hold my hand when they pull this thing out?"

I nodded, unable to speak around the lump in my throat. I had a sneaking suspicion the dominant wolf didn't need his hand held. He was trying to make *me* feel better.

Nathaniel crouched on Xander's other side. His eyes were all wolf.

"You ready?"

Xander's gaze automatically flicked away, but he nodded. Nathaniel glanced at our hands. "He squeezes too hard, and he'll turn your bones to dust."

Little spots danced in front of my eyes, and both men cursed.

Nathaniel was at my side an instant later. "I'm sorry, darling. I shouldn't have said it like that. Come sit near his head so he can scent you. He needs to be surrounded by pack."

I nodded, hideously embarrassed. Nathaniel could likely feel that embarrassment, but thankfully, he didn't comment on it.

"How about a kiss for luck?" Xander gave me a wink, startling a laugh out of me.

"I don't think so," Nathaniel said.

Ignoring that, I leaned down and pressed a kiss to Xander's cheek. Nathaniel gave a mock growl.

Several wolves had gathered, and I realized they were about to hold Xander down. Neana waited, ready for when the steel was removed.

"Don't need a healer," Xander told her. "Help the others."

"I'll just stop the worst of the bleeding," she told him. "You can heal the rest."

I couldn't bring myself to watch them pull the steel from Xander's thigh, so I pressed my face to his neck, hoping my scent would help. He let out a low growl, turning his head, and for a moment, I was worried he was about to rip out my throat.

But he buried his face in my hair instead.

Finally, I felt the others let him go. I raised my head.

"Thank you," Xander whispered.

"Anytime."

Nathaniel lifted me to my feet. His eyes were tender as he wiped at my tears. For the next half hour, we went from wolf to wolf, ensuring they were healed enough that their bodies could take over. Miraculously, no one had died.

Still, I wanted to impale Gabriel with something sharp and pointy in the worst way.

Ryker appeared, his face covered with grime and dust. "You think that's the worst of it?"

Nathaniel's expression was terrible as he stared at the rubble in front of us. One room had been unaffected by the explosion. A dare if ever there was one.

"We need to check it out," Nathaniel said.

"I'm coming with you."

He opened his mouth to argue, and I slammed my palm over it. He raised one eyebrow. Behind us, one of the wolves laughed.

"I'll ward all of us. Now that we know what to expect, I can keep us safe."

A sick feeling took up residence in my gut. I should've warded all of us when we arrived.

"Hey. There was no way to know he'd arranged for the building to explode out the way it did. Explosives don't do that—the building should have pancaked. Now we know not to underestimate him."

I nodded. "Okay. Let's go."

In the end, Nathaniel, Hunter, Ryker, Aubrey, and Kyla went with me. Nathaniel ordered everyone else to move back at least a hundred feet. I spotted Neana coaxing Virtus out of the car.

Digging deep, I poured every drop of my magic into my ward. Any further explosions, and my friends and family would be safe.

The room was standing untouched. Even the door was still on its hinges—making it obvious just how much Gabriel wanted us to see whatever horror he'd left in there.

Aubrey opened the door. We followed him into the room, and all of us were silent for a long moment as we surveyed the seelie on the wall.

Nathaniel glanced at Aubrey. "One of yours."

Aubrey nodded. Bile rose as I took in the seelie, who'd been torn into several pieces, those pieces arranged in a macabre pattern that didn't come close to resembling a humanoid body. This explained why Gabriel was usually a hermit. The guy was a psychopath.

"What was the seelie doing here?" I got out.

Aubrey rolled his shoulders. "His name is Mydian. And he must have been betraying me. Taraghlan has infiltrated my people with his own. Since he is working with the mages, he obviously instructed Mydian to tell Gabriel our plans to take him down."

And now Gabriel was on the run, likely with complete knowledge of those plans.

"How much did this guy know?" Nathaniel asked, reading my mind.

Aubrey sighed. "I gave him limited information. He knew about our plans for Gabriel, but nothing else. I suppose some part of me knew to be careful."

Aubrey looked depressed as hell. I couldn't blame him. There were few things worse than being betrayed by someone you'd trusted.

NATHANIEL

Evie was quiet as we drove back toward our territory. She'd tightened her hold on the bond between us, shutting me out.

It was normal. We weren't *supposed* to be able to feel our mate's emotions every second of every day.

That didn't mean I didn't miss it.

I didn't exactly need the bond to guess how she was feeling anyway. We all likely felt the same. Frustration, fury, and wrath.

Now Gabriel was in the wind. And—if the seelie he'd left behind was any indication—he was pissed off.

"At least he doesn't know we're planning to hit HFE," Evie said softly.

I glanced at her. "Exactly. We might get lucky and find something in one of the labs that leads us to him."

"How is it going with blackmailing the guards?"

"All of them have agreed to open the first gates except one. And one of Samael's demons took him out. His replacement was more than happy to cooperate."

Evie stiffened. She slid her hand into her pocket, and she pulled out the lapis lazuli.

It was glowing.

"Get me home," she breathed. "I need a map."

I put my foot down. By the time we pulled up outside my house, the stone was glowing so brightly, it almost hurt to look at it. Evie shot out of the car and into the house. I was a few steps behind her. Within a couple of moments, Tobias had found her a map of the United States and placed it on the table.

"What if they've taken her somewhere else?"

"Then I'll need a world map. But we'll try this first."

Tobias's eyes widened as Evie placed the stone on the map. It immediately moved eerily across the paper.

"West Virginia," Evie breathed. "But there are two labs there."

The stone stayed where it was, planted in the middle of the state. Kyla walked in and tensed.

"We've found it," she said.

"Not yet." Evie was glancing between information

on her phone and the map below us.

"There are two labs in West Virginia. That we know of. One of them is on the outskirts of Morgantown, in the northern part of the state. The other is in what was once a Walmart Supercenter in Summersville. I was right, and the labs are warded. At least, the main lab is. We have no way of knowing exactly where they're taking her."

"We're hitting all the labs at the same time anyway," Kyla said.

I considered our options. We'd planned for the most powerful of us to target the main lab since it would be the most secure—and the most dangerous.

"Two teams," I said. "We hit the lab in Summersville. Danica and Samael hit the one outside Morgantown. We'll need an even split of fae, demons, and wolves for each lab."

Evie nodded. "All the other teams continue as planned."

"They'll be monitoring the airspace," I said.

Evie frowned. "So, how do we get in?"

"Leave that up to me."

22

EVIE

I gaped at the armored black bus outside Nathaniel's house. Although, calling it a bus was like calling a fighter jet a plane. I could already tell that this thing was *equipped*.

The bus was surprisingly sleek, and if I knew Nathaniel, it was also bulletproof. In fact, I wouldn't be surprised if it could take a hit from an Uzi and continue on as if nothing had happened.

"Where the hell did you get this?"

Nathaniel's grin was smug. "I've had a few of them for a while. Unlike demons, wolves can't fly—unless we're using planes. And only the most powerful among us can use the portals. That limits us. Thankfully, I've got these beauties."

"How fast can they go?" The thing was built like a tank.

Nathaniel's grin widened at the suspicion in my

voice. "Much, much faster than they look. The biggest issue will be avoiding human police."

Right. We didn't have time for sirens and cops.

I wasn't worried about driving faster than what was legally allowed. The wolves' reflexes were hundreds of times better than a human's. Besides, lives were on the line.

"The FBI have set themselves up in a white van just outside our territory," Kyla announced. "I think that's their version of being under the radar."

I heaved a sigh. "They want us to know they're there and they don't trust us. The moment they see us moving out of wolf territory, they'll be attempting to figure out where we're going. If I could trust them to follow us, that would be one thing, but if they learn which lab we're hitting, they'll get their local people to go in first. They'll justify it because HFE are supposedly *humans*. And it'll be a bloodbath."

"I'll go scare the shit out of them," Nathaniel said.

I laughed, shaking my head. "We need to notify them when we're already close enough to the labs that they can't prematurely crash our party." I studied the bus and thought about our options.

"I think I have an idea."

Nathaniel pressed a kiss to my temple. "Have I told you how hot it is when you get all witchy?"

I just grinned, watching Hunter yell orders as everyone continued the loading of weapons, water, medical supplies, and everything else we needed.

"What kind of idea are we talking?" Nathaniel asked. Curious wolf.

"It involves a spell I created a while ago. Similar to a look-away spell. But I've only ever held it for a few minutes at a time. This will allow us to get out of Durham, and I can use it wherever there are most likely to be traffic cops and when we enter West Virginia. I thought about trying to use something similar the other day when HFE was after me, but there's no way I could concentrate *and* focus on the spell. Also, it'll drain me. I won't have much power left when we get to the lab."

"We'll have Aubrey on our team, along with several demons and our wolves. I'm pretty sure Finvarra will find a way to end up at one of the most important labs as well. Hiding the bus is the smartest use of your power—we won't get near the lab if we tip them off. And we don't have time to drive the speed limit." He leveled me with a hard stare. "But if you're going to be drained when we arrive, you stick to me like glue. No exceptions."

I ground my teeth, annoyed at the order. Nathaniel just waited me out. Thanks to the bond, I knew he wasn't flexing his Alphaness. And he wasn't ordering me around simply because he felt he could.

No, he was worried.

"We go in together," I agreed. "But if you try to shove me behind you like you did at Eachann's, I'll kick your ass."

He shook his head at me. "There will never come a day when you walk into danger ahead of me."

"Then walk next to me. Partners, remember? Plus, last time I checked, *I* was the one with the magic."

"Magic which will be drained."

"I'll still be able to ward." I eyed him. "Are you going to be a dick about this?"

He sighed. "No. I'm trying. We'll walk in together. Partners."

I beamed at him, and his eyes softened. "Partners."

EVIE

The wolves moved like a well-oiled machine. Within an hour, the bus was loaded with weapons; I was strapped into Kevlar—hot and heavy, but unlike the wolves and the demons, I wouldn't shake off a bullet wound—and Aubrey had gathered the team he was taking into this lab with him.

Samael had sent Asmodeus, Bael, Abaddon, and Vas with us. They'd take to the air once we passed over the West Virginia border. The demons were our scouts for all of the labs, ensuring we would immediately know if someone tipped off HFE. They'd also pick up the unseelie from the closest portal, so our team would be intact by the time we needed to move.

Each of the demons needed two seats to themselves,

thanks to their wings. None of them looked pleased to be confined to the bus, but they were dealing with it.

Meredith was sitting next to Vas, who wore a backward baseball cap and a content smile. It was good seeing him so happy. Things had gotten dark there for a while.

Mere waved at me. She'd be staying on the bus, but she'd use her tech magic to take down the HFE communication systems.

Hannah boarded, ignoring the way the wolves stiffened at the scent of her black magic. Nathaniel had already made his expectations clear, and none of them said a word as she chose a seat halfway down the bus and gazed out the window like someone's grandma on the way to bingo.

I took a seat at the front of the bus. Kyla snorted at me as she boarded the bus. "Nerd."

"I get car sick, asshole."

Nathaniel sat next to me and wound his arm over my shoulders. If I ignored the ruckus from everyone else as they filed past us and sat down, I could almost pretend we were taking our own road trip.

"I was always into the nerds," he murmured into my ear.

"Oh yeah?" I smirked at him, but the smile dropped from my face as Aubrey stepped onto the bus with several of his seelie behind him. They continued walking, and he took the seat across from us.

I'd never seen him look so desolate before.

"Are you…okay?"

"I will be. It's difficult, knowing my king has been sending our people to be tortured. It explains why so many were terrified of speaking their minds. He used to have a council who would give him their opinions. Each of them was an expert in a different part of seelie life. But one by one, they disappeared, replaced by sycophants. Now it's easy to see why. But…there are few things worse than betraying your own people, especially to a human hate group. It's difficult to see how we can come back from this."

"I'm sorry. But the actions of a few don't represent the many. Taraghlan is rotten at his core, and his rot has spread. But you can remove that rot and save your court. You, ah, may want to talk to Samael."

Surprise flashed across Aubrey's face, immediately followed by understanding. "Because so many of his people were loyal to Lucifer."

"Yeah. And while some of them are still causing problems, there are plenty who were only loyal out of fear. Now that Samael is in charge, they've happily switched their allegiance."

"Do you think he'll talk to me? Historically, demons and seelie…"

"I think he'll do anything to make Danica happy," I said.

Nathaniel leaned down and nipped at my ear. "I can't imagine what that must be like."

I squeezed his hand.

Hunter boarded, plopping himself into the driver's seat, and I narrowed my eyes at him. *"You're driving us?"*

"Sure am. Hold on to your asses, 'cause we've got places to be."

The bus went quiet as he pulled out. I took a deep breath. The moment we hit the outskirts of wolf territory, I needed to make us invisible to human eyes.

Hunter handled the bus expertly, and within a few minutes, we were approaching the turnoff. According to our spies, the FBI was sitting in their van monitoring us just around the next corner.

"You ready, Evie?"

I took a deep breath and nodded. Nathaniel held up a hand, and the bus went silent. Cool trick.

Feeling all the eyes on me might have made me nervous, if I'd had the time to pay attention. But Hunter was waiting to turn, and my uncle, Hellaphine, her sister, and everyone else who'd been kidnapped and tortured were waiting in those labs.

Sometimes, I had to coax my magic to life. Today, it was a case of cracking open the floodgates, just enough for my power to pour into me.

"Her hair is floating," someone whispered.

"Creeeepy." That was Kyla.

Nathaniel turned, and I knew he was sending them a warning look. Silence reigned once more.

I could do this. People were counting on me to do this.

My mind threw me back to the way I'd constructed the spell last time. And I pushed it farther out until it surrounded our bus. The power drain was immediate, but I nodded to Hunter.

"Did it work?" Naomi asked.

"Of course it worked." That was Xander. "We wouldn't be driving past the FBI if it didn't."

"Are you okay?" Nathaniel murmured into my ear.

"Fine. We expected this."

Nathaniel got to work, opening his laptop and continuing to coordinate with the other teams. Just looking at his screen made me queasy, so I kept my gaze firmly on the wide window in front of me.

Danica, Samael, and their team were loaded into a bus just like ours, only they'd left an hour earlier. I'd told her how I'd come up with this spell, and she'd gently told me that thanks to Lucifer's untimely death, she didn't need a spell to turn an entire bus invisible. It would happen because she *willed* it to happen.

"We need a road trip song," I announced.

Groans sounded. Someone threw a wadded-up piece of paper at my head, and I lifted a hand, incinerating it while it was still in the air.

"Show-off." Nathaniel smiled.

Behind us, Bael and Vas started talking shit to Xander and Ryker. The wolves responded, and the bus erupted into jeering. Within a few minutes, Naomi and Kyla slid into the empty seats behind us.

I turned and raised an eyebrow. "Oh, *now* you

want to sit with the nerds?"

Kyla scowled. "Better than the jocks."

"Soon they'll be having wrestling competitions and bragging about the women they've banged," Naomi sniffed. "Men are all the same."

Nathaniel chose to ignore that. I snuggled into him and focused on keeping the spell around our bus, my stomach churning at the thought of what would come next.

NATHANIEL

By the time we made it into West Virginia, we were all on edge. Hunter had shot up highways, past cops, and over the border with no problems, thanks to Evie's spell. We were right to be prepared as we crossed into West Virginia, as Hunter pointed out the HFE van at the state line.

"Not only are they monitoring the air, but they're keeping an eye on anyone coming across too. It's a good thing we have Evie here, because this bus is suspicious as hell."

Evie smiled, but it was faint. It was clear she was feeling the drain on her power, and the bus had slowly quieted as we got closer to West Virginia, allowing her to focus.

Bael muttered on his phone behind Aubrey. He was

one of Samael's most trusted people and was ensuring all the other demons were in place. He nodded at me, and I waved at Hunter, who pulled the bus over.

"Anyone with wings, out," I said.

"Gladly," Vas muttered, kissing Meredith on the forehead. He got to his feet and glanced around. "This bus smells like wolf farts, black magic, and Ryker's meatball sub."

"Hey," Ryker said, "Tobias made me that sub."

"You should've told him to skip the onions."

Hannah just watched Vas like she was contemplating removing his wings.

Evie smirked at me. "This is weird."

It *was* weird. Before Danica and Evie, my pack would never have been caught in the vicinity of demons. Now, we'd worked together enough that they were ragging on one another.

The demons got out of the bus, immediately taking to the air. According to Samael, they didn't need to worry about being seen by HFE. If they didn't want to be seen, they wouldn't be.

By the time we arrived at our assigned spot three miles from the lab, my wolf was closer to the surface than he'd been in some time. Not only was he tired of being in a confined space with so many others, but our mate was pale, clearly tired, and determined to be one of the first people in when we stormed the lab.

"I told Danica I'd call her before we both went in," she told me as we filed off the bus.

I nodded, and she stepped away to make the call. As much as I would've preferred the sisters were together—knowing they'd protect each other with their lives—it made strategic sense to have one going into each of the last two labs.

"Ten minutes and counting," Hunter announced.

"Love you too," Evie murmured to her sister. She ended her call and nodded to me. "They're ready. What's the status of the other labs?"

Now that she'd dropped the spell around the bus, some of the color had returned to her cheeks. But she would need to keep us hidden again as we approached the lab.

She leaned close. "Stop worrying."

"I'm not worried."

She just looked at me.

"I'm concerned. It's different."

"Uh-huh. It's going to be fine. We're lucky the guard on the main gate was feeling particularly chatty." She smirked.

I reached out and tugged on one of her curls, watching it spring back up. We *had* gotten lucky with the day guard, who'd already had misgivings about the lab—and the horrors he'd heard were happening inside it. The demon in charge of blackmailing him hadn't had to do much threatening. All he'd had to do was guarantee we wouldn't kill him when we went in, and the guard had told us everything he knew about the lab. It wasn't much since the guards on the gates didn't go farther than the main door. But it was something.

"Five-minute count. Time to roll, boys and girls," Hunter called out.

I could feel Evie's nerves, along with *her* worry. "We're going to find Eachann," I told her. "Either our team or Samael's. No matter what, this ends today."

She took a deep breath and gave me a faint smile. "I love you."

"I love you too."

"Yeah, yeah, we all love each other. Can we get this show on the road?" Kyla grumbled, stalking into the bus.

"What's wrong with her?" Evie asked.

"Finvarra's meeting us at this lab. It turns out, your uncle is more important than he let on."

She winced. "Ah."

Kyla glanced over her shoulder at us as we climbed onto the bus. "I can't escape the unseelie bastard. Everywhere I turn, there he is. Just like Ryker's onion breath."

"Seriously?" Ryker growled.

I got to my feet and stood in the aisle as Hunter navigated to the lab. "The moment we step from this bus, we will be visible. Evie can't hide us all at the same time. The guard should open the gates, but we need to be prepared just in case."

Xander pointed down toward the explosives, which had been carefully packed and wrapped in the specially designed, armored storage beneath the bus.

"They don't let us in, we'll get in with force," he said. "But we don't want to risk hurting the prisoners if at all possible."

"FBI is on the way," Ryker said. "They're pissed."

I nodded. We'd gone over this plan multiple times, but I wanted to be sure we were all on the same page.

"Stay with your buddies. I don't want to hear about any stupid accidents," I said as Hunter parked the bus directly outside the gate.

Evie batted her eyes at me. "Are you my buddy?"

"Always." I grinned at her, then turned to the rest of the team. "Go."

We filed out. Demons dropped from the sky, each of them hauling one of the unseelie. Bael dropped Finvarra a few feet from the air, and he landed like a large cat.

Xander's job was to protect Hannah. He hadn't complained, although I could tell the thought of protecting a black witch didn't sit well with him. But we needed her to help Evie ward us as we entered. I glanced at him, and he grimaced but nodded. He'd do his job.

Otherwise, he wouldn't be one of my dominants.

The gate slid open.

Bullets flew through the air. Evie shuddered, and Hannah took her hand. Together, their ward encompassed all of us, and we sprinted through the inner courtyard. The demons launched into the air, taking out the HFE members positioned several floors up shooting down at us.

The moment we got to the first room, we split into our teams, each taking a corridor. None of us knew what we would find at the end of each hallway, which was why each team had a mixture of demons, fae, and wolves.

Finvarra and his team peeled off to the left. We went straight, while Aubrey's team headed to the right.

We hit the first door. Kyla lifted her leg and kicked it down.

Evie sighed. "My toxic trait is thinking I could do that."

I couldn't help it. I leaned over and pressed a kiss to her forehead.

Then we stepped through the door.

Together.

23

EVIE

Unlike the last lab I'd explored—the one that still gave me nightmares—this lab wasn't empty. And that meant I didn't have the luxury of giving in to the terror and rage that churned in my stomach.

That was for later. Right now, it took everything in me to keep the ward around my team. I'd be forced to drop it soon—hiding the bus had drained me. But HFE members were jumping out of hidden corners, crouching behind doors, and firing at us with everything they had.

Their bullets sank into my ward. I lowered it strategically, allowing the wolves to dart out and slash throats.

"Surrender and live." Nathaniel's voice carried over the sound of screaming. "Fight and die."

Several HFE members put their hands up. They

were instantly handcuffed and pushed toward the door. Xander escorted them to the parking lot, where the FBI had arrived.

We were going straight down to the cells. Nathaniel stepped in front of me when the hall narrowed. I didn't complain, but I did push my ward out until it enveloped him once more.

The light was dim, and the cells had been built beneath the ground. It was damp and chilly, and by the time we got to the bottom of the stairs, I was shivering with a mixture of cold and adrenaline.

"You came," a hoarse voice said.

I spun. Hellaphine sat in the closest cage, a woman who looked similar enough to her to be her twin next to her. That woman was covered in bandages, her face pale. "I need a healer," I called.

Tears were dripping down Hellaphine's face. "They were going to kill her today," she said. "Now that I'm here, they figured they didn't need her anymore. I had more *life* in me."

"We're here now."

I glanced around, but Naomi was already stepping forward quickly, a set of keys in her hand. "One of the men who surrendered had these," she said. Nathaniel grabbed them and unlocked the cage, but Hellaphine's sister froze.

"Too many scary men." Hellaphine gave him an apologetic look.

He just nodded.

Naomi stepped forward. "I've got this," she said, her eyes filled with pity as she took in the seelie women. "You guys keep moving."

Some of the prisoners didn't even stir when we freed them. I took a deep breath. "We need more healers."

Aubrey was leading a group of seelie men toward the exit, and he nodded at me. "We have more on the way. There are ambulances pulling into the parking lot, too."

Nathaniel went still. "Evie."

I whirled, my heart thudding at the way he'd said my name. But he'd moved several feet away and was staring at my uncle.

Eachann sat in the cage, his face bruised so badly, he was barely recognizable. I was standing in front of his cage before I realized I'd moved. I choked out a sob, and he opened his eyes.

"Evie. What the hell are you doing here?"

"You must be okay if you're lecturing me. We're breaking you out."

He shook his head, but I caught the pride in his eyes. "Lorcan," he said gruffly. "Meet your daughter."

My breath froze in my lungs.

"It's okay," Nathaniel whispered in my ear. "He's here, Evie. And he's alive."

I turned and looked at my father for the first time.

He smiled at me. "I should've known you'd be the one breaking us out. You're a spitfire. Just like your mother."

The world narrowed until all I could see was his face. He needed a shave. His eyes burned into mine, and his long, dark hair was matted with blood.

"Hi."

His mouth curved up. "Hi."

And then Finvarra was there, his magic burning away the lock on my father's cage. "Lorcan," he growled. "Next time you want to go off on some dangerous, mysterious job, the answer is no."

Lorcan grinned, but his gaze immediately returned to mine. I looked at Finvarra. "You knew he was here." *That's* why he'd decided to come.

"I'd hoped. He was powerful enough that it made no sense for them to kill him."

Nathaniel's phone beeped. He glanced down at it. "Kyla and Vas have Lennox."

"Go," Eachann ordered me.

"Are you crazy? I'm not leaving you guys."

"We'll help get some of the other prisoners out."

My lower lip trembled. Now that I had Eachann and—holy shit—my *father* back, I was terrified they'd disappear. After all, Danica's father was murdered mere days after she met him as an adult.

Eachann leveled me with his most stubborn look. "Go. Make sure he doesn't get away."

I nodded, suddenly unable to speak. Finvarra was helping my father out of his cage, and Lorcan smiled at me again. "It's okay. We'll talk soon."

My pulse raced as we filed up the stairs.

My power sparked to life, fueled by rage. Vengeance was flowing through my bloodstream like poison.

I wanted Lennox Rees *dead.*

My mother was caged in a lab just like this. I was born in a lab just like this. My father was *tortured* in a lab just like this.

"Breathe," Nathaniel murmured in my ear, and I realized I was hyperventilating.

I nodded. "You go first." I couldn't guarantee I wouldn't kill Lennox on sight. If Nathaniel was standing in front of me, I knew I'd hesitate before striking the HFE leader down right where he stood.

Nathaniel pressed a kiss to my forehead, then stepped in front of me. Following him up the stairs, I focused on all the reasons Lennox needed to stay alive.

He may have more information. He needs to be questioned properly. There could be other HFE cells in this country—hell, even in other countries around the world.

"I need you to make sure I don't kill him," I said.

Nathaniel slowly turned, his eyes almost white. I'd underestimated just how much *he* wanted Lennox dead.

"He sent those men to take you from me," he said, his voice quiet.

I knew that tone. When Nathaniel got quiet, it was a sign he was fighting for control.

Maybe he shouldn't be the one in charge of

keeping Lennox alive.

I shut my mouth, and he slowly turned, prowling up the rest of the stairs. Hunter was standing guard outside the door, and he nodded at us. Blood was splattered across his face, and Nathaniel took a moment to step closer to him.

Hunter dropped his eyes.

He was fighting for control himself.

"Do you need a minute?" Nathaniel asked him.

"They have kids on the floor above us." Hunter's voice was hoarse, more wolf than man. I caught a flash of teeth that were longer than they should be. "Babies," he snarled and glanced at me.

My heart twisted. I hadn't realized the pack knew the details of my early life. Hunter would've been outraged the moment he saw those kids, but he was taking it especially badly, knowing I'd been one of those babies.

Surprisingly, it was seeing Hunter fight against his wolf that helped me calm myself down.

I could feel Nathaniel's dominance creeping out along the pack bonds. It made me shiver, but it was necessary. As Nathaniel's number two, if Hunter lost it, he could kill far too many people before he was contained.

Stepping closer, I ignored the warning glance Nathaniel sent in my direction. Hunter wouldn't hurt me. Instead, I squeezed between them and wrapped my arms around Hunter. He froze.

With a sigh, the tension left his body, and he leaned against the wall, hugging me back.

"Sorry," he muttered.

I could feel Nathaniel's approval. He loved that I was able to comfort his pack. "You okay?" I asked Hunter.

"Yeah." Hunter ruffled my hair, and it was my turn to sigh. Another male intent on making me walk around with frizzy curls. Awesome.

"Ryker says our people have secured the building. Any guards left alive are in cuffs in the parking lot. The FBI is about to enter, so you don't have much time with Lennox."

"We've already told the FBI we're keeping him," Nathaniel growled.

Hunter just shrugged. "Every paranormal faction is going to want him too. I suggest you get as much as you can out of him now, before someone like Finvarra tries to steal him out from under our noses."

Drawing back, I took Nathaniel's hand. "Let's go."

24

EVIE

I didn't know what I'd expected Lennox Rees to look like, but it wasn't like a guy who coached Little League in his spare time. He had light-brown hair, a wide chin, and gray eyes. But those eyes were eerily empty.

They'd tied him to a chair, and Vas loomed over him, while Meredith sat a few feet away at a computer station. I wasn't surprised she'd insisted on ditching the plan for her to stay on the bus so she could take a look at Lennox's electronics herself, instead.

"Evie Amana," Lennox said, the hint of a smirk tightening his lips. "You would have been an excellent addition to my lab."

"I certainly *am* one of a kind." I strolled toward him. "But your labs are done."

Lennox's smirk became a grin. I shivered. Ted Bundy had probably smiled like that. "You'll never find them all."

"Actually," Meredith said, "we just did."

Lennox's gaze flicked to her, and Vas stepped in front of his view.

"There's one more in Florida," Meredith said. "It was on our *maybe* list. I shut down all communications, so they won't know about the raids. We have enough time to get a team in there."

Vas held out his hand, and Mere high-fived him.

"Where's the closest team?" Nathaniel asked.

"St. Petersburg," Ryker said, walking in behind us. "I'll let them know." He turned away again.

"You're done." I smiled at Lennox. "All of your little labs are destroyed. All your HFE members are either arrested, dead, or being hunted like dogs."

"You're making a mistake."

Nathaniel had gone still. He was looking at Lennox as if the man only had moments to live—and he was going to enjoy every second of his death.

Lennox instinctively dropped his gaze, making himself as small as possible in his chair.

"And why is that?" I asked.

Lennox swallowed. "Because I'm not the one you should be worried about."

I dropped my gaze to Misty, which hadn't reacted. Lennox believed what he was saying.

"And just who should we be worried about?"

Kyla stepped into the room with Hannah. Hannah looked pleased. Serene, even. Kyla's face was ashen.

"What's wrong?"

"There's something you should see."

NATHANIEL

It took every ounce of my self-control to leave Rees breathing. But the book was no longer riding me, which meant I could restrain myself from killing our prisoner before he gave us every detail he had.

I glanced at Hannah. The black witch looked like she'd shed ten years after sucking up all the misery in this place. My wolf was offended at the thought of allowing such a thing. He didn't care for politics.

She met my eyes and instantly dropped her gaze.

"Watch the prisoner," I ordered.

Rees glanced between us. He wasn't stupid. Even if he couldn't feel the black magic pouring from the witch, he knew she was dangerous.

"Wait," he called as I turned and walked away. "Wait!"

Ignoring him, I followed Evie and Kyla to a panel in the wall, which was propped open.

"Creepy," Evie said, taking in the wall, which led to some kind of secret room.

"Yeah," Kyla said. "If I hadn't smelled one of Lennox's men back here, I would've walked right past it."

That man was lying on the floor, his head located several feet from his body. Evie winced but continued walking into the hidden room.

"These are Rees's secret blackmail folders." Kyla waved a hand at a stack of files on the metal desk.

That hand shook, and Evie reached out and squeezed her shoulder.

"Whatever it is, we'll deal with it," she said.

"You don't understand. This is bad."

Leaning over the desk, I picked up the folder she'd clearly dropped before she found us.

I scanned the file on top and clenched my jaw. I'd been around for a while. I'd seen the worst of what humans—and every other paranormal faction—could do to one another. I'd seen war and power plays and betrayals.

But I'd never expected this.

"Share with the class." Evie's voice was tight.

I sent her an apologetic look. "If these files are correct—and not the ramblings of a madman…"

I considered that option, but the files had been handwritten, and it was clear that multiple people had worked on them.

Kyla shifted on her feet, as impatient as ever. "Okay, so you know how the McCormick coven woke the demigod in Guatemala, and the power influx opened portals to our world?"

"Of course."

"The way the mages tell the story, Colin Smith

happened to be volunteering in Guatemala. He was close enough that when the portals opened, that power hit him. For whatever reason, it didn't kill him. The demigod went back to sleep, and Colin began his task of saving humanity from the evil paranormals."

"Yep."

"So, he shared that power with ten other humans, who became the Mage Council."

Evie nodded, clearly impatient. Despite the topic, I smiled.

"We've always wondered exactly where the Mage Council got their power from," I said. "They are, after all, humans. Unlike the witches, there's no evidence that they *ever* had power in their bloodlines. And yet they pass varying amounts of magic down to mages who move up the ranks."

"Yeah." Evie turned to pace. "And those mages take vows which literally prevent them from breathing a word about where their magic comes from."

"That's right. But most paranormals know the mages are full of shit."

She went still.

"Ooh, story time," a voice said. Finvarra leaned against the open wall, the hint of a smile playing around his mouth, although his eyes were cold.

Kyla opened her mouth, and I shot her a look. She scowled.

Evie looked at Finvarra. He shrugged. "Long have I wondered where those humans were getting their magic. I believe Samael had several of his people working on it full time at one point." He glanced at me. "And wolves are known for their inability to leave a mystery alone." Turning his attention to Evie, he angled his head. "If I asked you to give some of your power to a human, could you do it?"

She frowned. "Not that I know of. The more powerful witches have attempted to share magic with less powerful coven members before, and it has never worked."

"That's because power is intrinsic to its owner," Finvarra said. "Ever since the portals opened, we've been attempting to find out where the mages were getting their power."

"And?" Evie narrowed her eyes, clearly out of patience. "Where are they getting it?"

Finvarra glanced at me, and his gold eyes lit with understanding. "From the demigod. The portals opened, and paranormals flooded this world. The McCormick coven died instantly. But Colin Smith survived. Didn't he?"

I nodded, glancing down at the notes. It all made a sick kind of sense.

"The witches didn't expect to die. But even though they were stupid, they weren't complete idiots. They'd brought Naud chains with them."

Evie shivered, and I couldn't help but run my hand over her back. Naud chains were one of the few ways to prevent a paranormal from using their magic.

"Colin Smith was close enough that he followed the trail of death to the place where the demigod had been sleeping. The witches had used their magic to uncover the cave, and while the demigod was technically awake, he was too weak to function—likely confused after being woken from thousands of years of sleep."

"The bastard used the Naud chains, didn't he?" Kyla asked.

"Yes."

Evie's face drained of color. "But how did Colin steal the demigod's power?"

"Rees's people don't yet know. If they did, they probably would have tried to do it themselves."

"Just what we need," Kyla muttered.

"So, all this time, they've had a demigod in Naud chains while they steal his power." Evie's hair began to do that eerie thing where it ruffled in a silent breeze. She started glowing again too. Something we'd thought she'd gained control over.

Finvarra gave her a cold, considering look that made me want to tear out his throat.

She just shot him her I-dare-you smile in return, her eyes turning witchy.

"As much as I wouldn't mind seeing you take out Finvarra, can we get back to the point?" Kyla muttered.

Finvarra flashed his teeth at her. She held up her middle finger.

I pinched the bridge of my nose.

"We have to do something about this demigod," Evie said.

Kyla nodded. "Fuck those mages. We'll cut off the source of their power and watch them scatter like rats."

Evie's eyes brightened at the thought.

Hunter leaned his head in. "A secret room," he said. "Cool."

"Get a group together and pack it up," I told him. "I want every scrap of paper, every file, and anything electronic. We'll go through all of it. And then we'll come up with a plan."

EVIE

For as long as I lived, I would never get the sight of the kids out of my mind.

I didn't want to. The more people who witnessed what had been done to them, the better.

Thankfully, the FBI had brought along medics and social workers. That didn't stop Vas from scooping up a crying three-year-old who had been experimented on in an effort to give him magic. Vas shook with rage, even as he smiled at the boy, but everyone went quiet when several tables toppled over—a sign that his wings were out and spread. The boy jumped at the sound, and Vas allowed his wings to appear, distracting him from the noise.

"You're going to be such a good father," I murmured to him when I walked past.

"I want to rip everyone who had a hand in this to pieces," Vas said in a light, singsong voice.

Eventually, I made my way to the parking lot, where seelie healers and human medics worked together to treat the prisoners. At some point, a team of reporters from the local news had shown up, although the FBI was keeping them behind a hastily erected fence.

My father was currently sitting in the back of an ambulance as a seelie healer I didn't recognize treated the worst of his injuries. Eachann stood next to him, his hand on his shoulder, as if he couldn't bring himself to let him go.

My father was *alive*.

I wanted to talk to him. Wanted to learn about him. But I'd give him some time to get used to his freedom first.

Kyla leaned against the building next to me. At some point, she'd become silent and withdrawn.

"What's going on?"

"Nothing."

"Uh-huh. No, but really, what's going on?"

She studied the ground. "I need to go on a trip. Alone."

"Good luck getting Nathaniel to agree to that."

"I need you to convince him."

I gaped at her. "While my pussy *is* magical—"

"Evie. This is important."

"If it's that important, I'll come with you."

"No. I need to go to Guatemala." Her gaze darted away. "And I'm going alone."

"The fuck you are."

She showed me her teeth. I scowled right back at her. "Just tell me what's going on."

"I can't. You'll tell Nathaniel."

I flinched. She rolled her eyes. "It's normal, Evie. Mates don't keep secrets. But I need this one to be on the down-low."

I studied her face. "When will you be back?"

"Once I've figured some stuff out. I'm just going to do a little spying for now, I promise. But, if I'm right..." She swallowed, her expression haunted. "We'll figure that out when we have to."

"Nathaniel's going to lose his mind."

"He hasn't ordered me not to go."

So that's how she'd get around it. She couldn't defy Nathaniel's orders, but he hadn't specifically said, *You will not go to Guatemala alone to spy on the bad guys.*

"Not bad," I admitted. "But I doubt it'll hold up. He hasn't ordered you because it wouldn't occur to him that you'd run off to Guatemala alone. If we're right, the cave where the demigod is trapped will be crawling with mages."

"I know. That's why I need your ring."

I glanced down at my hand. Technically, it was Danica's ring. Slipping it off my finger, I handed it over without a word. "*Please* let me come with you."

"If I need you, I'll call. I promise. But I'm not planning on doing anything crazy. I just want to get the lay of the land. Then I'll let you guys know what I found."

"Nathaniel's going to kill me," I muttered sullenly.

"Use your pussy power."

I glowered at her, and she grinned. "I'll be fine, and as soon as I'm back, we'll all figure it out together."

I didn't have to be a wolf to know she was lying. But Kyla was going to do what she thought she had to do. All I could do was support her.

Throwing my arms around her, I squeezed her tight.

"Go now, then. Before he notices you missing."

She nodded. "See you soon."

She was gone before I could tell her good luck.

"Evie."

I turned to find Eachann glowering at me. "Why aren't you talking to him?"

I glanced past him at where my father was talking to Finvarra.

"I...thought he might need some time..." It sounded stupid when I said it, and Eachann shook his head at me.

"He doesn't need time. He needs the daughter who was stolen from him."

Tears pricked my eyes. "What if... What if I'm not..."

Enough. What if I wasn't enough?

Eachann shook his head. "When I was dumped in that cage, do you know what he said to me?"

"Probably something like 'How the fuck were you stupid enough to get yourself kidnapped?'" I asked.

He gave me one of his rare grins. "Yes, pretty much word for word."

"How *did* you get yourself kidnapped, anyway?"

He scowled, his cheekbones flushing. "I thought I had a lead," he muttered. "But it was a trap. That's not the point. After we got reacquainted, your father told me the thought of you being out there somewhere and living your life was what kept him alive all these years. Just talk to him, Evie. Please."

I sucked in a breath. "Okay."

He let me go, and I turned, walking toward my father.

Finvarra nodded at him when he spotted me approaching, stepping away to speak to a group of scary-looking unseelie who were dressed in black and armed to the teeth.

Lorcan looked at me. He had such kind eyes. They were a pale blue, with the tiniest lines when he squinted into the sun.

"Are you okay?" he asked me.

"I should be asking you that, I think."

He dismissed years of torture with a wave of his hand. "You look so much like her."

My mom. My mouth trembled, and Lorcan got to

his feet. "May I hug you?"

I nodded, my throat suddenly so tight I couldn't speak. He was thinner than Eachann, likely from years of a nutrient-deficient diet. But his heart pounded beneath my ear, racing in a way that told me he was just as nervous as I was.

Strangely, it was that knowledge that steadied me.

"My brother told me you were a brave, beautiful woman. And he was right. I'm sorry I couldn't escape with your mother all those years ago. I can't regret the lives I saved, but... More than anything, I wanted to see you take your first steps. I wanted to hear you talk for the first time. Wanted to teach you to read..." He trailed off.

Tears were rolling down my cheeks now. "We'll never get that time back. But we have plenty of time now. I'm mated to the werewolf Alpha, which means I'm gonna live for a lot longer than I'd thought."

Lorcan stiffened, and I eased back.

"Eachann didn't tell you that?"

"No. The Alpha is the werewolf who was with you when you freed us."

"Yeah."

"Does he make you happy?"

"So happy," I said, my voice hoarse. "I never imagined I could be this happy."

He smiled at me, those tiny lines appearing next to his eyes. "Then I've gained both a daughter and a son."

25

EVIE

While I'd been talking with my father, Nathaniel had left to organize our team, ensuring the kids had trusted people with them and everyone was getting the medical attention they needed.

"What will happen to all these people?" I asked when I finally saw him next.

"I've chartered a plane. We're taking most of them back to Durham."

I blinked. "Durham?"

He just nodded. "I get anyone paranormal. That means the smallest amount of paranormal blood. A lot of the kids have parents here. They were just downstairs in the cells or elsewhere in the lab. I'm lending them a slice of my territory. We're going to build some cabins so they can recover there."

My heart melted. "I love you."

He leaned down and nuzzled my temple. "Finvarra agreed to lend some of his people to help with the build. Apparently, they're pretty good at using their power to construct buildings." He angled his head at Finvarra, who was walking past.

Finvarra just nodded.

Nathaniel glanced around. "Where's Kyla?"

I cleared my throat. "Uh, she had to do something."

He tensed, studying my face. "She had to do what, Evie?"

"I don't like your tone." Mm-hm. Going on the offensive was sure to help the situation.

Nathaniel just waited me out. I couldn't blame him. Over his shoulder, I saw Finvarra moving toward us.

"She went to Guatemala to check out the demigod situation," I mumbled, the words rushing out over one another.

It wasn't often that I saw Nathaniel speechless. Finally, he recovered, a low growl spilling from his throat. "You let her go?"

"I'm not the boss of her."

"That's exactly what you are."

Finvarra had gone still in that unnatural way of his. "Taraghlan will have some of his best people watching all three of you, waiting for a moment to strike in retaliation for the sword. If they find the wolf, she's dead."

With a shake of his head, he stalked across the

parking lot. Nathaniel let me go and walked away, obviously too mad to talk about it. I swallowed around the lump in my throat. That could have gone better.

I'd give him some space and talk to him when he'd cooled down a little.

My phone buzzed. Danica was calling.

We crowed about our victory. And I told her about Lorcan.

"Your father is alive?" She let out a low whistle. "Wow."

"Yup. We're insanely awkward with each other, but…he's alive."

"Wow. That's amazing, Evie. I can't wait to meet him."

My stomach churned, and Danica cleared her throat. "You better not be thinking what I think you're thinking."

"I just… I wish your father had lived too."

She sighed. "I know. But do you honestly think I'd resent you? Or be jealous? Sure, I wish he were here too, and that they'd both meet and we'd all hang out together. But that's not how life works. Now why don't you tell me why Kyla's not answering any of my messages?"

I filled her in. She was silent for a long moment.

"Are you pissed at me?" I asked. "'Cause I really can't take another—"

"No, I'm not pissed at you. I'm pissed at Kyla. But I also know that if she left suddenly, it's because she put something together. I think we need to try to figure out what that was, so if she doesn't come back, we know where to find her."

"Shit."

"Let's look on the bright side for now. We got them. All of them, Evie. HFE is dead."

I'd tell her about the mages another day. We'd had so few opportunities to celebrate recently.

We hung up soon after that, and I helped sort the paranormals into groups, ensuring everyone had received medical attention. Seeing how thin some of them were, not to mention the bandages, and the way they clutched at their children…

I was glad Nathaniel had moved Lennox already.

It took another few hours before everyone was organized. Nelson arrived at some point, clearly satisfied with the way things had shaken out, although he was still pissed at me. He'd gone into the lab with Danica and Samael.

Finally, it was time to board the bus once more. Eachann had insisted on taking portals back to Durham with my father. They were going to live together while Lorcan recovered. I could see him every day if I wanted. I still had to pinch myself occasionally.

I sat next to Nathaniel, both of us silent the entire way home. Everyone else was celebrating, but Nathaniel was clearly terrified for Kyla. I was scared too, but I was also convinced that she knew what she was doing. Kyla was impulsive, sure, but she wasn't suicidal.

The pack had embraced me. Even when they were pissed at me, it was more the way siblings were mad at each other, and not like the outsider I'd been when I'd first started working for Nathaniel.

It was the Alpha who worried me. Nathaniel clearly thought I'd undermined him with Kyla.

But he'd sworn we were partners.

I couldn't ignore the fact that, deep down, part of me wondered if this was it. If Nathaniel was realizing just whom he'd chosen as a mate.

And regretting it.

By the time we pulled up outside Nathaniel's house, I could feel his fury.

The moment Hunter parked, I shot to my feet. Nathaniel's eyes met mine, and he smiled.

It was the smile of a hunter.

I didn't have it in me to fight right now. Instead, I tucked tail and fled.

"Evie," Tobias greeted me, although his smile dimmed a little when he took a good look at my face. "How did it go?"

Even my shitty mood couldn't touch the fact that we'd killed HFE.

"They're dead," I said. "We've got Lennox—he's going to be kept in our prison here until we're satisfied he's told us everything he knows. Nathaniel had to roar at the FBI for that to happen. The other HFE members were arrested, and we'll have access to anything they say. It was part of the deal Nathaniel made when he brought the FBI in."

"Excellent." Tobias smiled. He glanced at Nathaniel, who had stalked in behind me. With quick fingers, Tobias untied his apron. "I believe I need a walk. We're having Greek for dinner, but there are leftovers in the fridge if you're hungry."

"Thanks, Tobias."

I turned and ducked around Nathaniel, heading upstairs. Maybe I could cry in the shower for a while until I felt like I could deal with all these emotions.

I should've known better. The moment we were in our bedroom, Nathaniel closed the door in that careful way of his—the one that told me he wanted to pull it off its hinges and throw it through a window.

"Why don't you explain to me why you look like the world is ending every time you look at me?"

I could barely breathe around the lump in my throat. My lungs had seized up, and all I could do was shake my head at him.

"Oh yes, you *will* tell me." His voice was a dark promise. He stepped close to me, cupping my cheek with his huge hand.

"I'm sorry about Kyla," I said. "But I don't regret it."

"If you don't regret it, why is your heart pounding so hard it sounds like it'll jump out of your chest?"

I scowled. Surely using his werewolf senses while we were fighting had to be cheating.

"You're angry," I began. My voice trailed off, and he frowned down at me.

"I have no doubt that you're going to piss me off in a million ways throughout our lives together. And I'm going to do the same to you. That doesn't explain why I can feel your dread and fear."

"This isn't being mildly pissed off."

"So, what? You imagine one day you'll do something that angers me, and I'll be done with you?"

My eyes burned, and I pressed the heels of my hands to them. Nathaniel caught my wrists, pulling them down and holding them firmly.

"Hey. Look at me."

I immediately wanted to cover my face once more. To hide. Nathaniel was perceptive enough to pick up on all my insecurities. And that was before he'd had access to my emotions.

"You still think I'll leave you," he said, jaw tightening. His hands let mine go, and a tiny, broken sound left my throat.

Then I was in his arms, and he was stalking toward the bed. He laid me down and leaned over me, trapping me with his weight.

"You know mating is for life."

"Yes. I do know that. But just because you're stuck with me for life doesn't mean you'll always *want* to be with me. We could end up in the paranormal equivalent of a bad marriage, where you resent the hell out of me for undermining you."

I swore I would rather he leave me. At least then, I wouldn't be able to feel him pulling away a little more every day.

His mouth dropped open. "The *paranormal equivalent of a bad marriage?*"

"I can't... I can't deal with the silent treatment, Nathaniel. You could barely look at me today, and that's fine, but—"

"You think I was giving you the silent treatment? And I couldn't look at you?"

Nathaniel looked so appalled, I blinked. When I opened my mouth next, nothing came out.

He tightened his hands on me. "I was sitting there trying to figure out where I'd gone wrong with Kyla. And why she felt the need to sneak off, rather than talk to me about it. And why I'd lashed out at you, like you could stop her when she had her mind made up. And I was also trying to understand why the fuck I couldn't feel anything except desolation and grief from your end of the bond."

"I..." I had nothing.

Nathaniel just leaned even closer, until our faces were inches away. "Why didn't you reach for the bond?"

Because if I'd felt how disgusted he was with me, I wouldn't have been able to handle it.

He shook his head at me. "I'm sorry you thought I was giving you the silent treatment. I would've discussed my thoughts with you, but we were on a bus filled with paranormals."

I felt like an idiot.

"I'm sorry. Thank you for letting me know."

I pushed against his chest, and he slowly shook his head. "You're not going anywhere. Perhaps I'll keep you chained to this bed forever, hmm? Continually out of your mind with pleasure? Would that convince you I'll never leave you?"

I knew he'd never consider such a thing, but my mouth still fell open at the thought.

He took advantage, crushing his mouth to mine. He kissed me until I was breathless, until I was aching for him. And then he backed away.

I hissed out a protest, but he was already pulling my sweater and tank top off together. My bra followed, Nathaniel's movements so fast, I could barely keep track of where his hands were.

My shoes and pants went next, underwear fluttering to the floor directly after. I shivered at the lust in Nathaniel's eyes. There was something incredibly erotic about being naked on his bed while he was fully clothed.

He turned and opened his closet. Our closet now. Pulling open a drawer, he grabbed something that glinted in the light.

I craned my neck, but he was already prowling toward me. He lifted his hand, and I gaped. Those weren't sex handcuffs. Those were *real* handcuffs.

"You gave me the green light," he reminded me.

"Is that light still green?"

"Yeah," I got out, my mouth suddenly dry. "It's green, all right. Fluorescent green. Glowing green. So green."

He grinned at me, and then he was leaning over my upper body, hooking the handcuffs through the headboard. He kissed my right hand, then closed the cuff around my wrist, repeating the motion with my left.

"Pick a safeword, darling."

I gaped at him. "A safeword? How about 'let me out'?"

He shook his head. "I'm going to teach you why we'll never have the *paranormal equivalent of a bad marriage*," he said. His expression had turned blank, but not before I caught the flicker of hurt in his eyes.

I'd really pissed him off with that. But even worse, I'd wounded him too.

Shit.

"Um, okay. My safeword is amethyst."

"Done this before, have you?" he asked silkily.

I frowned at him. "I don't ask about *your* ex-lovers."

"No one mattered until you."

I wrestled with that while he stripped off his shirt. My mouth watered as my gaze caught on his upper body. Then he stepped out of his pants, and I went instantly hot all over.

"Come here," I said, needing him.

He just gave me a very male look. "I'm in charge here. You know how I know that, sweetheart? Because you're the one in handcuffs."

God, I'd never wanted anyone like I wanted this man. My gaze was glued to his every movement as he climbed onto the bed, leaning over me. I arched my hips, already desperate for him, and his eyes laughed at me.

"I don't think so."

"Please."

"I like your manners, but they won't help you today. You've been a bad girl."

I cracked up at that. He smiled. It was an evil smile.

Then he was kissing me, and I sighed against his mouth, soaking in the feel of him. He pulled away too soon, and I scowled, but he was already kissing his way down my neck, paying special attention to all my most sensitive spots.

I moved restlessly under him, automatically attempting to reach for his head and hold him to me. But the handcuffs kept me his prisoner, and the sensation of wanting to move them but not being able to, all while Nathaniel cupped my breasts in his large hands...

I was going out of my mind with lust.

Nathaniel rolled my nipples between his fingers, watching my face. I sucked in a sharp breath, and he squeezed a little harder.

My core went molten.

"Well, well, well," he said. "That's interesting."

My cheeks heated, and he just shook his head. "There's no shame between us. Not ever. And *especially* not when it comes to your pleasure."

He removed his hands, and I whined. But he was already leaning over me, his expression serious.

"I need you to talk to me when you feel this way," he said. "Please."

"I don't want to be that needy, insecure person. We've been over this. You've promised not to leave me."

"A fear of abandonment doesn't go away overnight. Even with a mating bond. It takes time and trust, and seeing for yourself that no matter what you do, no matter how badly we argue, I will always love you. And I will always stay."

I nodded, unable to talk around the lump in my throat.

God, I loved this man.

He nuzzled my neck, and I sighed. I was moving restlessly under him, desperate to feel him inside me, and the cuffs around my wrists ratcheted that desperation higher until I was letting out tiny sounds of want. Nathaniel gazed down at me, his eyes dark.

"Do you trust me to make you feel good?"

"God, yes."

He smiled at that, and my mind went blank as he lowered his head, running his mouth along my breast. His tongue circled my nipple, and my breath caught in my throat.

"Breathe," he murmured, turning his attention to my other breast.

My breath shuddered out, and I felt him smile against my skin.

And then there was nothing but feeling. Each time I attempted to move my arms and couldn't, my mind turned foggier, my body needier. Nathaniel drove me crazy with his mouth, nipping and licking and blowing air over my most sensitive spots. He kissed me everywhere, from my forehead to my little toe.

He was cherishing me.

He was also driving me crazy, refusing to kiss me where I needed him the most.

Finally, *finally*, he pushed my thighs open. I watched as he surveyed me, and my cheeks heated at the hungry expression on his face.

His eyes met mine.

Then he was rolling off me.

"What—oh, wait—"

He was tying a dark T-shirt around my head, ensuring my eyes were covered.

"Why?" I managed to get out.

"Because I want you focused only on the pleasure I can bring you."

And then his mouth was on me, licking and teasing and driving me out of my mind.

His tongue slipped inside me, and I moaned. Then he replaced his tongue with his finger, his tongue circling my clit, and I gasped. They moved together, and I let out a choked sound that seemed to please him, because he growled against me, and just that noise nearly threw me over.

"Shall I keep you on the edge just like this for hours?" he mused, and I let out a garbled string of curses. He laughed, nipping at my inner thigh, and I almost kicked him. But I also wanted his mouth on me again.

He moved off me, and I almost cried, I was so desperate. "Shh, darling," he crooned. Within moments, he was positioning himself at my entrance. "I want you to come around me when you're this needy. So you remember I'm the only one who can make you feel this way."

I had no argument for that. He *was* the only one who could make me feel this way. I arched my hips. "Please."

He took his sweet time, torturing both of us. When he was finally seated within me, he pulled off my blindfold, and I blinked up at him.

"Need to see your face," he muttered. His lips found mine, and he began to thrust. Once. Twice.

"Ahh…"

"That was quick," he said as I clenched around him, writhing through my climax. But his voice was tight, and he closed his eyes for a moment, making it clear he was fighting for control.

I gasped as he thrust deeper. I wanted to hold him

to me, and yet the feeling of him taking my body as he saw fit, the feeling of not being able to do anything except enjoy what he was doing to me...

"Almost there again?" He sent me a shit-eating grin. "I sense more bondage in our future."

I would have laughed, but his cock was caressing my G-spot and his pelvic bone hit my clit with each thrust. My breath caught in my throat, and he gave me a look of such dark satisfaction, my body exploded with pleasure. My climax went on and on, ripping through me until I felt like I was flying. Distantly, I was aware of Nathaniel cursing, and then he slumped, both of us panting.

His mouth found mine, and he unlocked the cuffs. I wound my arms around him and held him close, my heart pounding.

I was right where I was supposed to be.

26

EVIE

I cracked open my eyes the next morning, smiling at the feel of Nathaniel's arms around me, his body spooning mine.

He shifted, the hardness against my butt letting me know he was awake. I arched into him. But something else caught my attention.

"What's that?"

He nipped my ear. "If you haven't learned by now…"

I burst out laughing. "No, you fool. *That.*"

A huge basket was sitting on my bedside table. A basket filled with chocolate.

Gourmet truffles, chocolate pretzels, brownies, cookies, chocolate-covered strawberries…but it was the center of the basket that made me gasp.

Chocolate wolves, made with such incredible detail…

"Oh my God, that one's Ryker." I cracked up. Only

Ryker had a tail that bushy. I recognized more wolves as I peered at them. Of course, the white chocolate wolf was Kyla, who was the color of snow when she shifted.

"This is incredible," I breathed. I could feel Nathaniel's pleasure radiating down the bond, and I glanced over my shoulder at him. "Did you do this?"

He shook his head. "I had nothing to do with it. But when Ryker thanked you for saving me from the book, you told him to say it with chocolate… From the look of this, the pack *did*."

Warmth spread through my chest. Someone must've snuck in here and put it next to me. Of course, Nathaniel would have woken up for that, but he'd allowed them to surprise me.

I got out of bed, leaning down to examine the gift basket once more. Each time I looked at the wolves, I noticed more details. "That one is you." I pointed at the wolf in the middle. "It's the biggest of them all."

Nathaniel was watching me, a satisfied smile on his face.

"I need to thank them," I murmured. It was such an incredible gesture.

"We have a pack lunch," Nathaniel told me. "Hunter and the others invited your father and your uncle, too."

Because they were now considered family as well. I practically purred with contentment, right before anxiety took over. Nathaniel got out of bed, wrapping his arms around me.

"It will be fine. Your family will fit right in with the

chaos. You'll see."

I nodded, but my mind was on the one person no one had mentioned. "What are we going to do about Gabriel?"

"According to our spies, he's on the run. He'll be mobilizing the mages and likely planning to wage war. Now that we've taken down HFE, he'll know we've discovered how he's getting his power."

I reached for my robe. "His back is up against the wall. The best way to neuter him is to remove his access to that power."

"Yes. As much as I'd prefer Kyla hadn't gone running off to Guatemala, she had the right idea. We free that demigod from the mages, and they'll be powerless."

Anticipation clawed through me at the thought. All these years, and the mages had presented themselves as the good guys, keeping humanity safe from the paranormals. When really, they were power hungry liars.

"Enough thinking about our enemies," Nathaniel said, pulling me into his arms. "Let's go have lunch with our pack."

Our pack. My family. My *mate*. It sometimes all felt too good to be true. But it wasn't. This life was mine.

We showered, and by the time Nathaniel was done with me, I was a sated, limp, and sleepy. I dropped my towel, reaching for jeans, and he went still in that wolfy way of his.

"Don't even think about it. I'm starving."

He prowled toward me. "I want to see you chained

up for me again. I want to hear you *beg*."

And just like that, I no longer cared about lunch.

Someone banged on the door. "Hurry up, you two," Ryker growled. "Tobias will punish us all if lunch gets cold."

Smiling up at Nathaniel, I looped my arms around his neck. "Go tell them I'll be right there, so I can get dressed. And then later, maybe I'll cuff *you*."

His eyes darkened, but Ryker was knocking again. Nathaniel slid an irritated look toward the door, and I chuckled.

"Don't be too long," he said, stalking out the door.

I reached for my jeans and T-shirt. Downstairs, the pack were gathering to celebrate the fact that we were all still alive.

Growing up in the coven, I could never have imagined this life. And when they kicked me out…a part of me had floundered—no matter how badly I wanted to pretend I was okay. The pack wasn't a family of secrets and lies, determined to keep me small and ignorant about my power. It was a family who had already welcomed my father and uncle to lunch. A family who protected innocents. A family who would never turn their backs on me.

My eyes burned, and I took a deep breath, murmuring a final goodbye to my previous life.

Then I slipped my feet into flip-flops, shoved my hair into a messy bun, and followed my mate downstairs.

Epilogue

KYLA

Getting to Tikal was no joke.

It involved a portal to the Middleground, another portal to Antigua, a small colonial town in Guatemala, a chicken bus to Guatemala City, and a flight—on a plane that was little more than a lawnmower with wings—to Flores.

By the time I landed, my wolf was pissed. She hadn't enjoyed any part of the trip, and I couldn't exactly blame her.

After all, neither had I.

As soon as I landed in Flores, I focused on filtering every scent I came across. I had no doubt this place was filled with mages, keeping an eye out for any other paranormals who might be looking into their activities.

My wolf wanted to run to Tikal. I wanted to do the same. But we didn't have the time. Instead, I a private transfer. The driver's name was Juan, and he spoke much better English than my bad Spanish. The drive went faster than I'd anticipated, thanks to his history lesson about the Mayans, who'd inhabited the area from the sixth century BC to around the tenth century AD. Apparently, a good chunk of the archaeological remains were still underground.

While I'd assumed the demigod would've been buried beneath one of the huge temples, I was actually headed *away* from the temples. Juan dropped me on the outskirts of the site, clearly concerned about leaving me.

"I'll wait for you," he told me.

"No thank you. I'm meeting some friends." A lie, but relief crossed his face and he nodded.

"Enjoy your time here."

And then I was alone. Glancing at the map I'd lifted from Lennox Rees's little information room, I got my bearings, shoved Angelica's ring into my mouth, and took off at a steady jog.

The mages had stationed guards in nondescript clothing all over the area. Several of them were wearing giant cameras around their necks, while a few more wore fanny packs and baseball caps. A sad attempt to fit in with the tourists, but I could see—and smell—their magic a mile away.

Their presence reinforced that I was in the right place.

The demigod was located outside the national park, deep in the forest. He'd originally gone to sleep far beneath the earth but was now in the cave that had been created when the McCormick coven raised him from his coma-like sleep.

It took me an hour to hike to the cave, keeping my footsteps light. Finally, I heard voices.

I caught sight of twenty or thirty mages, all armed with guns. I had no doubt they were also armed with that stolen power. I crouched, watching the area for a few hours, while I stored away everything I noticed about the guards, their shifts, and just how much attention they were paying to their surroundings.

I couldn't just check out the security. I had to know what we were working with.

My wolf liked that idea, and I padded toward the cave. I'd expected it to be warded, but that likely would've stopped them from being able to access their stolen power.

I crept into the mouth of the cave, and my eyes adjusted to the dim light.

I'd once seen photos of the Reclining Buddha in Thailand. The demigod was large enough that he reminded me of those pictures. Only he wasn't gold, and he wasn't reclining with his eyes open.

Even with him lying down, his shoulder ended far above my head. His feet were as long as my body and crossed at the ankles, while his wrists were encircled with what seemed like miles of Naud chains. My wolf snarled at the sight.

I couldn't even attempt to soothe her. I wanted to rip out these mages' throats in the worst way.

The guy had tried to take a nap for a few thousand years and woke up in chains, surrounded by humans who were feasting on him. I was betting he was *pissed*.

Unfortunately, as much as I wanted to do a little slaughtering, this was supposed to be a reconnaissance mission. Even if I hadn't promised Evie that I'd just come to spy, I was massively outnumbered by these fuckheads.

Soon, I soothed my wolf.

We'd once been trapped just like this. A soundless growl left my throat.

And that's when the ground began shaking.

Little wolf, why are you here? A voice sounded in my head.

I went still. I was invisible. But this guy was a demigod. The mages were running for cover, but from what I could see, the earthquake wasn't unexpected. Obviously, it was one of the few ways the demigod could show his displeasure.

"I'm here to figure out how to free you," I whispered, hoping he'd hear me. I wasn't sure if the whole talking to him in my head thing would work.

I wish to sleep.

"I know. I'm sorry they woke you up."

Come closer.

I padded toward him, and even though his eyes were closed, I had a pretty good feeling he could see me.

Other side, he instructed. Pushy bastard.

A low laugh sounded in my head, and I froze. Could he—

Read your mind? Of course. Why do you think I spoke to you? You're the only one here who isn't attempting to suck my power dry.

"Yeah, sorry about that." I crossed around those massive

feet, aware that his toenails were the size of my face.

This side of his body was closest to the cave wall. I took a good look and went still.

Ah, you see it.

Yes, I fucking saw it.

Strapped to the demigod's side, looking absurdly small given how big he was…

Was an empty sword sheath.

Return my sword and remove these chains so I can sleep. Please.

The last word sounded foreign. He likely hadn't ever used the word before.

I stared at the demigod and forgot how to breathe. My suspicions were correct.

Selina had been clear. Steal the sword from Finvarra and return it to its owner. Or the worlds burn. Well, I'd found the owner. But if I returned the sword and sent him back to sleep…

The portals to our world would close.

Forever.

THE END

Thank you so much for reading Unbroken Magic! The final book in the Bargains with Beasts series is Unending Magic which is Kyla's story.